MURDER AT HAGGBURN HALL

An addictive crime mystery full of twists

ROY LEWIS

Arnold Landon Mysteries Book 13

Originally published as
The Shape-Shifter

Revised edition 2022
Joffe Books, London
www.joffebooks.com

First published in Great Britain in 1998
as *The Shape-Shifter*

This paperback edition was first published
in Great Britain in 2022

ISBN: 978-1-80405-176-4

PROLOGUE

The Northman came out of the west, storm-sped, and his brow was dark as the storm. He beached his longships on the muddy shores of the wide estuary and with twenty of his strongest men he swept inland, taking swine and cattle from the outlying homesteads, seizing what they willed. Two days later the rest of his forces joined him on the long hill called Ardrath and there they built a palisade for they had come to stay. The west had been denied them by their fathers and the Northman had led them here.

In the days that followed he led his warriors from the long hill and they raided the villages that lay fat below them. They took women and food, and the night was alight with fire. The outlying villages were destroyed and the shadow of the Northman lay along the coast and deep into the narrow valleys, dark and violent and menacing.

It was an unpropitious time along the coast and in the valleys, for the clans were riven with dissension. The Clan of the Boar had long been dominant but now there was a weakness in the leadership with the death of the Old One, and the Clans of the Eagle and the Hare were in dispute. It seemed as though it was a time for talk and no deeds. Long discussions were held around the night fires and the shamans

1

consulted endlessly, their incantations drifting up to the silent trees. There was mischief in the air, uncertainty as the entrails showed no discernible prediction. The frightened, cowed villagers in the turf-protected settlements shivered as wolves howled on the hill and the brooding menace of the Northman was dark on Ardrath. They knew he waited as the clans gathered courage, called together their warriors to attempt the storming of the long hill, and the recapture of their women and plunder.

They marched on an early autumn morning.

There was the cold sharpness of winter in the air and their feet rustled softly on the gold of the fallen leaves in the woods. The clans had reached an uneasy compromise, accepting the need to fight together if they were to regain their own, but there was mistrust in their ranks, a nervousness about the insecurities of the shamans, and clan marched uneasily with clan.

The shamans had been contradictory, they seemed confused by the night sky and the sparks that showered about their incantations. They muttered amongst themselves and seemed afraid: they spoke of a new coming of an old curse, the return of an ancient war deity, untrustworthy as only a war deity could be, cunning as only a woman could be, who ate at the heart-strength of men.

A raven had sat on the roof of the Hare Clan meeting house and had croaked thrice before flying away; the mists that had crawled insidiously along the valley floor had been dank and cold, and from their wispy depths snakes had slithered, blind-eyed and deadly; eagles had whirled soundlessly above their heads as the remaining women, old and toothless, keened and wailed in the dimness of the enclosures. Dark clouds had gathered about the shoulders of Ardrath, presaging violence and death and wings of storm, but the stones of its slopes had glittered like weapons unsheathed and there was a feeling of great change in the air.

No man seemed to know his neighbour; husband and wife were strangers; the certainties that had bound the clans together in mutual support seemed to have been eroded and a great mischief lay over the land. When the warriors gathered there was no sense of the group: petty disagreements flared into quarrels, and quarrels into violence. The shamans muttered of an old religion returned, of a dark influence that had been cast out, of the war deity who came in the shape of a woman, or a bird, or an animal but who could change shape at will to the confusion of men.

And the man on Ardrath lay at the centre of the confusion.

The shamans finally agreed that it was the Northman at Ardrath who had been responsible for the heaviness in the air, the doubts and uncertainties, the mischief that was ripping the heart out of their warriors, and that only in the extirpation of his influence could they see a return to the softer, clearer days they had latterly enjoyed.

So they marched through the rustling beech woods of autumn, the Clans of the Hare and the Eagle and the Boar, and as odd shafts of light glanced down through the dying canopy above their heads the hollowness of their cheeks was picked out, the madness of panic and fear in their eyes, the leaden pallor of their skin as they moved silently, uncertainly, towards Ardrath and the violence that waited for them, brooding on the hill.

Between the beech woods and the granite outcrops on the shoulders of Ardrath there was an open space, a wide bare clearing of slippery rock and shale, and it was here that the clans were caught. They heard nothing, saw no warning signs, but as they crossed the clearing there seemed to be a rush of wings, a cleaving of the air about them as though something malign circled above their heads. And it was then that they saw him.

He stood, legs braced apart on the crag in front of them, and he was tall, broad and black-haired. He wore a dark helmet of fur, eagle-beaked, clamped with bands of iron; the pelt of a bear was slung across his shoulders and it was stiff with the dried blood of many battles. His brows were black and heavy, his eyes, sharp either side of the iron nose-guard, seemed to pierce the heart of each man of the host that advanced across the clearing towards him. They felt a shudder in their chests. They felt their hearts move, sinking at the terror he promised them.

In his right hand the Northman wielded a shining battle-axe. The targe that protected his muscular left arm was made of wood strengthened with a layer of metal, centred with a spiked boss that glittered a deadly menace. He spread his arms wide and he was no longer a man. He was a bear, roaring silent defiance; he was a malignant, mocking raven; he was a black eagle under the skullcap, its predatory beak curved to tear and rend at the courage of every man facing him.

It was only then that they heard the susurration, saw the swift, deadly movements at their flanks — became aware of the silent, powerful warriors who materialized out of the woods and stood there, half crouching, awaiting the signal to kill. The Northman held his hands wide, shaking the battle-axe and the shield, and then in a sudden, violent movement he clashed them together. Next moment he swung his battle-axe high, threw back his head and howled like a wolf before he leaped forward, rushing down the slope towards the clans like a ravaging animal.

The flanking warriors surged in, howling in their turn. Disembowelled by fear, the clans swung about uncertainly for their war gods had deserted them. Their enemy seemed to take on new shapes — wolf, bear, leaping stag — and the clans gave way, throwing down their arms, tumbling back towards the useless shelter of the woods. There they were cut down like hunted vermin. The Northman who led the hunters seemed to be everywhere, cutting, slashing, smashing with his gory axe, thrusting with his terrible shield, dancing from one group to another in a blood-lust that seemed endless, and ceased only with the darkness that finally folded the hill. It was a darkness scented with the sweet smell of death, cloaking the sprawled, smashed limbs, allowing the nocturnal rustling to begin as the scavengers crept out of the darkness to feast on the blood and torn flesh, wet and still warm among the golden leaves . . .

The villages were silent thereafter. As the days passed, Ardrath brooded darkly above them, the Northman and his followers taking the produce of the fields and silently accepting the gifts of the terrified population of the valleys. For five years the men on Ardrath laid waste to the villages and then, almost as quickly and silently as they had come, they left the long hill, and the sharp-prowed boats moved away from the wide estuary, nosing their way up river, into the heartlands and the towering fells whose shoulders glittered with snow.

The clans regrouped but remained broken in spirit. They watched Ardrath and its storm-clouded shoulders and they told and retold the story of the Northman and the return of the Ancient One. The shamans cast their stones, chanted their runes, called high the flickering flames of their fires with time-steeped incantations, and explained to the clans how it had been and how it would be.

It was the time of the Old Ones again, the storm gods; it was the return of the terrible female war deity who had come out of the west in vengeance for their disbelief in her power and her strength and her viciousness. She was the Oldest; she was the Ancient One who stole the hearts of men with her mischief and her malice; she was the enemy who was seen and never seen, who shrouded her form and translated herself into many shapes. She was the deity who lived among men and could be a man, or a wolf, or a boar; who could promise but could never be trusted, who could offer riches and glory but would in the end deliver only sand in their mouths.

They could only watch Ardrath with the death of hope in their hearts for they knew she was there and the Northman would come again. He was her weapon, the terrible tool in her hands, the harbinger of her coming, the bringer of her terror. He was the upholder of her law.

She was the Mórrigan.

CHAPTER ONE

1

The Boeing 747 sat solidly, glittering in the sunshine on the tarmac at Newcastle Airport as at the far end of the runway a Cessna took off fussily, taking its cargo of businessmen down to Manchester, or London, or Dublin, to make deals, or money, or mistakes.

Arnold Landon turned away from the terminal window and rejoined Jane Wilson as she sat in the small café that overlooked the runway. She had clasped her hands together, supporting her chin, elbows on the table. As she stared at the coffee he had bought her, there was a slight frown on her face.

'They should be calling your flight soon,' he said. 'That's one advantage with provincial airports, you don't get interminable waiting times at check-in desks and airport lounges.'

She made no reply. He took a seat opposite her and sipped his coffee; they sat quietly for a little while. At last, he ventured, 'I think it was a sensible idea to stay at the airport hotel last night. I doubt whether I'd have stirred myself in time to see you off here if we'd had to drive up from Durham.'

'I'm pleased you stayed with me,' she replied. There was a short silence. 'Arnold—'

He could see she was troubled but he felt helpless. He was reluctant to discuss with her what he guessed was on both their minds. He could hardly explain his reluctance to himself, let alone her, and he shifted uneasily in his seat.

'Arnold — last night, at the hotel I . . . I said certain things.'

'Yes.'

'I don't know what came over me. I guess it was tension . . . an early homesickness maybe—'

'Before you've even gone.' He smiled wryly.

She flushed. It had been the wrong response to make. She looked at him levelly. 'Well, it's all been so rushed. I've hardly had time to turn around, to think things through. The speed of it all . . . and when the offer came—'

'Jane, there's no need to go into this. I think the whole thing is great — it's too good an offer, too good an opportunity to miss. I'm delighted for you that your last book did so well and now, with the New York thing coming through . . .'

She stared at him and he was unable to read the expression in her eyes. He suspected she wanted to speak of matters other than the New York offer and was hurt that he was so defensive in his responses. She sat quietly, her left hand toying absent-mindedly with her coffee cup.

He knew there should be something he could say to fill in the gap that had yawned in their relationship last night; he knew there was something still unsaid this morning, the remains of a conversation that had begun in the darkness of the hotel room. But the words wouldn't come. He feared it would be dishonest to say what she wanted to hear, and he felt ill at ease, out of sorts with himself.

When Jane's book, *Dark Dragon*, had come out last year it had been an instant success. Her agent had advised her that there was considerable Continental and American interest in the novel, not least because of the sweep of its theme ranging from London to Paris to New York and Washington in the mid-nineteenth century. The auction the agent had conducted thereafter had been immensely successful: a bid came in from a leading publisher in the States and the film rights were snapped up by a New York production company. But they had wanted her out there, soon: a lecture stint to promote the publication, discussions with the scriptwriters, the raising of her author profile for a book that they felt was going to storm into the best-seller lists.

Her initial excitement had been infectious, and Arnold had been delighted for her. There had been much to do by way of preparation: travel arrangements, someone to look after the bookshop on the Quayside in Newcastle, provisions to ensure the security of her bungalow in Framwellgate. But for the last week or so a change had come over her, she had been somewhat withdrawn; he had seen little of her, she seemed to find excuses not to meet him for dinner, and when he had finally suggested taking her to the airport, for her flight to London and then onward to New York, she had seemed oddly reluctant.

'I'm not sure it's a good idea,' she had said. 'I hate goodbyes.'

'I know what you mean, train stations and airports and all that. But we have to say goodbye at some stage and I'd rather do it at the airport than earlier. I'd like to see you off. It's an early-morning flight, so maybe I could pick you up at Framwellgate — so you needn't worry about making arrangements for your car — then we could drive to the airport, check in at the hotel and spend your last evening together. That way I'd be on hand to see you off in the morning.'

He had finally persuaded her. But the evening had not been a great success. Their conversation had been somewhat brittle, they had both felt awkward without quite knowing why, and there was an inexplicable difficulty in finding anything to say to each other. And then later, in the darkness of the hotel room, they had lain side by side, silently, for a long time before she had talked, words tumbling out, seemingly oblivious of his silence. In the dark they could barely see each other, but they were touching, close, and yet oddly distant.

The coffee cup rattled as Jane pushed it aside and glanced up at Arnold. Her eyes were shadowed and serious. 'Look, I'm sorry that I was a bit, well, pushy last night.'

'I wouldn't have said—'

'I was *pushy*,' she interrupted him with determination. 'And very female, for God's sake! I suppose it's all down to the flurry of the last few weeks. I just haven't had time to get my act together. All the rushing around, arrangements to be made, phone calls from the States, trying to set up this damned lecture tour, all that sort of rubbish. It just isn't me, and I guess it got to me, made me edgy. Maybe it's all been a bit too much, a bit too frenetic.' She observed him carefully. 'I think I was panicking a bit. I said things I shouldn't have said — made requests that were unfair.'

'There's no need to panic,' Arnold replied evasively, shaking his head and failing to meet her glance. 'I'll be here when you get back. We can talk then . . .'

'It's going to be three months, Arnold.'

'So? We've been friends for three years or more — what's three months?'

Even as he said it, he knew the words and the tone were wrong. It was true they had been friends for years, albeit a somewhat prickly friendship for some of that time, but they had recently become lovers and the relationship had changed in consequence. Possibly not enough, though. In the warm darkness last night Jane had talked, and her emotional defences had come down. While not asking him directly what their future together might be, she had made it clear, if somewhat hesitantly, that she felt there was a gap in their relationship, on her side an understated desire for some commitment — and that perhaps it was time for a declaration of just what they meant to each other.

He had sensed that the moment she'd asked the question she had regretted it. His own silence had made matters worse, but the confusion in his mind made it impossible for him to answer her immediately. He was fond of Jane, he enjoyed their lovemaking, but their friendship was important to him. To go further, to talk of a commitment at a time when she was leaving for the States for a three-month stay, during which anything might happen, had seemed to him unwise. In his silence, she had turned away and her back was stiff. He had watched the dawn break, sleeplessly.

Jane glanced up at the monitor display, the flight was being called. Arnold took her hand. 'There's no rush. They'll just be sitting in the holding lounge. Jane, I'm sorry there's this tension between us. It's my fault—'

'No, it's mine,' she interrupted firmly. 'I was being particularly stupid last night. I know you well, Arnold, maybe better than you know yourself. We've been friends, we are still friends, and it's not necessary that we should attempt to redefine that relationship just because we've got closer these last few months. I'm being a typical woman — tearful at a parting, fearful of the future uncertainties — and I despise myself for it. As I despise myself for my weakness last night. I know you'll be here when I get back — whenever that'll be — and there was no need for me to ask you what you felt for me. I know how you feel . . .'

She knew him for what he was, he thought glumly. Introverted, controlled, unwilling to expose his innermost feelings to anyone because that way lay injury and hurt. Maybe it was something he had learned, inadvertently, from his father. The long walks they had taken together in the dales of Yorkshire, the seeking out of quiet places, delving into the ancient hearts of long-dead communities, it had all had an impact on him, moulding his character and fixing his flaws to such an extent that while most people seemed at ease with him, he remained doubtful and wary, careful in his relationships.

The thought made him uneasy. Jane was rising, reaching for her hand luggage. 'I'd better go. I'm always nervous at airports. They make my knees turn to water.'

He took her bag from her and walked her down the stairs to the control desk. She looked at him, smiled, then took him by the shoulders. She kissed him. 'I'll see you when I get back, Arnold. And don't look so downcast. I'll ring you when I reach New York.'

'I'll look forward to hearing from you.'

She stared at him searchingly. 'And good luck with the inquiry.'

He nodded. There seemed nothing more either could say.

Their eyes were seeking an escape from the tension of the moment; she took her hand luggage from him and he kissed her again on the cheek. 'Take care.'

She walked briskly past the desk and was hidden from sight. Arnold hesitated, then after a few minutes he walked up the stairs and made his way to the café window. He stood there silently for almost twenty minutes until at last he caught sight of her among the other passengers, making their way up the steps to the Heathrow-bound flight. He watched it take off glittering brightly in the sunshine and he turned away.

He returned to the main concourse, made his way to the car park and drove north, back to the office. There was an emptiness in his chest. The sad thing was that he could not be certain whether it was due to Jane's leaving, or his own disappointment in himself.

2

Some things at least never changed.

Miss Sansom, private secretary to Mr Brent-Ellis, Director of Museums and Antiquities, had never made any secret of her dislike for Arnold or, for that matter, of any member of the staff who somehow contrived to make her employer's life more difficult than she would have wished. Miss Sansom was of Valkyrian build, her mouth was like a steel trap and she wore a perpetual scowl, it seemed to Arnold. Her manner was that of a Teutonic Cerberus: tough, sharp-tongued, protective and uncompromising. Her dreams were probably full of stock whips. When he entered her domain, the small ante-room between the twin offices of Simon Brent-Ellis and Karen Stannard, she usually made a point of ignoring him; now, she barely glanced up from her word processor.

'He's not in,' she growled ferociously, as though blaming him for the event.

'I wasn't really expecting to see Mr Brent-Ellis,' Arnold offered. 'It was just a matter of checking with you.'

'Me?' The effrontery of it made her swing her chair to glare at him. 'What do you want with me?'

'You'll have the timetable for the inquiry, I presume, since Mr Brent-Ellis will be called. I understand I also will

14

be interviewed and since I suppose they'll take departmental staff in sequence—'

'The Director,' she interrupted glacially, 'will be presenting himself before the committee at ten this morning. He will be followed by Miss Stannard.' She almost spat out the name. She had conceived a vast loathing for Karen Stannard, not least because she saw the deputy director as having interposed herself between Miss Sansom and Mr Brent-Ellis. The fact that Karen Stannard was also extremely beautiful may have had something to do with it. She glowered at Arnold. 'You'll be called in after their interviews are finished.'

'This afternoon?'

Miss Sansom swung back to her word processor. 'I've no idea. You'll be called when you're required.'

None the wiser for his brief discussion with Miss Sansom, Arnold returned to his office. He glanced out of the window at the car park below, Karen Stannard's car was there so she was in early enough, waiting for her call to the inquiry. Arnold sighed, it was a bad business, and getting worse. But it was pointless worrying about it, trying to work out which direction the inquiry would head in. There was still work to be done, files to immerse himself in, a backlog to clear.

He settled down to check the file on top of the pile on his desk, a list of a collection of Mesolithic flints and artefacts which had been offered to the museum service. The donor was an ex-Army colonel who had inherited the collection from his father, a somewhat eccentric amateur archaeologist who had spent thirty years burrowing on the upland moors and in the deep-cut valleys of Northumberland for remains of prehistoric settlements. He had been surprisingly successful until arthritis had cut back his activity — 'too much working in wet bogs' he had scribbled in an addendum to his will. His son, the colonel, had kept the collection intact but had never been particularly interested in it and now wished it to be held in one of the town museums for which the department was responsible. There were three conflicting claims on which

Arnold had to adjudicate, from museums who felt their status might be enhanced by the collection.

He was immersed in the file when he became aware of someone standing in the doorway. He glanced up and mentally groaned. Jerry Picton was universally disliked in the department but seemed to possess a protective shell that left him impervious to slight. He was a small man, lean, with pitted skin, narrow eyes and a weasely mouth. His teeth were badly stained: nicotine, Arnold guessed. Arnold was always cool towards him, for the man was a dangerous, malicious gossip, but his obvious disdain seemed to have little effect on Jerry Picton. The man was not easily dismissed or discouraged.

'So, Arnold, what's new?'

Arnold shook his head, saying nothing.

'Big day today, isn't it?' Picton went on, unabashed. 'Start of the inquiry and all that. You think there's any significance in the fact that they're starting with us — our department, I mean?'

'I haven't thought about it.'

'But Brent-Ellis is first in, after all, and the beautiful Miss Stannard after him. Then I guess it'll be your turn.' He grinned wolfishly. 'Better you behind her than having her at your back, you reckon, Arnold?'

Dejectedly, Arnold leaned back in his chair and folded his arms. 'Is there anything in particular you want?'

'Passing the time of day, that's all! You a bit grouchy this morning, Arnold? Had a bad night? Or have you got an uneasy conscience about the inquiry?'

'What's that supposed to mean?'

'Hey, just testing! But it is a bit queer, though, isn't it, that they start with Brent-Ellis and his department when all the signs were that it was going to be an investigation into leaks from the council departments as a whole. Or have I missed something?'

The man's nostrils seemed to flare in anticipation. Arnold stared at him with distaste. 'I think it's extremely unlikely you've missed anything.'

'Thanks for the compliment. Tell you what, though, my guess is it won't be an easy ride for any of us. You heard who'll be in the chair?'

'No.'

'Councillor Mulberry,' Picton announced triumphantly. 'And we can all guess what that means, can't we?'

'Can we?'

'If we've got two short hairs to rub together, we can! You know he's got a boat to row and this inquiry could give him just the muscle he needs on the council. I tell you, Arnold, I'm bloody glad I'm not among those who are being carpeted by the committee. I'm anaemic, me — I can't afford to lose the sort of blood that Mulberry's like to howl for. Flaming vampire, that one. Still, who knows? Maybe Miss Karen Stannard might do her tart-of-the-month trick on him. It's felled lesser men. But you know all about that, don't you?'

There was a veiled insinuation in his tone. Arnold chose to ignore it. 'I've work to do,' he said.

'Ain't we all, my friend . . . But these are interesting times, don't you think? I mean, what would happen in the department if Brent-Ellis and Karen Stannard got censured? The powers that be would have to look for a replacement, wouldn't they. Makes you wonder who'd be the natural . . . and what he might do to get placed in the running.'

A stab of anger flashed through Arnold's chest at the innuendo. He glanced up in irritation but Picton was raising a hand, grinning with stained teeth as he backed away into the corridor. He whistled as he walked away, back to his own office. There was a sour taste in Arnold's mouth.

Councillor Mulberry. Jerry Picton could be right. Mulberry was coming up for re-election in a month or so. A forty-year-old successful small businessman, he had joined the council some six years ago and had shown himself to be an aggressive councillor and a sharp-tongued commit-teeman. He was known to be ambitious. He had sold his business interests to a large company just before he entered politics and had since made no secret of his desire to rise in the party. There was gossip in the town that Mulberry would want to use his position on the council as a stepping stone to Parliament in due course. He kept the right company, joined select dinner parties, showed off his somewhat flashy wife — twelve years his junior — and cultivated all the right people. There was sufficient evidence from his committee work to suggest that he was not above undermining other people's interests to further his own: he was recognized to be ruthless, able and committed. Arnold understood he could also be charming, but he had never been sufficiently closely involved to make a judgement on the matter.

And Picton's gossip was that he'd be chairing the inquiry. That could mean trouble for someone, Arnold guessed. And Brent-Ellis hated being in any firing line, anywhere.

He worked on at his desk and lunch time came and went.

Brent-Ellis's car had arrived shortly before ten and was still there at four. By four thirty it had gone, though Karen Stannard's vehicle remained in the car park. She was probably undergoing her grilling at the inquiry session. The committee room where the inquiry was being held was still blazing with lights when Arnold finally went down to his own car at five thirty. It seemed that the committee was taking its job seriously, and both Brent-Ellis and Karen Stannard would be having a rough ride.

Arnold did not sleep well that night. He was in a strange, indeterminate mood. Thoughts of Jane on her transatlantic venture were confused with consideration of what he would be asked at the inquiry, when it came to his turn. When he went to work next morning he felt jaded, and his eyelids were sore. He did not feel in best form to face Mr Mulberry and his committee.

In the event the call did not come until late that afternoon. Miss Sansom rang him. 'You're required in the committee room,' she snapped.

Arnold went immediately.

They were ranged in inquisitorial fashion along one side of the committee table: Powell Frinton, the cold, ascetic chief executive; a committee clerk called Edwards, there to take the minutes; and two councillors — Franklin and Jerrold both of whom Arnold knew only slightly. As Jerry Picton had predicted, the chairman was Councillor Mulberry, and seated on his immediate right was a thickset, pinstripe-suited man with a sour mouth and hooded eyes. There was a single chair placed in front of the group. At the chairman's gesture, Arnold took it. Mulberry stared at him, grim-visaged.

'Mr Landon . . . I think you'll know everyone in the room with the possible exception of the gentleman on my right. He is here by my invitation, Mr Perriman, of the legal department of a large commercial firm who specialize in cases of this kind.'

Arnold was not sure quite what was meant by 'cases of this kind'; perhaps Mulberry caught some of his uncertainty. The chairman smiled thinly. 'I have been advised that the best way to commence proceedings with each witness is to spell out precisely what the scope and aims of this inquiry are to be. So I'll begin by explaining that you are here in the capacity of a witness only, at this stage . . .' He paused, and there was a hint of menace in the air. 'Of course, your status might change as the inquiry proceeds and other witnesses are called. You will be aware we have already interviewed Mr Brent-Ellis and Miss Stannard.'

Mulberry's eyes were a sharp blue, intense and glittering. He was broad-shouldered, well dressed, and possessed an air of controlled antagonism, like a snake coiled to strike. His nose was fleshy and there was a hard dissatisfaction about his mouth that suggested life had still not given him all he desired and thought he deserved. He exuded confidence and the illusion of power; his fingers were thick, clenched on the tabletop as he held Arnold's glance with a cold calculation, probing for weakness, and ready to take advantage of any he discerned. His voice was deep and resonant, trained for the hustings.

'There has probably been enough speculation in the newspapers of late,' he was saying, 'for you to have at least some idea of what this inquiry is about. It's as well, however, that I give you some further detail. You'll no doubt be aware that considerable disquiet has been expressed in the council chamber of recent months concerning the standard of support that councillors feel they are getting from the senior salaried officers in this council. Issues of incompetence have been mooted — but these can very largely be dealt with. What is of greater moment is the question of executive staff loyalty . . .'

He paused, glanced sideways towards Powell Frinton as though expecting the chief executive to say something. Powell Frinton remained silent, his cold, elegant features impassive, his mouth a thin grim line. After a brief pause, Mulberry continued.

'We shall be directing our attention in this committee to a number of specific issues which have caused concern. One, clearly, is the leaking of details of the proposed development up at Hawley Spur. It led to an ill-informed demonstration that resulted, unfortunately, in the withdrawal of our commercial partners who were frightened off by the environmental issues that were erroneously raised by certain . . . activists. Then there is the matter of disclosure of commercial contract details from the Department of Legal Administration — the department from which our chief executive was promoted some years ago.'

Again he paused; Arnold gained the impression he was baiting Powell Frinton, but the man made no response. He was holding himself in. It was possible he had already been scarred by the rasp-edge of Mulberry's tongue during the interviews with Arnold's superior officers, and had developed stoicism in the face of veiled malice.

'You'll forgive me,' Arnold said in the brief silence, 'but I'm not sure that I'd have anything to say that would be of assistance in your deliberations on the matters you've mentioned.'

'I was filling in background,' Mulberry sneered, 'as I've been advised to with all witnesses. However, I'll take your point. Enough of generalities. In the interests of expedition, perhaps we should move on to those areas where it's suggested you would have something to offer by way of information. I refer, of course, to the Cossman International affair.'

A coldness gripped Arnold. It was perhaps inevitable that the Cossman business would be wound into this rather more wide-ranging investigation — witch-hunt, some of the staff were calling it — of the relationships between staff and councillors that seemed to have soured of recent months.

'For the record,' Mulberry stated, glancing at the committee clerk, 'I'll outline the facts. The construction company Cossman International entered into a relationship with a trust company to purchase certain land for the construction of leisure-centre facilities. They demonstrated considerable regard for interests which are covered by your department, Mr Landon, when they allowed, and indeed enhanced access to the Ravenstone site for archaeological purposes. We needn't go into the unfortunate incidents that then occurred but will confine ourselves to those matters which affect your department and this inquiry. We have reason to believe that during the course of those events there was a deliberate leaking of information from this department which has led directly to the commencement of legal proceedings against the council.'

They would have raised this with both Brent-Ellis and Karen Stannard. Arnold could guess how Brent-Ellis would have reacted: sweating, panicked, seeking to lay blame anywhere but at his own door, effusive in his stammering denials and protestations of innocence. Karen Stannard would have been cold, controlled, maybe even showing some icy fury . . . but what would she have said?

What line had Karen Stannard taken? It would have been useful to know.

Mulberry riffled through some papers on the table in front of him and grimaced. 'What has happened, of course, should have been foreseen at the time . . . and maybe Mr Powell Frinton should have taken appropriate steps to stifle the whole problem at source. But there is no doubt now as to the outcome: we are to be involved in a lengthy and possibly financially crippling lawsuit as a result of events that took place in this department.'

'Mr Mulberry—'

'I'll continue,' Mulberry interrupted coldly. 'You'll get your chance in a while. I think the facts are not in dispute. You, Mr Landon, were instructed by your superior officer, Miss Karen Stannard, to produce a report on the involvement of Cossman International in the development of the site at Ravenstone — a development which your department was overseeing.'

'That's right, but—'

'The report should have been factual, accurate and non-libellous. However, you chose to stray from the strictly professional path laid out for you and you interviewed the solicitor advising the trust involved, and as a result of these discussions you chose to make certain statements and assumptions which you included in your report. The find-ings — which in my view strayed beyond your brief — were then transmitted to a television company which saw fit to give wider utterance to the statements — unsubscribed, of course, like all gutter journalism — in the report by way of hints and insinuations. It is in respect of those statements that we now find ourselves, as a council, made party to a lawsuit for libel. I think, at that point, I might ask you to comment, Mr Landon.'

Arnold's throat was dry with anger. He could see where the investigation was headed, and he knew that Brent-Ellis would have run swiftly for cover, whatever Karen Stannard had said. 'I'll just make this comment, Mr Mulberry. The report that I wrote was made in good faith and was not libel-lous, because the statements it contained were accurate.'

The grim-faced solicitor, Perriman, leaned forward. He permitted himself a wintry smile. 'A matter yet to be deter-mined, I believe, in the relevant court of law.'

'Nor was it libellous,' Arnold insisted, 'in that it was delivered to persons who had an interest in receiving it.'

'The television public?' Mulberry scoffed. 'Rumours that had not been proved founded in fact?'

'No,' Arnold replied coldly. 'The officers in the department. My report was an internal document, submitted inter-
nally and discussed only in the department. They had an
interest in receiving it so as far as I'm concerned the "libel",
as you call it, was not disseminated.'

'Until you leaked its contents to the television company.'

'No.'

'Then who did? It was your report. Very few people
saw it otherwise. Mr Brent-Ellis; Miss Stannard; maybe a
copy typist. The fact is, Mr Landon, the contents of your
report were used by the television company . . . with unfortunate results, as we know, for the female presenter who used
them. But we are not concerned with her subsequent death.
Our concern is to discover exactly what happened to that
report, how that information came to be placed in the public
domain, and how it all seems to fit into a pattern of diso-
bedience, malicious intervention and professional incompetence, not only in this department but throughout the whole
authority!'

Mulberry's voice had risen; the lawyer at his side leaned
towards him and whispered something in a low tone. Powell
Frinton remained impassive, while the other two councillors
shifted uneasily in their seats. Mulberry glared at Arnold. 'I
ask you once more. Did you leak that report to the television
company, Mr Landon?'

'I did not.'

'Then who did?'

'I cannot say.'

'Or won't say?' He paused, his lip curling unpleasantly.
'What is your relationship with Miss Stannard, Landon?'

'I don't understand the question.'

'Do you admire her?' Mulberry sneered.

'She is my senior officer and I have considerable respect
for her professional competence.'

Mulberry glowered. 'That's not what I was asking.'

'Then, with respect,' Arnold responded icily, 'I would
suggest you be more specific — just what *were* you asking?'

Mulberry was nettled. He opened his mouth to speak and Perriman leaned towards him again, whispering urgently. Mulberry grimaced and shook his head in frustration, but he was in control again. He leaned forward, staring at Arnold. 'All right, let's be clear. This committee is investigating the behaviour of senior departmental officers in the authority, both for their incompetence and their malicious subversion of council policies. This department is being investigated first of all, because there is an additional element — a lawsuit against the television company by Cossman International. The fact that their chairman is in prison is irrelevant. The company exists apart from him and is now seeking damages from the television people — and we've been joined in the action since it was your report which seems to have sparked the whole thing off. Now I want the whole truth, Landon, every step of the way. I want for the record a full statement of what you said and did, what you found out, who you gave that report to and who you discussed it with. You can start right now — and give me all the detail.'

And after that they'd check it against the statements of Simon Brent-Ellis and Karen Stannard. Arnold had the sinking feeling that he was going to be all alone in this, alone and hung out to dry.

An hour later he passed Jerry Picton in the car park. 'Really pissed off, ain't they?' Picton called out cheerfully.

* * *

The next thirty-six hours dragged by. Arnold felt unsettled. He received a phone call from Jane but it was brief and she sounded tired, probably still suffering from jet lag. She had been given a schedule of interviews and meetings with script-writers and she was already concerned about the amount of activity she was to be involved in. She made no mention of their last evening together.

Rumours in the department were shuttled about by Jerry Picton, but Arnold tried to keep well away from them and their purveyor. He had plenty of work to occupy him, and yet he found it difficult to concentrate. He kept going over what he had said to the inquiry, concerned that while he had told the truth generally, there were some things he had not disclosed. But they had been matters of confidence between him and Karen Stannard, and he owed no loyalty to Mulberry, had little sympathy with what the man was doing. It all smacked of electioneering and Arnold had no doubt that when the time came, a great deal would be made of the inquiry, to put Mulberry in a favourable light with the electorate.

Three other people were interviewed from the department but Arnold heard nothing that concerned his own part in the Cossman International affair. It seemed that the inquiry had moved on to the question of general morale in the department. On the Friday afternoon he had managed to get through most of the backlog of files on his desk — even though he felt that his powers of concentration had failed him in dealing with them — when one of the young girls who worked in the front office tapped on his door and entered with an armful of additional files.

'What are these?' Arnold asked in surprise.

'Dunno, Mr Landon. I was just told to bring them to you, like.'

'Where did they come from?'

'Miss Stannard, I think.'

Arnold frowned. He glanced at a few of the covers. They were files he had not seen before, and some of them concerned the kind of policy issues that Karen Stannard normally kept jealously to herself. He nodded to the girl, who stood waiting there uneasily. 'All right, I'll find out about this myself.'

He glanced through a few more of the files. One of the committees serviced by Karen Stannard figured prominently. He frowned, puzzled. There was only one way to find out what was going on. He walked along the corridor to the ante-room where Miss Sansom reigned with her word processor.

She raised her head as he entered. She seemed to be in as good a mood as she had ever experienced, to his knowledge. She almost smiled, and her normal growl had turned to a malicious purr. 'Mr Landon . . . the files have arrived then?'

'The files?' He stared at her, annoyed that she had guessed the reason for his visit. 'Is Miss Stannard in her office?'

There was a gloating element in Miss Sansom's voice. 'The deputy director is in, yes. For the moment. And I'm sure she'll want to see you.' She pressed the buzzer on her desk and announced his presence. There was a short pause, and then he heard Karen Stannard's voice.

'Send him in.'

Miss Sansom waved a negligently triumphant hand and Arnold, still puzzled and not a little nettled, tapped on Karen Stannard's door and went in.

Karen Stannard was standing behind her desk, leaning against the windowsill. The sunlight streaming in through the window behind her struck natural russet-gold highlights in her hair. He was reminded again of the difficulty he experienced in categorizing anything about her: the colour of her hair and of her eyes, what motivated her, the nature of the relationship between them — part competition, part dislike, but always unpredictable. She wore a dark skirt that accentuated the curve of her hips and length of her legs; the formal, almost severe white blouse, buttoned high at the throat, oddly emphasized her femininity. Her wide mouth was half smiling, though it was an enigmatic smile in which Arnold detected a degree of cynical contempt. He had always found it difficult to read her mind or predict her behaviour. She was utterly beautiful, and he had seen her warmth, had even felt her respect from time to time — and yet there was still a barrier between them, a prickly hedge of uncertainty and wariness. And now, contempt.

'Mr Landon,' she said, in a carefully modulated tone, 'I thought you might want to call in to see me today.'

'I've received some files—'

'I'm sure you'll be able to handle them,' She folded her left arm across her breasts, raised her right hand to caress her cheek thoughtfully. 'After all, you've worked hard to get them.'

'I don't understand,' Arnold looked at her desk. It was clear of papers. He glanced at the filing cabinet: its drawers were opened, as though they had been cleared. 'What's going on?'

'Surely,' she purred, 'you of all people can guess. You probably had a hand in it — you might even have been the major mover.'

He stared at her. 'I don't know what you're talking about.'

Her smile became hard-edged. Her eyes glittered, and there was an angry bitterness in their depths. 'You mean you haven't heard? Come, Mr Landon, you must know.'

'Know what?'

'I've been suspended.'

Arnold stared at her in surprise. He was silent, unable to muster his thoughts beyond a panicked attempt to recall precisely what he might have said to Mulberry at the inquiry. It was as though Karen Stannard guessed what he was thinking; she came forward, rested her hands on the desk and fixed him with a contemptuous glance.

'You must surely have guessed it would come to this, and fairly quickly. After all, you told them what happened in the Cossman business didn't you? How you gave me the report. How you weren't the one to break confidences. How you certainly couldn't vouch for your deputy director, on the other hand. And how Karen Stannard was friendly with the woman who was presenting the television programme—'

'I said nothing of the sort,' Arnold interposed angrily. 'I was pressed to suggest how the information might have leaked out, but I made no such remarks. I denied leaking the report details myself, certainly, but I made no comment—'

'You're a bloody liar, Landon.'

He was surprised by the coolness of her tone. She was clearly unimpressed by his protestations and convinced that he had pointed the finger at her in front of the committee. 'I'm not lying,' he insisted, quietly.

She smiled cynically. 'Why bother with the charade, Landon? I know perfectly well what makes you tick. I've always known you were one to watch. You want the job that was given to me, and although there was a time when I thought . . . Well, no matter, it's unimportant. In time all things are revealed, and you've shown what a little worm you are. Well, I've been suspended, and the way is clear for you to wheedle your way into this office.'

He was silent for a while, staring at her. The smile faded on her lips after a few moments and she betrayed a certain unease; the hostility in her glance changed, became tinged with uncertainty. 'I say again,' he remarked, 'I did not implicate you before the committee.'

The denial seemed to inflame her once more. 'You know damn well it was I who gave the information to that woman!' she flared. 'But I gave it as a friend, not expecting her to use it. And only you knew about it — I damn well told you, after all. But that was in confidence!'

'And I kept the confidence.'

'Until you told the committee!'

'I swear to you—'

She shook her head impatiently. 'What the hell is this all about, Landon? I knew you'd come in here to gloat, but I didn't expect this weaselly attempt to deny that you're to blame. What the hell do you expect to gain by it? My thanks? My goodwill? You've won, dammit — why go through this pretence? The committee have decided to suspend me until they've talked to all witnesses in all other matters that are bothering them — but I'm the first casualty, and I bet I'll be the only casualty in this department.' Her voice had risen, as bitterness took root. 'I've no illusions about any of this, Landon. I've not been liked here, because I was an outsider, because I'm efficient and because I'm a woman. None of you like it, me being here, running the damned department while that idiot of a director spends his time on the golf course!'

There was some truth in what she said, although her own attitudes had contributed to the fear and dislike in which she was held.

'And I can guess how you'll be feeling,' she raged, 'now I'm side-lined. You can feather your own nest, take my job—'

'This is foolish,' he interrupted hotly. 'I have no brief for the committee — I don't like the way Mulberry is going about things. I suspect it's all politically motivated, the whole inquiry. And as for wanting your job, I've never wanted it, never sought it. It's your own damned insecurity that's causing the trouble in this department, and your misplaced feminism that's now seeking to place blame on me and maybe other men in the department, for your own failings and lack of popular support!'

She was astonished. Her eyes widened, they suddenly seemed very green. She was silent, her tongue flickering over her lips as though they were suddenly dry. She gave a light grunt of disbelief. 'Well, well . . . You've never spoken to me like that while you've been working for me, Landon.'

'I've never had reason to.'

She smiled, edgily. 'I would have thought I've given you plenty of occasion.'

'You haven't called me a liar before.'

'I've called you sneaky, untrustworthy, active behind my back . . .'

'There's a difference,' he replied doggedly. 'You've held opinions about me, based on an interpretation of my behaviour. You're entitled to those — even if they were wrong — as I'm entitled to my opinions about you. But to call me a liar is different. I've not lied to you. And I didn't implicate you in front of the committee.'

Her eyes were fixed on him, searchingly, and as the anger in his veins slowly died he became aware of how incredibly beautiful she was. It reminded him of a moment, a few months ago, when she had been aroused by the violence around her, shaken from her normal control and in a moment of heady triumph she had kissed him . . . and he recalled the sensation of her mouth on his. Perhaps there was something in his eyes that communicated his thoughts to her because suddenly she turned away, confusion bringing a frown to her face.

'I'm not convinced,' she muttered. 'But it doesn't matter, anyway. I'm out of here, suspended on full pay until they can make up their measly political minds. As to what part you played in it, what the hell does it matter?'

It mattered to him. He hesitated, then shrugged, realizing further protestations were useless. 'I'm sorry.'

She laughed mockingly. 'Now *that* I certainly can't believe. But if I'm wrong in my interpretation and you really are sorry, don't worry about me. I can always get a job. In fact, during my suspension, I've no problem. I'd already been asked to undertake some consultancy for the university, at a dig beyond Alnwick. So what the hell — I can enjoy myself, and get paid my full salary in the process. Until I get back here.'

Her mood changed again, the mockery suddenly giving way to defiance as she fixed him with a fierce glare. 'And you can be damned sure I *will* get back, believe me, my friend! Suspension is one thing — sacking is something else again. I might be a woman but I can kick, scratch and bite with the rest of you. I tell you, I don't give up a fight easily!'

'Of that,' Arnold said quietly, 'I'm already well aware.'

3

The local newspapers were quick to give coverage to the inquiry. The taking of witness statements by Councillor Mulberry and his committee had been in camera so there was no direct reporting of what had been said or done. This, Arnold noted cynically, gave Mulberry free rein to make statements to the press, in portentous, ostensibly guarded but nevertheless damaging tones. As chairman he was the obvious person to give out statements concerning the conduct of the inquiry. On the other hand, it was clear he was milking the situation for all it was worth and gaining a higher political profile for himself in the process.

The culmination came on the following Thursday.

Arnold had heard little during the course of the week about the proceedings themselves; interviews with staff of his own department had concluded, and he understood the Legal Administration department had been put to the knife thereafter. He wondered what Powell Frinton would be thinking about that.

But there was nothing emerging from the committee room — in that at least Mulberry was keeping a tight rein on tongues. Even Jerry Picton had been unable to glean anything and was walking around the department with a mournful look in his eye, his *raison d'être* gone for the moment.

Karen Stannard's departure had, naturally, caused a stir. Once she had cleared her desk the story had flashed around the department like wildfire, and yet, to Arnold's surprise, after the initial chattering the reaction was somewhat muted. She had been feared rather than popular, disliked rather than respected, but people seemed disinclined to talk much about her now that she was on suspension. It could have been a 'don't speak ill of the dead' attitude, but Arnold doubted that. He guessed it was because there was a feeling she wouldn't be so easily got rid of. She could yet be reinstated — and unguarded comments now could lead to painful repercussions later.

It was on the Thursday evening that Councillor Mulberry gave his views a wider airing. Arnold had returned home from the office at six thirty and was busy making himself a meal. He had prepared the vegetables and opened a bottle of wine; he was tasting it with reflective pleasure as he turned on the television set in the sitting room. He had switched on to a current affairs programme, beamed from Newcastle. The interviewer wore a dark suit and serious frown to denote the importance both of the programme and himself.

'Various suppositions have appeared in the media of late about an internal inquiry set up by the local authority to investigate, it seems, its own organs. This evening,' the interviewer intoned, 'we've been able to persuade Councillor Frank Mulberry to come along and explain just what's been going on in our local political world recently. We've all seen the reports in the newspapers this last week, and read, shall we say, rather terse and uninformative statements of the "No Comment" variety from Mr Mulberry. But he's come along to the studio tonight prepared, we hope, to tell us a bit more about the inquiry than we've been told so far . . .'

The camera switched to Councillor Mulberry, looking rather heavier than he did in the flesh; dark-suited, matching the interviewer's serious frown, with his sandy hair carefully groomed and the wings of grey above his ears prominent, shining in the arc lamps of the studio. He looked as distinguished as he would have hoped, Arnold thought sourly as he went back into the kitchen to check on the chicken Kiev he was heating in the oven.

Through the open door he could hear the interviewer sketch in Mulberry's background.

'Mr Mulberry was, as we all know, one of the bright successes of the Thatcher era — a prominent entrepreneur who built up a business here in the north-east, serving the community needs at the same time that he made, may I say, a well-deserved fortune. A local man, of course, Durham born and bred, he was elected to the council about six years ago . . . Mr Mulberry, you were seen as one of the exciting prospects at the time, for the council, I mean. A successful businessman in your own right, you were heralded as bringing a breath of fresh air into the local political scene.'

Mulberry emitted a sincere laugh and waved a self-deprecating hand. 'I don't know about that. You exaggerate, I suspect. But I suppose there was a certain amount of staleness in the development of council policies, a feeling of stagnation. I certainly came forward with the intention of opening a few windows. As to whether I've succeeded, that's for others to say.'

'So you gave up the world of business to devote your energies to local politics.'

'Not quite . . .' The chicken Kiev was browning nicely, so Arnold returned to the sitting room, sipping his wine. '. . . I'd come to a sort of watershed in my life: I'd achieved all my objectives, reached my goals,' Mulberry was saying. 'I'd built a number of nursing homes, there were systems put in, and when a likely purchaser made me an offer I couldn't refuse . . .' He tapped his fleshy nose and gave a knowing wink, backed up by his sincere laugh again. 'Well, it seemed to be the right time for a new challenge, though by then I had decided I was totally committed to politics and doing what I could for the community, other than in the area of community nursing which is where my previous business interests lay.'

33

'And now you have no business interests?'

'None. I don't think it's compatible with the kind of work I want to do on the council.'

'How do you mean?'

Mulberry leaned forward, his brow furrowed, and he stroked his heavy chin thoughtfully. 'Well, let me put it like this. Politicians need to be Caesar's wife, you know what I mean? They can't afford to say one thing, and do another. Too many politicians get their fingers grubby while they're in office, that's not my style. I have an advantage, of course, I don't need to make money. I've done that, been there. Now, I can serve the public with a clear conscience. And that means I can speak my mind, without fear or favour.'

Arnold took a long, cynical sip of his wine, and shook his head slowly. A hint of garlic reached him from the kitchen.

'Does this in any way amount to a reflection of what you're doing at the present inquiry, Mr Mulberry?' the interviewer asked.

'You could say that, yes,' Mulberry replied, leaning back easily in his chair. He waved a confident hand. 'I was responsible for setting up this inquiry. I saw a problem; I decided something had to be done. By me. I've always been a front-runner and a man who speaks his mind. I was born in Durham, but I had a Yorkshire pitman father. That explains a lot in my character. Not all politicians are like that, prepared to speak up for what they think is right — they're too concerned with looking over their shoulders, protecting their backs. Me, I've got a broad back and I don't mind the occasional knife.'

'Are you suggesting that your colleagues—'

'I'm not talking about political colleagues,' Mulberry interposed swiftly. He grinned in conspiratorial fashion. 'Of course, there are those on the opposition benches who would dearly like to plant the odd political blade between my shoulders.'

Or put a gag in your mouth to stop the flow of self-serving platitudes, Arnold mused.

'No, in a sense I'm talking about something more serious. It's a matter of gravity for the local political scene, really. You see, things have been going wrong up here for some time. There's been a sort of creeping disease that's affecting the working of our democratic principles here in the north. And it needs stamping on, because it's deadly like a snake, and it denies the power of the people.'

'This is what you're dealing with in the internal inquiry, then?'

Here we go, thought Arnold, the political pitch.

Mulberry was silent, frowning, as though he was considering his words with care. Arnold didn't believe it. The man was a demagogue; he would have prepared every word he uttered, and he would have insisted on knowing in advance the questions he was going to be asked. Not that they were much more than gentle leads, so far. But the programme was not known for its hard-hitting deflation of local luminaries.

'I cannot, of course, go into details as to what we are probing into in the inquiry that I have the honour to chair. It's a matter of pleasure to me that my colleagues have seen fit to place the task in my hands, though that might be a reflection of the fact that it's well known I don't pull my punches when I see things are going wrong. But I can only generalize, you understand, when I talk to you of the committee work.'

'We understand that, Mr Mulberry.'

Arnold clucked his tongue in despair.

'The fact is,' Mulberry continued, 'I have seen a sea change in the relatively short time I've been in local politics. My understanding — which I'm sure is shared by the vast majority — is that politicians are the servants of the people. Our job is to give the public what they want and deserve — and to that end we put forward policies and, if the voters don't like them, they can throw us out of office at the next election.'

'Which is coming up soon, as we know,' the interviewer interrupted.

For a moment Mulberry lost his stride. A certain balefulness came into his glance as he glared at the interviewer, but his recovery was swift, and he managed another sincere smile. 'Sooner than some of us are prepared for, believe me. I always leave my own campaigning until it's almost too late — too much business to be done, you know? However, the disease that I'm talking about lies not in what's happening among the politicians — even my opponents on the council. Rather it lies with the officers — those senior people in the departments who have been appointed to salaried, well-paid positions — to implement the policies that are laid down by their masters, the politicians. You see, these officers — unelected, undemocratic, faceless in their bureaucracies — have come to believe they hold the reins of power; they have the controlling voice; and that is what the inquiry is about. To find out exactly what is going on; to expose the malice, the chicanery, the undermining of authority, and the undemocratic putting up of barriers to the decision making of the council.'

'By senior officers employed by the council! These are strong words, with serious implications, Mr Mulberry.'

'Unpalatable truths! Look here, I'm already uncovering evidence that would suggest there's an organized conspiracy among the senior officers to deliberately oppose some of the policies we're keen to implement for the public good. Things are haggled over in committees; points of order are adjudicated on by officers, not members; advice to proceed slowly is given; unnecessary referrals back to committee are suggested; there are leaks to the press, intended to damage our progress; pressure groups are fed information by disaffected officers in the hope that the democratic process will be slowed down. That's what I'm investigating with my committee; that's the kind of thing I intend to expose. That, and other matters where negligence and incompetence have, additionally, led us to face legal proceedings that could be damaging financially to the authority at large.'

'I presume you're in no position to name names, Mr Mulberry.'

The councillor gave a healthy growl to demonstrate frustration that would yet be overcome by innate determination.

He stuck out a Churchillian under-lip and adopted a statesmanlike tone. 'I'd dearly love to do just that. But I'm a fair man. I believe in waiting until all the evidence is in. And it's going to take time, of course. But in the end—'

'Will you be reporting before the next election?'

Mulberry shook an honest, doubtful head. 'That I can't guarantee. These things take time — and I believe in doing a thorough job. That's the sort of man I am . . .'

Arnold groaned. He had had enough. He turned down the sound and drained his glass, then poured himself another with a feeling of despondency. Mulberry's motivations were as clear as a cloudless sky but far more sinister. He would drag out the inquiry until the election, take advantage of the high profile he was getting, and only come out with his findings afterwards when, if it all turned out to be a damp squib, a gerrymandered structure of hints and insinuations and unsupported claims, he would be back with a secure seat again and careless of the strains he might have put on the system, and on the relationship between the paid officials and the politicians who relied upon them.

Arnold was depressed by the thought. And the chicken Kiev was burned.

* * *

On Saturday morning he was in a better mood. He had decided to drive up to Ravenstone Fell to discover how the dig was going under the direction of Dr Rena Williams. It was the kind of drive he really enjoyed taking since it led him high on the fells, past ruined bridges and dark-earthed embankments, the residue of the railway line that had been cut in the Victorian era and abandoned a hundred years later. There were narrow, high-hedged lanes to drive through, an ancient drover's road to follow, and a long sweep of fell to traverse where he caught distant views of The Cheviot and the thin, blue line of the sea. The scars of the old cuttings were green now, dotted by browsing sheep, and a blue-grey haze hung over the tops of the fells, lifting as the sun rose higher. From the heights he could make out distant patches of mist in the deep-cut valleys, and he drove slowly, taking pleasure in looking about him.

The dig at Ravenstone Fell had been interrupted for a short period when government aid had been withdrawn from the project begun by Cossman International. The original intention had been to use new technology to allow a team of archaeologists to work at the site uncovered by the company's activity. Cossman International had come up with a fascinating proposal: they would erect a huge slab-like structure under which the people at the dig would work in safety, protected from the elements, while construction work on a new leisure centre went on above their heads.

The collapse of government support for the project meant that the only funding came from Northern Heritage and there was no question of the new technology being available. The dig had resumed, however, once the political fallout had ended. Now, as Arnold came over the hill and found himself looking down on the abandoned concrete piles, gaunt reminders of a ruined dream and monuments to a man's ambition, he recalled with a slight shiver the atmosphere they had experienced that day some months ago, when looking at the Celtic icons the workers had uncovered.

Celtic icons in a Saxon grave: it had puzzled the team. There was a small sandstone figurine of a woman, with a horse, distinctive in its anthropomorphic form. In Celtic iconography the horse, dog and bull were god forms, dependent on the animal for their identity and well recognized in the archaeological world. But there had been other, more puzzling sandstone carvings depicting a torso with a boar superimposed; galloping horses with human heads; deities with horns, hooves and animal ears.

He recalled Jane picking up one of the figurines and shuddering. She had turned to him, pale-faced, and said, 'There's a feeling of something almost . . . evil, here.'

Suddenly they all felt it. The small group around the table had fallen silent and the hairs had prickled at the back of Arnold's neck as he had taken the figurine from her. The others were all staring at him, and he had felt that they were experiencing the same images that had begun to dance in his brain: a swirling haze out of which he seemed to hear harsh breathing, the rumble of powerful hooves, the death-cry of a dangerous animal. The thin chanting of long-dead shamans and the cold high whistling of the wind across the ancient fells had rung in his ears as he handled the figurine, the female torso with a bull's head.

And he remembered the excited light which had come into Rena Williams eyes when he had said, 'The great Bull of Cooley had the power to reason and understand, as a human being.'

She had started, nodded. 'That's right. I remember . . . The divine bulls of the Ulster Cycle reached their final form after a series of metamorphoses. Originally, they were divine swineherds but the phenomenon of metamorphosis always played a prominent role in Celtic vernacular tradition. The great Bull of Cooley . . . But to find evidence of such a tradition, here, at Ravenstone . . .'

She had told him she hoped he would help at the site. He knew he wouldn't be able to stay away. It was fanciful, but his head was full of a light singing in the thin, clear air: ancient voices, lost languages, the keening of a decayed culture, dead gods awaiting resurrection in the minds of men.

Rena Williams had put the puzzle into words, 'How does a Celtic cult with its origins in ancient Ireland find its way to the high moors in a Saxon grave?'

And it was only then that it had become clear to Arnold. 'The Mórrigan,' he had said. 'The Shape-Shifter.'

The coldness of that moment, as the legend of the female war god of ancient Ireland had touched them, returned again now to Arnold as he drove down the winding road towards the site, at the far end of the railway cutting that had been driven across the fell a hundred years ago to serve the grey stone-roofed village of Digby Thore. The construction site was now deserted, the single-storey stone and timber huts built for the workmen already showing signs of dismayed dilapidation. The Cossman International dream was over. The financial collapse of the company had left only these decaying buildings — and a lawsuit threatened against the council for statements made in a television programme.

But he did not want to think about the Mulberry inquiry. He parked his car on the gravel and cinder parking area. There were four other cars there; one he recognized as belonging to Rena Williams. He turned away and began the short walk up the slope of the field towards the cutting in the hillside.

The railway navigators had swarmed here a hundred years ago, hacking out the cutting, building the embankment, armed only with picks and shovels. Human muscle had torn into the fellside to create a great black scar, but now the embankment was covered with fern and bracken, shrubs, alder, ash, young, stubby oaks. The line had long disappeared, but on the northern edge of the cutting, where the rock face curved out in a great overhang, there was new digging being carried out, for it was there that the ancient burial ground had first been discovered by Irish navvies who had downed tools in panic. Now it was where the archaeological team worked, uncovering an area the railway had not wished to disturb, because it would have delayed their cutting of the line down to Digby Thore. The commercial decision taken then meant that the burial ground had been left largely undisturbed; saved for modern excavation.

As he approached the site of the dig, Arnold caught sight of a middle-aged, white-haired man with flyaway eyebrows who was engaged in discussion with four young men. Sam Loxton had been in charge of the dig when the project had been part-funded by Cossman International; when the project collapsed Rena Williams had been put in charge by Northern Heritage, but Arnold understood that no animus had resulted between the two: Loxton was happy to continue under the direction of the university professor. He looked up now and spotted Arnold. He grinned, scratching his grey-stubbled chin. 'Hey, it's good to see you! Come to add to the muscle?'

'It's about all I'm good for,' Arnold replied and shook hands with him. 'How are things going?'

Loxton shrugged. 'Pretty slowly at the moment. Dr Williams has managed to dredge up this lot to assist—' he jerked his head in the direction of the dispersing group of young men 'first-year archaeological students at the university. They need some teaching for this fieldwork, but they're all keen. We've hit some problems with the grave sites, though. It looks as if the Victorians did a fair bit of damage here, rather more than we'd first realized. But Rena can tell you more about it. She's over at the hut.'

After a brief conversation with Loxton about the latest finds, Arnold moved away towards the wooden hut where artefacts were stored, cleaned and examined on a long pine table. He found Rena Williams there, leaning over the table studying some materials. She turned as he entered and smiled warmly.

'Arnold! I'm pleased you've managed to make it this weekend.'

She was a tall, handsome woman in her late thirties. She had thick dark hair which was greying at the temples, but she made no attempt to change its natural colour. She had fine features and a broad, generous mouth. There had been the odd occasion when he had felt she was developing a certain warmth towards him, but it had remained unexpressed. He regarded her as a good friend and an interesting colleague. She looked at him quizzically now. 'You've not brought Jane with you?'

Arnold shook his head. 'She's gone to the States. She's had a film offer for her last book and she's on a lecture tour, all that sort of thing.'

'How long will she be away?'

'Three months, more or less.'

'Then she might miss some of the excitement here.' Rena Williams turned away and gestured towards the table.

'They're still coming to light. We've come across some further interesting, though somewhat confusing finds. There's been quite a wide range of animal burials — we've got bones of sheep, lambs, goats and, of course, pigs.'

'The meat of warrior champions,' Arnold murmured. 'I suppose these would have been sacrificial offerings?'

'I would imagine so. And we've got some dog and horse bones too, so it seems to me that in one section of the burial ground we've got evidence to suggest a link with the worship of the Apollo Cunomaglus — the Hound Lord.'

'And the confusion you mentioned?'

Rena Williams shrugged. 'Well, we know sacrificial burials were a major part of Celtic religious activities connected with death — they were fascinated by animals and their links with man. And we also know that the sacrificial habit continued unabated in Romano-British society. But evidence of that kind is usually to be found in temple sites rather than burial grounds like this one — although we know the site was in use for several centuries, extended and re-used over generations. But I'm beginning to suspect that the graves we've uncovered recently were used to inter criminals or other outcasts.'

'Why do you reach that conclusion?'

'There's some evidence of impalement, burning — and we've found one skeleton with a stone knife which seems to have been thrust in above the man's diaphragm. And all the burials in this last group have been males.'

'Disembodied skulls?' Arnold queried.

'Two.' Rena Williams frowned, leaning on the table with her fingers splayed and looking over the artefacts displayed there with a dissatisfied air. 'I'm just not getting a pattern, you know? I would have expected to form some idea of a settled religious practice over a period of time. But we're not getting that. I could understand that changes would take place over a period of time. We're well used to seeing occasionally rapid changes in religious practices when we investigate an old grave site. But here the evidence is of a series of changes, as though something happened to disturb cult practices that might have been settled for centuries, leaving confusion, receptiveness towards new cults that perhaps flourished only for a short time — a kind of uncertainty. Am I being too impressionistic, Arnold?'

Arnold shook his head. 'You're the site director. You're closest to it. But what about the bull-headed torsos? Have you uncovered any more of those?'

'No. We came across a crouched burial where a complete pot was lying between the arms, and beside the pot was a horse figurine. I feel there's a link with the bull-headed torsos, and I think you're right about the Mórrigan cult. But it's something I can't yet put my finger on. We had that brief section where the cult figurines were coming out like crazy, and then nothing, except the odd one like the horse. But I have a strong feeling that the cult persisted, and we'll find more yet. Although how the hell it got here, I don't know . . .' She turned away. 'You want a coffee?'

'That would be welcome. And then you can tell me how I can help this weekend. I've booked in at the Mason's Arms down in Digby Thore and I needn't leave until early Monday morning. So, my time is at your disposal.'

She switched on the electric kettle and put some coffee in a chipped mug. 'And how are things going on with the Mulberry inquiry?'

'The witch-hunt?' He sighed. 'I've had my interview. And so has Karen Stannard. I don't know whether you've heard, but she's been suspended.'

'Because of the inquiry?' Rena Williams swung round to face him. 'So what's happening?'

Arnold shrugged. 'I don't know the full story. She's been suspended because of the part they suspect she played in leaking information to the television people. And . . . well, she thinks I told them it was her. So, she's blaming me for the suspension.'

'Hmmm.' Rena Williams stared at him for several seconds, frowning slightly. 'You and Karen . . . you've always seemed to have a rather . . . curious relationship.'

'How do you mean?' Arnold demanded, unaccountably nettled. 'It's true I find her difficult to work for — in common with most of the department — but I've never been disloyal or attempted to undermine her. Much as I'd have liked to, on occasions.'

'I wasn't talking about loyalty, or professional relationships,' Rena Williams said firmly. She seemed about to add something, but then shook her head. 'Anyway, apart from that, I'm surprised she hasn't been in touch with me. She's expressed great interest in this site in the past; I'd have thought that since she's suspended, she might have wished to come up here and continue the work she started with us when the Cossman dig began. Or is the Cossman connection too sore a point for her?'

'I don't think it's that,' Arnold replied. 'She told me she's been given some kind of consultancy or commission by the university to work at a dig north of Alnwick. She intends doing that until the suspension thing is all sorted out.'

'North of Alnwick,' Rena Williams mused. 'That's likely to be Haggburn Hall, I'd guess. Interesting . . . Well, I wish her luck.' She flashed him an odd glance. 'As you do, I imagine . . .' She poured the hot water into the coffee mug. 'I don't think the department's heard the last of her yet.'

'I'm inclined to agree with you.'

'Anyway, you take milk but no sugar, I believe. This do you?' She handed him the steaming mug and gestured towards the table. 'Come and have a look at my location map of the finds. Here you'll see delineated exactly the problem we face: evidence of face-down burials; equipment placed next to bodies as offerings. Here's the two decapitations, and here the north-south grave alignments. Find me a pattern, Arnold, and I'll give you more than a cup of coffee.'

Arnold leaned over the sketch map and began to study it. He was looking forward to the weekend. It would be interesting working at the site with Rena and Sam Loxton, and it would help take his mind off the Mulberry inquisition. And the fact that he was missing Jane.

44

It might also help him get rid of the odd feeling of guilt regarding the suspension of Karen Stannard.

When he happened to glance at Rena Williams she was staring at him thoughtfully. He had the strange feeling she knew exactly what was on his mind. And was analysing it in a way he seemed incapable of doing.

CHAPTER TWO

1

Detective Chief Inspector Culpeper had managed to get in a pleasant weekend at Seahouses. He recognized himself for what he was: a big, broad, thick-waisted copper with grey hair, a discontented mouth and dinosaurian attitudes. He mourned the passing of the old policing system, withdrawal of bobbies from the heat, the use of panda cars in street policing, and the decision to remove promotional opportunities for coppers by collapsing the ranks into fewer grades. And he liked Seahouses and the cold Northumberland coast, whereas the younger policemen enjoyed holidays in France, Germany, Spain, or Italy.

He was a man who was going nowhere, except to retirement, but he made no apologies for his views or the fact that Seahouses suited him for holidays. He could prowl along the narrow harbour wall, inspecting the fishing fleet; take a boat trip out to the Farne Islands and observe the seals; do a bit of desultory fishing; sit in the snugness of the Ship Inn with a pint of beer, and have a plate of haddock and chips in the Pinnacle restaurant, just up from the harbour itself. It was an old-fashioned man's world and he enjoyed it.

His wife Margaret — a strong-minded and outspoken Durham lass — had put up with Seahouses for years. There had been a revolt of sorts last year, when she had booked a holiday for them in Greece, but he had been called away by duty, so she had now resigned herself to the fact that she should accept the availability of Seahouses while she could. At least he had managed to get away there for a few weekends with her, and on this occasion in good weather too.

So he felt relatively refreshed when he returned to headquarters at Ponteland on the Monday morning. The sea breezes at the coast had cleared his mind, and he felt there was a possibility he could remove from his desk some of the files that had been accumulating, annoyingly, without result. Some of the feeling of relaxed confidence was dissipated however when, climbing the stairs, he came face to face with Detective Inspector Farnsby.

Culpeper did not like Vic Farnsby.

It wasn't that he thought Farnsby was a poor copper. In fact, Farnsby could be perceptive and quick, as one would have expected of a fast-track graduate entrant. Possibly, that was the problem, the difference between Culpeper — who had come up the hard way, serving his time on the beat, working the pit villages, struggling through the exams to make sergeant, and then inspector and finally DCI — and the young graduate Farnsby, who had made detective inspector when he was still wet behind the ears. There was also the fact that Culpeper always suspected Farnsby's career was being watched carefully by the Chief Constable. He'd wondered whether there were family connections. Anyway, he didn't like Farnsby and that was that.

He managed to grunt a sour 'Good morning' and tried to brush past. Farnsby blocked him.

As Culpeper scowled, Farnsby said, 'There's a message on your desk, sir. You and I are called to a meeting at nine thirty.' He hesitated. 'I thought I'd better warn you.'

Culpeper glared with distaste at Farnsby's lean, saturnine features and his pale, washed-out blue eyes. Farnsby always seemed to be trying to keep a step ahead of him: he knew about the meeting first; he took it upon himself to tell

Culpeper even though the message was on the desk. Did the man think he wouldn't see the message, for God's sake? He grimaced. No matter. There were always ways of putting Farnsby in his place. That was one of the advantages of experience, being streetwise, knowing how to play the systems.

'It's with the Chief,' Farnsby added.

'What the hell does he want?' Culpeper asked, in surprise. 'We don't normally see hide nor hair of him this early in the week!'

'It's called for nine thirty,' Farnsby replied stiffly. He was always cool when there were criticisms made of the Chief Constable. 'No mention of what it's about.'

Disgruntled, Culpeper stumped past Farnsby to the top of the stairs and made his way to his office. The message was there, on his blotter. He glanced at it briefly, humphed and sat down, scowling at the papers on his desk. So much for his hopes of clearing files. If the Chief was calling both him and Farnsby in, it would be to load them with some rubbishy job, seen as important to the powers that be, but likely to fizzle out into an indeterminate report at the end of the day.

Unless, Culpeper thought with a groan, the Chief wanted them to go on another course. The Chief hadn't been long in post and still had new brooms to wield. He had certain enthusiasms: one was that he believed in training and computers and was fond of seminars. He thought it was a good idea to put the police in close touch with other professionals.

If it was to be another course, Farnsby would be delighted, naturally: a chance to glitter among the dross of disillusioned, half-asleep, ageing officers, an opportunity to cross intellectual swords with psychiatrists, psychologists, management gurus and the rest of the pack that knew nothing about down-to-earth, honest policing but had plenty of theories on how it should best be done.

Culpeper hoped it wasn't another course.

At nine twenty-five there was a tap on his door. Bloody efficient Farnsby, checking that Culpeper wasn't dozing in his chair. Bad-temperedly, Culpeper threw aside the file he had been reading and then cursed as the papers were scattered to the floor. Annoyed, he lumbered to his feet and was picking them up when Farnsby poked his head around the door. 'Can I help, sir?'

Culpeper's expletive was as short as his temper. He thumped the papers down on his desk and then led the way down the corridor. They were kept waiting for three minutes only, before they were allowed to join the presence.

'Gentlemen. Sit down, if you please.'

They took seats while the Chief Constable remained standing, hands clasped behind his back, rocking slightly on his heels as he gazed out of the window in the vague direction of Morpeth, away to the north-east. He was a hulking man, but smart and precise in his dress. He had heavy jowls and young eyes, hair still dark apart from a frosting at the temples. He was reputed to be a bit of a ladies' man and could be charming at parties. He certainly went to enough of them, since he had quickly made his mark with the people who mattered in the county.

He was from Melton Mowbray originally, though he had worked in the Met and in Lancashire at various stages in his career. His accent was carefully modulated; Culpeper suspected he didn't care for the north-east. Well, that was his problem.

'Have you seen or heard very much about this inquiry that's being held in the local authority?' the Chief Constable barked suddenly, dispensing with preliminaries, as usual.

Culpeper frowned. 'I've been up at Seahouses—'

'The Mulberry inquiry, sir?' Farnsby asked eagerly. Culpeper uttered an obscenity under his breath.

'That's right. Councillor Mulberry.' The Chief Constable's eyes bored into Culpeper's as he turned away from the window. 'Perhaps you'd like to tell us what you know about it, Farnsby, for the DCI's benefit.'

Farnsby was unable to avoid a grimace. Culpeper guessed that Farnsby knew what he was thinking. 'Well,' Farnsby said in a somewhat reluctant tone, 'it seems that there's been a degree of dissatisfaction lately about the performance of senior departmental officers in the local authority and an inquiry has been set up to take evidence of incompetence and . . . disloyalty, I think was the phrase used by its chairman, when he appeared on television last week.'

'That would be *before* you took the weekend off in Seahouses, Culpeper,' the Chief Constable remarked dryly. 'Have the media not penetrated to your area yet?'

'Didn't have time for television last week, sir. The Roberts case—'

The Chief Constable wasn't interested in the Roberts case, or any of the other files on Culpeper's desk. 'Yes, yes, go on, Farnsby.'

The detective inspector shot a nervous glance at Culpeper, guessing he'd pay for this later, in some way. 'There's not much more I can add, sir. Councillor Mulberry is leading the inquiry and he was pretty severe in his statements. It's caused quite a flurry on the council, but he's got the backing of the majority party, and though I don't think he'll report until after the elections—'

'Hah! But that's it, Farnsby! You've hit the nail on the head. There's a view about the county that the whole thing is just a matter of personal politics.'

'Sir?'

'Mulberry's up for election shortly. By getting elected to the chairmanship of this inquiry, holding press conferences, making a noise on radio and on television, he's improving his chances in a seat that he only held by the skin of his teeth last time around.'

The room was silent. Culpeper closed his eyes, wearily. Here we go, he thought.

'I had dinner with the Lord Lieutenant last night,' the Chief Constable began.

Exactly, Culpeper thought.

'And he was telling me there's a great deal of uneasiness around, in respect of this inquiry. Mulberry isn't a popular man, and there's a view that he may be getting too enthusiastic, rocking too many boats for comfort. Bringing people to heel is one thing — but to damage the whole structure and relationships within a group of committed professionals . . .' The Chief Constable paused, relishing the smoothness of the phrasing. 'I listened to what he said — it was a casual conversation, you understand — and then I asked around a little bit more during the course of the evening; there were various other people there — the Chief Executive from Gateshead, Chairman of Planning from Teesside . . .'

A masonic do, Culpeper concluded. The Great and the Good. He'd never joined, himself; laziness really. Maybe that's why he'd never got beyond DCI. Or had he wanted to anyway? He wondered whether young Farnsby was a Mason.

'There's a sort of general view that this is going to be a witch-hunt that might just fizzle out after the election. Or it may turn up some rather unpleasant toads, crawling out from under stones.' The Chief Constable paused, reflectively. He seemed rather to like the simile he'd just come up with. His lips moved, as he repeated himself silently. 'Anyway, be that as it may . . . I thought a lot about it last night, couldn't sleep, because I've got a feeling it could have repercussions. The kind I wouldn't be happy about.'

They had no idea what he was talking about. It showed in their faces. Impatiently, the Chief Constable sat down, tugging at his jacket. 'Let me spell it out to you. There are two possibilities arising out of the Mulberry inquiry. First, he finds evidence to support his assertions; second, he doesn't — and it's all just farting in the wind.' Culpeper blinked. The Chief didn't usually express himself so graphically. 'Now, in the latter case, it just means it's all a waste of public money, and that's nothing to do with us —we've got our own financial problems to worry about. But what if he does turn something up? What then, hey?'

Culpeper was silent. Farnsby leaned forward, frowning. 'I suppose it could mean that questions will be asked of us, and we might get involved — if there are any criminal implications in what he finds.'

53

'Exactly,' the Chief Constable exclaimed triumphantly. He glanced at Culpeper and scowled. 'You following this, Culpeper?'

Culpeper shifted his bulk uneasily in his chair. 'I'm not sure I am, sir. Mulberry, from what you said, is investigating senior officers in the departments of the local authority. For incompetence and . . . what was it — disloyalty? What's criminal about incompetence? And disloyalty in one direction can be seen as support for another group. How would all this affect us?'

'We don't know,' the Chief Constable replied impatiently. 'You must be as well aware as anyone else, with your experience: once someone starts turning over stones, all sorts of things come to light. Now what if Mulberry comes up with evidence of corruption? What if the witch-hunt starts spreading? What if criticisms are levelled against us, that there were things going on under our noses that we didn't know about, but should have had sorted?'

'I don't see—'

'Are you suggesting, sir, that the Police Authority might also begin to get ideas?' Farnsby asked.

'It has been known,' the Chief Constable replied sagely. 'I think it's unlikely, my guess is we're still just dealing with a politically motivated witch-hunt that'll go down the plughole once the reason for it all — political insecurity — disappears. But I want to make sure . . . I think we need to be careful. We mustn't get caught out. Therefore, I have a task for you two. I want you to construct what we might call the . . . ah . . . the Mulberry Defence.'

'I don't play chess, sir,' Culpeper growled.

The Chief Constable gave him a withering look. 'We're not playing games here, Culpeper. I'm serious. I don't want this inquiry to expose anything that will put this force in a bad light.'

'Sir, with respect, I still don't see—'

'Consequently, I want to establish a parallel investigation low key, but serious. I want to find out two things, and you can give the matter priority.'

Culpeper was disgruntled; he folded his arms stubbornly and stared at the Chief Constable, his mouth turned down in displeasure. He had better things to do than chase the Chief Constable's wild geese. At last, he said, 'We have a great deal on our plates at the moment, sir. When you say this is to take priority, that means we'll have to shelve other matters which—'

'Priority,' the Chief Constable interrupted coldly, 'means just what it says. I want you to put your backs into it, and I want it concluded within two weeks.'

'And what exactly do you want us to find out, sir?' Farnsby asked in a hesitant tone.

'Firstly, as I said, I want a parallel investigation. If Mulberry's going to find out something that is in any way, shape or form a matter that could give rise to a criminal prosecution, I want us — you — to find it first. But you do it under wraps. I don't want the newspapers getting wind of it or all hell will break loose.' He paused. 'From what I hear, the first attack has already been made and a suspension has been placed on one of the senior employees in the authority. A Miss Stannard.' He fixed a cold stare on Culpeper. 'I believe you know her.'

Culpeper sighed. 'Karen Stannard. Yes, our paths have crossed. This suspension has arisen out of the Cossman International business?'

'That's right.'

'Well, I don't know what they're fussing about. We've got the guys who caused the problems at Cossman International banged up in Durham jail. But now Stannard's under the knife with the authority?'

'I don't know the details. You find out,' the Chief Constable said crisply. 'And find out who else is likely to be attacked where the allegations of incompetence, disloyalty, maybe criminal behaviour are coming from. We don't want to get caught short on this one. If Mulberry comes up with anything, I want to be able to say to the chairman of the Police Committee that we've already got our finger on the pulse of it. Understood?'

'Yes, sir.' Farnsby began to rise from his seat, assuming the interview was at an end. Culpeper stayed where he was, watching the Chief Constable carefully.

'You said you wanted us to do *two* things, sir, in this . . . Mulberry Defence.'

The Chief Constable grimaced, involuntarily. He rose from his chair and walked across to the window again, then stared out blankly for a few seconds. 'That's right,' he said at last. 'Two things. I want you to monitor the inquiry itself, keep a check as far as you can on what's going on. The other thing . . . well, I told you there's a deal of uneasiness among . . . certain persons of influence and authority in the country. They see Mulberry as ruthless, and careless. He could do a lot of damage. Occasionally, it's possible to undertake damage limitation by . . . being aware.'

'What's that mean, sir?' Culpeper pursued.

The Chief Constable interlocked his fingers behind his back, they twisted together in a nervous gesture. Culpeper waited.

'It's as well to be forewarned. So . . . I want you to carry out a check on Mulberry himself. He has a background of business interests; he claims he has none now. Mr Clean. But nobody's ever *completely* clean. There are always skeletons. I want a check made on him.'

All three men were silent for a while. At last Culpeper heaved himself to his feet. 'So the Mulberry Defence is really about trying to pin something on Councillor Mulberry; that way if he were to find anything of an . . . uncomfortable nature in his inquiry — uncomfortable to people that matter — he might be persuaded to back off. Is that what you're saying, sir?'

The Chief Constable seemed not to have heard him. 'Two prongs,' he said stiffly. 'Monitor the inquiry and try to get ahead of it; and run a check on Mulberry himself. We have to make sure we haven't missed anything — either side of the fence.'

Culpeper was breathing hard. He glanced at Farnsby. The detective inspector was a little pale; it was clear he was as unhappy as Culpeper about the nature of this assignment. But he was a young man with a career ahead of him, he wasn't about to argue with the Chief.

'Will that be all, sir?'

The Chief Constable disregarded the sourness in Culpeper's tone. He nodded. They turned and made their way to the door. As Farnsby held it open for Culpeper to walk through, the older man paused, glanced back to the Chief Constable. 'The Lord Lieutenant, sir . . .'

The Chief Constable turned his head. 'What about him?' Culpeper frowned innocently. 'Didn't I hear that his son was appointed Head of Financial Administration in the county last year?'

As he closed the door behind him the Chief Constable's brow was black as thunder.

2

The department seemed quietly subdued the following week. Karen Stannard's absence was not commented on. Arnold had the eerie feeling that it was almost as though she had never worked in the department. But there was an underlying tension nevertheless, a general nervousness humming in the air as if everyone was expectant, waiting, aware that there were more problems to come. The inquiry was continuing, and staff in the authority were unsettled.

The director did not appear on the Wednesday. A message was sent in by Councillor Mrs Brent-Ellis that her husband had been stricken with summer flu and was confined to his bed. Jerry Picton was of the opinion that it was a strategic illness.

'He's just in a panic,' he told Arnold. 'With the delectable Ms Stannard not around to pick up his problems, he's worried to death. And I hear he's also been talking to Nick Francis, the Director of Legal Administration, what he heard there has thrown him into a complete tizz. It seems Francis had a pretty torrid time in front of the inquiry — and if lawyers are being given a tough time of it, what chance for Brent-Ellis, hey?' He eyed Arnold with a cynical leer. 'Leaves you in an interesting position, though, bonny lad.'

'What's that supposed to mean?'

'Cold-eyed Karen out of the way; Bombastic Brent-Ellis in his sick bed . . . why, man, you're in line for stardom! Who can they turn to but you? You'll be favoured son. Mind, I always said you should have got the job in the first place . . .'

But Arnold didn't want the job. With Karen Stannard and Brent-Ellis away from the office he had to stand in for them at some of the committees they would normally have attended, and with extra files piling up on his desk he found he was forced to work late. He spent most of Friday evening working because he had no intention of taking files home with him at the weekend. He had enjoyed the fresh air up at Ravenstone, and he had promised Rena Williams that he would join her again. There was a casual holiday period coming up and the department offices would be closed for two days, which meant he would be able to manage an extended period at the dig. He completed the files at nine thirty and got home bleary-eyed.

He set off early on Saturday morning. The air was clear and sharp, the sun bright at his back as he drove west. On the climb to the fell he caught sight of a merlin hunting the unwary moor. The heather was in bloom among the rocky outcrops and there was a distant haze, blue and purple across the length of the fell, as he reached the crest. He drove past deep burns on wooded slopes that provided ample cover for badgers and deer, and then he crossed the last ridge before beginning the descent to the Ravenstone site above Digby Thore.

As he pulled into the car park he was surprised to see Rena Williams standing beside her own vehicle, its door open as she prepared to step in. He pulled in beside her and wound down his window. 'You look as though you're going somewhere.'

She squinted at him in the bright sunshine. 'Arnold — I'm glad you arrived early. I'd left a message for you with Sam Loxton, but no matter now. Don't bother getting out of the car.' She grinned at him. 'I've got a surprise for you. You've got a few days off, haven't you?'

'Till Wednesday next.'

'Excellent.' She hesitated, considering, muttering to herself. 'Maybe we could go in one car . . . No, better not. Just follow me, okay?'

'Where are we going?'

'Surprise, Arnold, surprise! Just follow me. It's a run of about an hour or so.'

Before he could argue she had got into her car and was heading out of the car park. He shrugged and swung his car out behind hers.

They took a narrow lane northwards, skirting past Digby Thore, and drove along the south-west bank of the river, looping through some fine oak and beech woodland until the valley opened out and they began to climb the hillside again. They had left the country of the lead men behind them and there were no more deserted, crumbling mine shafts and decayed stone cottages to be seen. They were winding their way along minor roads, over narrow stone bridges, and although Arnold knew the area well enough, he was unable to guess where they were headed. They drove past a group of young men, broken shotguns over their arms, probably out looking for rabbits or foxes, and then they were moving past meadows yellow with cowslips. He recalled a time when it had been thought that the days of meadow flowers had gone and would never return with the agricultural use of chemicals, but he had walked this riverbank of recent years and the fields had been yellow again, the riverside blue with harebells and sweet with the scent of rich water mint, scattered among pink valerian, wood sage, purple orchid and dog's mercury. He'd even found, one day, a bank with the pretty but dangerous white-flowered enchanter's nightshade.

Within half an hour they were driving north on main roads again. After passing close to Alnwick, they swung west again beyond the road to Coquetdale. Finally, he caught sight of the signpost to Haggburn, and Rena was turning right. She parked in the narrow street that comprised most of the village; as he pulled in behind her, she got out of the car and gestured to the old inn that stood squarely in the centre of the village. 'The only reasonable place around here, I'm told,' she said cheerfully.

'The Drover's Rest,' Arnold said, scanning the weather-beaten sign displaying a moorside scene with a solitary shepherd. 'Are we stopping for a coffee?'

'No, we're booking in for a few days.'

'But I thought we'd be working at Ravenstone—'

'Don't argue. I told you. Surprise.'

She marched in ahead of him and he followed, still puzzled. After they had booked rooms, he deposited his small suitcase on his bed and then went down to the bar, where he had suggested they meet for a cup of coffee. There was only one other person there when he entered: a slim, fair-haired man in his early twenties, sitting on a bar stool, nursing a gin and tonic. He glanced at Arnold but said nothing. He had dark eyes but seemed to lack eyebrows, so his face had a pale, washed-out look. Arnold ordered a pot of coffee from the barman; it had just arrived when Rena joined him. She slid into the bench seat opposite him and smiled. 'So. Still puzzled, my friend?'

'Enough even to get irritated if you don't put me out of my misery,' Arnold replied as he filled her cup.

'Tut, tut, impatient!' She shook her head and took a sip of coffee. 'Okay, I'll relent, and tell you. It's probably as well — the surprise might be too much if I spin it out longer. I had a phone call in the week.'

'And?'

'They've come across some more artefacts. Another bull torso.'

'Where? Up here? But it's miles from Ravenstone! I don't believe it!'

'True enough.' She was grinning again, broadly. 'Think about it. The cult of the Mórrigan at Ravenstone is one thing, but if we now have a second site where it seems the Shape-Shifter held sway, it could mean that the cult was more widespread than we believed. It's like the discovery in the sixties,

61

about the Mithraic cult. It had been thought to be a minor deity, but turned out to be widespread among the legions of Rome on the frontier.'

'Where exactly was the find made?'

'About a mile or so from here. Near Haggburn Hall — appropriate name, don't you think, for a female war deity?'

Arnold smiled. 'I don't think the connection is there. *Hagg* has nothing to do with sorcery, it's a Celtic word for an enclosed wood. Like the old Norse word "hogg", meaning a copse or coppice.'

Rena Williams grimaced. 'You're full of useless information, destroying dreams.'

'And you're still being economical with the information. So there's a dig going on at Haggburn Hall. I don't know this area particularly well. And the dig—'

'It's recent.' She eyed him with a hint of wickedness in her glance. 'It's a university project. I got a call about it . . . from an old friend of yours.'

Arnold stared at her, thoughtfully. He had the glimmering of a suspicion. 'And just who is this old friend?'

'Can't you guess?' The gleam in her eyes was obvious, she was enjoying the moment. 'Karen Stannard.'

Arnold leaned back and folded his arms. 'You're a malicious old crone.'

'Arnold! I'm not far beyond thirty-five!' She had raised her voice in mock indignation, and the young man at the bar turned his head, stared at them briefly.

'You *deserve* to be an old crone,' Arnold replied in a low voice. 'If you'd told me Miss Stannard was involved, I would never have come — I'd have stayed at Ravenstone.'

'Exactly. That's why I didn't tell you.' She was enjoying herself. 'And I didn't want you to miss the excitement of the new find.'

'You'd better start at the beginning.'

She leaned forward, elbows on the table, her face flushed with excitement and amusement. 'I got this call from Karen. She told me she'd joined the dig at Haggburn — it's under the direction of a man I've come across in the field, Fred Harkness — bit short-tempered but his heart's in the right place. Senior lecturer at the university. Anyway, she rang and said she'd recognized some of the early stuff they'd come across in a Saxon sacrificial burial — not unlike Ravenstone. And there it was, another torso with a bull head! She realized the importance of it and rang me straight away. She said she'd cleared it with Fred Harkness — they wanted me to come up and take a look, maybe do some checking with them at the site. So I had a word with Sam Loxton, and he's happy enough to carry on the Ravenstone dig by himself; after all, he was running it by himself earlier, before I was put in charge. And that was it.'

'Not quite everything,' Arnold said doubtfully. 'I can't imagine that the invitation included me.'

'Well, of course, your name wasn't exactly mentioned . . .'

'I'm in no doubt that Karen Stannard will throw a fit when she sees me in tow with you. Having me at the site is not what she would have had in mind when she rang you.'

'That's true, but as far as I'm concerned, for these next few days you're part of my team, and you have something to offer. Anyway, it'll be Fred's decision, not Karen's, and I think I can persuade him.' She paused, eyeing him carefully. 'There's always been a bit of an edge between you and Karen. What's it all about, really?'

Arnold shrugged. 'I don't know. I think maybe she feels she's in a male-dominated world, and so has to prove herself over and over. For some reason, she sees me as a threat.' But it was more than that, he guessed. She had disliked him from the start, and yet there had been times when there was something else in the air between them. Suddenly, confusingly, he thought of Jane, and realized he hadn't phoned her for the last few days.

'Well, I suppose I can appreciate Karen's feelings — and she *has* talked to me about them, a while back . . .' Rena Williams was lost in thought for a while and Arnold recalled the gossip that had been whispered at the site, about the nature of the relationship between Karen Stannard and Rena Williams. He had put little store by it himself, and he knew that Rena had been unhappy about it. They finished their coffee in a somewhat subdued frame of mind, and then Rena suggested they leave one of the cars at the inn.

Arnold followed her directions along rutted lanes, until they neared Haggburn Hall. To their right were some old ruins of an earlier building, a precursor of the fifteenth-century hall itself. They continued for half a mile along the track until it approached a rocky outcrop, looming above a gently sloping field in which a number of cars were parked and a rough shed and three tents had been erected.

Karen Stannard was walking at the edge of the field.

She had seen the car approach and was making her way across to meet them. If she had intended a welcome for Rena Williams it was now far from her mind. The wind had ruffled her hair, wild about her face. She was dressed in an anorak and jeans, and she wore boots but she still looked elegant, and beautiful. Her eyes seemed blue this morning, but it was the blue of jagged ice as she bore down on them with a purposeful stride. Her eyes were fixed on Arnold, getting out of the car.

'Good morning, Karen,' Rena Williams called out coolly. 'I met Arnold, thought I'd bring him along as well. He'll be able to help out in identifying your artefacts.'

Karen Stannard stopped and glared her displeasure at them both, but confined her remarks to Arnold. 'Have you nothing better to do than come up here?' she demanded. 'Surely, the department won't be able to do without you at weekends, now it's short-staffed.'

'The department's closed for a few days,' Arnold replied shortly. 'But if my presence here causes a problem—'

'Nonsense,' Rena Williams interposed cheerfully. She walked forward and linked her arm through Karen Stannard's, tugging at her, leading her away towards the shed. 'Let's go and have a word with Fred. I'm sure he'll appreciate an extra pair of hands, and another objective mind.'

Karen Stannard glared back at Arnold as she reluctantly allowed herself to be led away. Anger still stained her eyes, but Rena had handled the situation well. Even so, as Arnold trudged miserably behind them, he still felt this was not a good idea. Karen Stannard had been bruised by her treatment at the hands of the inquiry, and she saw Arnold as part of a movement against her. He was glad to have the chance to look in at the Haggburn dig, if it was to link up with the Mórrigan cult they had already discovered at Ravenstone, but his presence could cause problems in view of the tension that lay between him and the deputy director.

Fred Harkness was tall, lean, about forty years of age and almost bald. His skin was weather-beaten, his eyes intelligent, but there was an impatience about his mouth that suggested to Arnold that his students at the university would get short shrift if they displeased him. Karen Stannard stayed in the background as Rena made the introductions and told Harkness that she had brought Arnold along to help out with identification of the artefacts the Haggburn site had revealed.

'Another eye is always welcome,' Harkness said, nodding. 'So, glad to have you aboard, Mr Landon. I've heard about you from Karen, of course.'

Arnold was surprised. He glanced at Karen Stannard, but her face was averted as she leaned over the table that stretched the length of the wall. Her body language suggested anger, however, so Arnold did not follow up the surprising statement from Harkness. Any comments Karen had made about him would, he supposed, have been detrimental. But that was not implicit in what Harkness had said.

'So you'll be staying down at the Drover's, then,' Harkness was saying. 'I'm under canvas, myself, for this next week. University support isn't what it used to be. Anyway, come and have a look at what we have over here. Karen, where's the figurine you got so excited about?'

Wordlessly, she pointed to it on the table. She flicked a resentful glance in Arnold's direction, then turned away. Arnold picked up the object. It was made of sandstone, and was cruder in its carving than the figurine they had found at Ravenstone, but it possessed similar characteristics: a female torso, and the roughly carved head of a bull. He shook his head, considering.

'So you reckon it's further evidence of a cult?' Harkness asked. 'Similar to Ravenstone?'

Arnold handed the figurine to Rena Williams. 'Puzzling though it is, it looks like.'

'I don't know too much about this Mórrigan thing. Karen told me a little, but she suggests you know more about it.'

'I'm going out to the dig,' Karen Stannard suddenly interrupted. Her mouth was stiff with resentment. 'I'll see you down there later — once you've had your chat. I presume Mr Landon will be staying.'

'Oh, yes,' Harkness replied, oblivious to her clipped tone. 'It makes sense, if he knows about this cult, and has time to give us a hand. Now then, Irish in origin, you say, Landon?'

At least she doesn't feel able to pull rank at the moment, Arnold thought with a sigh, as he watched her stride out of the shed and down towards the exposed areas of earth under the overhang of the crag at the field's edge. The next few days were not going to be all sweetness and light; but then, when were they ever that, between him and Karen Stannard?

He and Rena spent the next hour poring over the items that had come to light at the Haggburn dig: it was interesting to hear Fred Harkness talk about the site. He described it in terms that struck a chord in both Arnold and Rena, albeit in a manner he had not heard before.

'I don't see the site as a physical thing, you know. Rather, I regard it as a sort of socially constructed web of values, categories and understandings that have been imposed upon the environment by the community that inhabited this place. It's a kind of cognitive map, always mutating, being contested, redefining itself as a result of changing relationships between people and the way they see things around them. The men and women who lived here constructed things in their heads, and then they structured and arranged things around them to reflect what was in their minds. That's why I was excited when Karen told me about the nature of this artefact, and explained about the site . . .'

The Haggburn site had only recently been subjected to excavation. The university had used it as a testing ground for students for some years: field-walking had been carried out, some test-pitting done and two target trenches had been dug before the team had finally been given the finance to open up an area below the crag which seemed interesting.

'We found some clay lining,' Harkness explained, 'lenses of charcoal interleaved with soil. The charcoal gave us a radiocarbon dating of about 4000 BC but, of course, the finds are much more recent than that. This was a place that was returned to over hundreds, thousands of years, and maybe had some religious significance. We've discovered evidence of heavy-blade flint working; then some narrow-blade traditions from a hunter-gatherer phase, but then we also have broken jars, implements, and, finally, we came across a small grave area. That's where we found the icons — we believe it's a Saxon grave, but hadn't recognized the iconography until Karen pointed out it was Celtic.'

'I look forward to making a closer inspection of the site,' Arnold said.

'That's excellent,' Harkness enthused. He clapped a boisterous hand on Arnold's shoulder. 'We can make a start after lunch. You'll join us, of course, splendid repast of ham sandwiches and lukewarm coffee.'

'Does the university own or lease this land you're working on?' Rena Williams asked, as they browsed over the artefacts on the table. 'I believe work has been carried on here for some time, before this dig.'

'Own it? Not at all,' Harkness replied. 'It's part of the Haggburn Hall estate, but we're extremely lucky that its owner — Mrs Delaney — is interested in our work here. At least, she *says* she's interested. I suspect it's more that she regards us as a somewhat odd group of people, in our enthusiasms. She's more than a little . . . unusual, herself. And she seems to collect odd people.' He paused, thoughtfully, glancing at them both. 'But, now I think about it, I guess there's no reason why you shouldn't find that out for yourself this evening.'

'How do you mean?'

'Mrs Delaney loves entertaining. As far as I can gather, she's lived up here for forty years or so but she's always enjoyed having people around her. In fact, she's hinted to me that as a young woman she had quite a life . . . and she misses it now, in old age. Anyway, she's invited us to dinner — Karen and me, that is — a couple of times. And we're invited again this evening. She's taken quite a shine to Karen and I imagine she'll be only too pleased if you and Rena were to come along as well.'

'But we haven't been invited,' Rena protested.

'She takes a more-the-merrier view. And her dinner group-ings can often be . . . interesting. There's no telling who'll be there this evening — and I'm certain she'd like the refreshment of some new faces around the table. Leave it to me, I'll fix it.'

'If you're really sure . . .'

'I'm more than sure. And in due course I'd be interested to hear what you think of Mrs Delaney,' Fred Harkness said with a grin.

They spent the rest of the day inspecting the site. The graves had been excavated at a location deep under the over-hang of the rocky outcrop and Harkness showed him where the icon had been found. The other artefacts, probably bur-ied in much older graves that had been weathered away over the centuries, had been discovered at the edge of the dig, and it was clear that Harkness was right when he suggested that the site had been one which had been used for hundreds of years. He introduced Arnold and Rena to the group of three young men and two women who were assisting at the dig, and they explained they were doing the work as part of their university research programme under Harkness's direction.

'We're awash with academics,' Rena said with a laugh.

'Of whom Mr Landon is not one,' Karen Stannard said coldly.

She kept her distance while they worked there. She was cool to Harkness, Arnold noted, and still out of temper at Arnold's arrival, even though Rena Williams engaged her in conversation and got her to laugh a couple of times later in the day. It reminded him of the time when they had seemed to be close friends . . .

At five they decided to finish for the day, since they would need to go back to the Drover's Rest to change. Arnold again inquired whether it would be acceptable for them to turn up unannounced. Harkness promised he would call in at Haggburn Hall to make sure it was all right. If he hadn't contacted them before six, he and Rena were to make their way to the hall for seven thirty.

Arnold had not brought a great deal with him in his small suitcase. He showered and changed into a clean shirt and slacks, hoping the meal would not be a formal one, since all he had with him was a light sports jacket. At seven there had been no call from Harkness so it was clear they were now expected at Haggburn Hall. He went down to the bar, to wait for Rena and Karen Stannard. The young man who had been there earlier was still on the bar stool. Arnold wondered if he had been there all day.

He went up to the bar and ordered himself a lager. He was aware of the scrutiny of the pale-faced man. He glanced at him and nodded. The man smiled.

'Hi,' he said, after a few seconds. 'You staying long here at the Drover's Rest?'

Arnold shrugged. 'A few days.'

'Working at the dig, are you?' the young man asked. 'I saw you come back with the women.'

'That's right. But casually, just for a while. The week-end, really, and a couple of days after that. You staying here long? On holiday?'

The stranger grimaced, and sipped his gin and tonic. 'Suppose so. Maybe a week or two. If I can stand the pace of

69

the place. Not very much to do around here.' He sounded disgruntled, as though he had been misled in some way. 'My name's Steve Quaid, by the way.'

'Arnold Landon.' There was a short silence. 'How do you spend your time here?'

'Walking. Just mooching around, I suppose. I'm resting, you know what I mean? Between work. I'm an actor. Not that you'd have heard of me. Edinburgh Fringe, that sort of thing. Alternative stuff . . .' He was silent for a while, then he glanced at Arnold, an odd curiosity in his eyes. 'You been up to Haggburn Hall, then?'

'Not yet. I'm going up there tonight, as it happens, but it'll be the first—'

'Give my regards then,' Quaid interrupted moodily, and with a grimace slid off the bar stool and walked across to a chair near the window. Surprised, Arnold picked up his drink, and then heard someone behind him. He looked round, it was Karen Stannard, staring frostily at him. 'So, you've managed to gate-crash Haggburn, then.'

'It wasn't my idea.'

'It's your *popularity*, of course.' She looked at him with a cool, raised eyebrow. There was some kind of challenge in her eyes, maybe it was because she wanted him to acknowledge that she looked stunning. But then, she usually did. She was dressed in a dark-coloured, low-cut dress that hugged her figure; small earrings sparkled a contrast to the russet tones of her hair, and the light make-up she had applied emphasized the line of her cheekbones, giving her a slightly oriental appearance. It seemed to Arnold that she had the capacity to change her appearance with the slightest effort, but the result was always breathtaking.

'A drink?'

She shook her head, eyeing him ironically. 'I'll pay my own way. I've promised to get one for Rena.' She called the barman and ordered a gin and tonic and a soft drink. 'That's for me,' she announced. 'I'll be driving the three of us up to Haggburn Hall. Give you the opportunity to indulge yourself. Mrs Delaney keeps a good cellar — or at least her nephew does for her. Or for himself.'

She leaned on the bar while she spoke to the barman, keeping her shoulder half-turned away from Arnold. When Rena Williams came in, she greeted her with smiles and compliments. Thereafter, until they went out to her car, she barely spoke to him.

Arnold had the impression it was going to be a long evening, and a tough few days.

3

'So you're the gate-crashers.'

Vita Delaney was perhaps five feet six in height, but somewhat round-shouldered and stooping now, in her mid-seventies. She was fighting the signs of age: her make-up was old-fashioned but carefully applied, though perhaps a little too heavily; her deep-set eyes shaded with mascara; her thinning hair defiantly tinted blonde. She wore an evening dress that was too young for her, exposing shoulders that were now thin and bony, and her earrings were expensive and jewelled. Her eyes were sharp and intelligent, nevertheless, capable of a certain mockery, a deep brown in colour and quick. She wore a flesh-coloured hearing aid in her left ear and her left hand fiddled constantly with its control, pinned to her dress. Her features were lean, but in her high cheekbones and generous mouth there were still signs of the beauty that she had once had and — Arnold guessed from the coquettishness of her manner — used to effect.

They were standing in the library of Haggburn Hall. It was a magnificent, high-ceilinged room, lined with expensive volumes which Arnold suspected had not been used for years. A polished oak table in the centre of the room had been laid with drinks. There were signs of opulence everywhere:

deep-pile carpets, expensive drapes, furniture of quality and taste, and Arnold had been amused to find that their entrance had been announced by an elderly butler. Mrs Delaney, it seemed, was seriously rich.

Their hostess held court from a deep armchair near the tall windows, a glass of straight whisky in her right hand; a middle-aged man in a sombre suit moved around the room quietly dispensing drinks to the dinner guests. Mrs Delaney had summoned each of them, with an imperious wave, to meet Arnold and Rena as they stood beside her wing-backed chair. First, she called forward a tall man in his late thirties, dark-haired, with discontented eyes.

'My nephew, Rick Newton. And this is his wife, Gabriella. Spanish, you know.'

Gabriella Newton was a natural blonde, the kind so often seen in northern Spain, somewhat plump, and dark-eyed. She gripped her husband's arm with a certain possessiveness; her English was perfect as she greeted them. Her husband was brusque, and his glance wandered towards Karen Stannard, who was standing a little to one side, talking to Fred Harkness.

Vita Delaney moved them on, to beckon forward a thickset, powerfully built man with thinning, sandy hair, grey eyes and a pleasant, easy-going expression. Arnold guessed he was in his early fifties, a man of solid, dependable appearance. 'And this is my estate manager. He's Irish, George Mahoney. It's so comforting to have an Irishman around the estate. My late husband was Irish, you know — or at least, Irish-American. But then, they're worse than those who really come from the old country, aren't they, in clinging to their Irishness. Like converted Catholics. More committed than the real thing.'

George Mahoney smiled. 'But I've never laid claim to an Irish accent. Though I've no doubt I could affect one. I'm pleased to meet you, Mr Landon . . . Dr Williams.'

Vita Delaney tapped him on the hand and smiled, waving him away. She gestured with her whisky glass to the tall, dark-suited man with tanned skin and distinguished-looking white hair, worn long and smoothed back carefully. His features were composed, his mouth primly set as he stood, slightly apart from the others, nursing a gin and tonic. 'And here we have my prize guest. He refuses to tell me his real name' he calls himself Vartek. So romantic, don't you think?' She smiled at him coquettishly as he shook hands with Arnold. 'He's after my money, of course. But then, so is dear Ricky. The question is, who should I leave it to? They're both such dear boys!'

'Madame exaggerates,' Vartek intoned in a deep, musical voice. 'I merely seek to show her the way forward—'

'Not just here on earth,' Vita Delaney interrupted, with a girlish giggle that was completely out of keeping with her appearance. 'He wants to point the way forward for me into the other world as well. Trouble is, I'm not yet ready to go.'

'The fate awaits us all,' Vartek said portentously.

'Oh, isn't he such *fun*!' Vita Delaney gurgled. 'But enough of him — you must tell me all about yourself, Mr Landon. And you too, Dr Williams. Come and monopolize me. I'm always excited at meeting new people. And dear Karen, too — I take it you know these bright young people already. Why are you looking so *miserable*, my dear?'

Karen Stannard managed a smile, but did not respond to the invitation to join her hostess with Arnold and Rena Williams. She gave Arnold a frosty glance and Mrs Delaney noticed it. The old lady made a small *moue* as she looked at Arnold, and he guessed that at some time he would be called upon to explain what lay between Karen and himself. Vita Delaney was a woman in possession of a large curiosity.

She insisted on Arnold telling her all about himself. He did it self-consciously, aware of Karen Stannard standing nearby, looking thoroughly bored, and not a little annoyed when Mrs Delaney crowed at receiving the information that they were actually both employed in the same department.

'Oh, how *romantic*! And you, Dr Williams — do you work there, too?'

Rena Williams explained that she worked in the archae-ological department of the university at York and had met both Arnold and Karen through their involvement in the digs at Garrigill and Ravenstone.

'And now you're all together again up here at Haggburn! How exciting. I bet you're all such good friends!' She glanced around the small group and giggled. Her eyes fixed on Arnold and he thought he detected a hint of irony in her gaze; for a brief moment he wondered whether she had already guessed at the tensions that lay between them. He dismissed the thought as she drained her glass of whisky and announced it was time to go in for dinner.

'The servants will be getting edgy if we keep them wait-ing too long. I have to rely on local staff, of course, and one finds it so difficult to get trained people out here in the wilds. Now then, Mr Landon, will you take me in? You shall sit on my right, and Dr Williams on my left, so I can absolutely drain you both of gossip. Karen, dear, you sit beside Mr Landon; that way, when I get tired, you can entertain him — since you're such good friends.' She took Arnold's arm as she rose from her chair and smiled demurely at him. 'Such a sweet child, Karen — don't you think so, Mr Landon?'

It was not the way he would have described her, and she didn't like it too much herself, either. There was a grim smile on her face as he held out a chair for her in the dining room.

Rick Newton had taken the seat opposite Karen Stannard, separated from his wife by George Mahoney. Fred Harkness sat beside Karen, while the man who called him-self Vartek made up the party by sitting at the far end of the table, facing Mrs Delaney. He appeared somewhat disgrun-tled; Arnold could not be certain whether it was his normal appearance, or whether he felt he had been pushed too far away from Mrs Delaney. Perhaps he was used to the place of honour that Arnold had been allocated.

The meal was splendid, the wines superb, and Vita Delaney dominated the conversation. Rena was amused by the tenor of the evening and was enjoying herself; Arnold remained fairly quiet, observing the gathering, responding to Mrs Delaney's quips and occasional jibes, but generally maintaining a certain reserve. He became aware that her nephew Rick Newton was drinking heavily, and suspected it was normal behaviour for him; as the dinner progressed, however, he caught sight of some of the impatience that began to appear in the features of Gabriella Newton. It was a while before Arnold identified the cause, Rick Newton was unable to keep his eyes off Karen Stannard, and directed most of his conversation towards her. He was making a clear effort to charm her, and, to Arnold's surprise, she seemed to respond. She engaged Newton in lively banter across the table in spite of the increasing discomfort evidenced in Gabriella Newton's demeanour. She became almost skittish in a way Arnold had never witnessed before, and her flirtatiousness was also visited upon Fred Harkness. She completely ignored Arnold.

Rick Newton basked in her attention, teasing her and saluting her with his wine glass while his wife sat grim and silent beside George Mahoney. The estate manager was clearly aware of the growing tension and attempted to engage Gabriella in conversation, but it proved difficult as Rick Newton continued to flirt with Karen Stannard. Arnold attempted to help out, speaking to Gabriella across the table, asking her about Spain and attempting, clumsily, to use a little of the small amount of Spanish he spoke and understood, but her reaction was muted as she seethed at her husband's behaviour. Her replies were monosyllabic and her attitude hostile.

The elegant Vartek remained distanced from the conversation. He picked at his meal, drank sparingly, and ignored Fred Harkness's attempts to discuss his background and work. He barely spoke, even though Vita Delaney upbraided him twice for not displaying his usual charm. 'One would have thought you were sulking, Vartek — is it that you expected to dine with me *tête-à-tête?*' she accused him archly. 'But you know I'm far too old for you, and besides, with other beautiful women in the room like Dr Williams, and dear Karen here, you really should be behaving better. Oh, and Gabriella, too — talk to her, Vartek; cheer her up.'

Arnold glanced sideways at Mrs Delaney; there was a certain mockery in her tone, and he thought he detected a glint of mischief in her eyes. He suspected that Gabriella and Vartek did not like each other and she was playing a game, sticking pins into them for her own pleasure. He sipped at his glass of the excellent Mouton Cadet and studied his fellow guests: Mahoney was at ease, Rick Newton infatuated, Gabriella Newton angry and Vartek settled in a haughty disregard for the company. Rena was enjoying herself, as was Karen Stannard, but in different ways. Rena seemed oblivious to the odd tensions in the room; Karen Stannard was happy fuelling some of them. He wondered briefly whether her reckless behaviour with Newton was in some way affected by his presence . . . though he could not fathom why that should be.

'Since you're interested in horses,' Newton was saying, 'you must let me show you the stables while you're here.'

'That would be delightful,' Karen Stannard gushed. 'I love horses.'

This was news to Arnold; it was bad news as far as Gabriella Newton was concerned. She glared at her husband, and then at Karen Stannard — there was pure hate in her eyes.

The dinner plates were finally cleared away, and they had been served with coffee and liqueurs. Vita Delaney, having partaken of the wine with enthusiasm, had ordered herself a large brandy and taken a cigar. She was puffing at it now with evident enjoyment. The only other person smoking was Rick Newton. 'Of course, in my heyday,' Vita Delaney exclaimed, 'it simply wasn't done for ladies to smoke. I think that's how my late husband first came to notice me — I was never one for the conventions, and I smoked then. Normally, the ladies retired to the withdrawing room and the men took their port and cigars and told dirty jokes until it was time to rejoin the ladies. So *barbaric*.' She inspected the glowing end of her cigar and hiccupped gently. 'I always liked the odd dirty joke myself, and all those years I was deprived. Still, one can get quite a lot of obscenity on the television these days. Do you watch much television, Mr Landon?'

'Not a great deal.'

'An outdoors man like you, though, I imagine you'd like those natural history programmes.' She wrinkled her eyes against the cigar smoke; she suddenly seemed very old and tired. 'I like those programmes myself, saw one the other day about kestrels. I love the way they hoover.'

Arnold looked at her and she returned his gaze, almost challengingly. 'Don't you?' she asked, and hiccupped again.

There was a short silence, and then George Mahoney stirred and began to rise from his chair. 'I wonder, Mrs Delaney, whether you'd excuse me now. I have an early start in the morning and there are still some things I need to check on, as I explained earlier.'

'Of course, George, of course,' the old lady replied, waving her cigar expansively. 'And you too, Mr Harness, I believe you said you're not one for late nights.'

Fred Harkness blinked. '*Harkness*,' he said, then wet his lips with his tongue nervously. 'If that would be all right with you, Mrs Delaney . . . those young lads up at the site, they need watching sometimes, and we have been getting a bit of bother . . .'

'Please feel free. I hope you enjoyed yourself.' She nodded as the two men left the room, and then she beamed around her. 'Now then, what was I saying a moment ago? Ah, yes, television . . . Vartek would love to be on television, wouldn't you, my friend?' Her voice was getting a little slurred, but her eyes were still sharp. 'Do your magic trips.'

'*Tricks*,' Vartek growled. 'And I'm concerned with neither magic, nor tricks. I am concerned with the quality of life here on earth and what will be destined for us in the—'

'Same thing,' Mrs Delaney cut in, yawning prodigiously. The slurring had become more obvious now, and she seemed

to have difficulty pronouncing some of her words. 'I've sheen
. . . seen some of the things he gets up to in the east wing . . .
Mr Vartek is staying here with me for a while, you see. Rick
doesn't approve. But I'm entertained by him. Which reminds
me — Dr Williams, Mr Landon, are you staying at the same
dreary hotel as Karen? I've got a good idea. I've plenty of
room here. Why don't you — all three of you — come to
stay?' She regarded Rick Newton. 'What do you think about
it, Ricky? We can afford it, can't we?'

He shrugged. His mouth was slack; he was close to being
drunk. 'Why not? More the merrier in the madhouse.'

'Now that's always been my shogun,' Mrs Delaney
announced, clearly taking no offence at the comment. She
beamed around the room. Arnold suggested they were perfectly comfortable at the Drover's Rest, aware that Karen
Stannard had stiffened beside him at Mrs Delaney's suggestion, and Rena Williams also professed her reluctance to
impose on Mrs Delaney's hospitality, but the old lady waved
the protestations aside.

'You shall all stay,' she affirmed. 'And then dear Ricky
can show Karen the horses and we can all have a good time.'
She shook her head as though she had lost track of what she
was saying, and some stray locks of her bleached hair fell over
her eyes. 'It's a bit late tonight, I guess; the servants haven't
been forewarned. And they'll play hell if I presume too much
on their goodwill — staff these days!' She blinked, and gazed
blearily at them, sitting stiffly at the table. 'But tomorrow
you all come here as my guests: Karen, Dr Williams — may
I call you R-Rena? And of course, Mr Landon. Arnold. What
a beautifully *old-fashioned* name.'

There seemed to be little they could do to dissuade her
from her invitation. Her eyes were getting heavy, but she
exuded an air of triumph. She called for another cigar, and
took another glass of brandy. Squinting around the gathering,
she smiled happily. 'We could then all dine together again like
this. And play games afterwards, like the old days. Charades

maybe. Or watch television. Watch games on television. Not that silly game they play . . . what's it called? The m-muscular one. They all take spheroids to get on the show. They all take them, you know,' she repeated, winking conspiratorially.

Rena Williams was embarrassed by the silence that followed. She glanced around and then leaned forward. 'Spheroids? What game show are you talking about, Mrs Delaney?'

Heavy-eyed, the old woman waved a dismissive cigar. 'You know the one. *Alligators*. That's what it's called: Alligators!'

Arnold flicked a glance around the table. Rick Newton was inspecting the end of his own, dying cigar; there was a supercilious sneer on his face. He had seen the old lady get drunk before. Gabriella Newton had moved to sit next to him in George Mahoney's absence and her lips were tight with disapproval. Karen Stannard was cool, inspecting her long fingernails with an exaggerated care. Rena Williams was nonplussed, not knowing what to say in response.

'At least,' Vita Delaney added, blinking away cigar smoke, 'you can get a good laugh with some of the programmes. Though with the s-sexual antics they get up to, you'd think most of the men would end up with a heroin. All that bonking! And I saw a show the other evening about transfertights!'

Karen snorted. Arnold shifted in his seat, uncertain, and then as he looked at Vita Delaney her eyelids began to close. She took a long sip of brandy and fiddled at her breast with her left hand. There was a slight clicking sound, and after a few moments her head slowly drooped until her chin lay on her chest.

There was silence for a few moments. At last, Rick Newton raised his hand to the waiter. 'I think we're all in need of a brandy now.' He glanced around the table, grinning unpleasantly. 'Don't all look so embarrassed. This is a far from unusual situation. There are times when she reverts to what she used to be. A music-hall tart. That's how she started you see, in a chorus line. It comes out when she's like this. She's just pissed, that's all.'

Rena Williams flashed an angry glance at him. 'I think—'

Newton held up a hand. 'Don't worry! She can't hear us talking. You can say what you please, now. She's switched off her bloody hearing aid. You know she does that every time the doctor comes to see her? She knows he's going to tell her that at her age she shouldn't drink so much, and she shouldn't smoke. So, she lets him come here and give her the once-over every month, and she plays the lady — tea in the afternoon and all that — and then as soon as he starts to give her instructions: click. She turns off her hearing aid. That way, she doesn't get to hear bad news.'

Newton cast a triumphant glance at Karen Stannard as he held his brandy glass out for a refill. 'After dinner she's usually well away, and then when the wine hits her she can't even get her words straight. Too much bonking — as she tastefully puts it — doesn't lead to a *heroin*. Doesn't even lead to a hernia, as far as I'm aware.' He grinned, staring meaningfully at Karen Stannard.

'Rick,' his wife warned. 'I think you've said enough. You should finish your brandy and then we all retire.'

'Well, she's crazy, isn't she? She's going gaga. And here she is, still running this estate, with a million in investments, and I work here for a pittance—'

'It really is time we were all leaving,' Gabriella Newton warned, rising to her feet.

Arnold rose with her. 'I think that's right. What about Mrs Delaney? Shouldn't we . . .'

'I'll call her personal maid,' Gabriella said shortly. 'She'll be all right.'

'Leave her to stew where she is,' Rick mumbled. He was staring at Karen Stannard. Slowly, he winked. 'When the old witch is away, the mouseketeers can play. Now that one's worthy of her, don't you think?'

Gabriella was speaking to the waiter; he nodded, and left. As they gathered near the door, Rick Newton muttered to Karen Stannard, 'Anyway, when you come up tomorrow I'll show you the horses. Tomorrow evening, maybe.' He leered at her, ignoring the furious presence of his wife. 'Better by moonlight, hey?'

A short, middle-aged woman entered the room. She nodded to the awkward group, seeming somewhat flustered herself, and then crossed the room to Mrs Delaney, shaking her lightly by the shoulder. Arnold joined her. 'Can I help at all?'

'It's all right, sir. I'm her nurse.' The woman shook Mrs Delaney again, then found the hearing-aid control, and clicked it on. Slowly Mrs Delaney opened her eyes. 'What is it — time for bed?' She looked up at Arnold and smiled. 'So nice to meet you . . . please come again.'

'She'll be all right now, sir, believe me,' the nurse announced firmly. She put her hand under Mrs Delaney's arm and helped her to her feet. The old lady smiled lopsidedly, and waved imperiously to the group at the door. 'Remember, you must all come to stay!'

As she made her way to the door, she looked at Arnold again. He could have sworn there was a dancing light of mischief in her eyes.

The night was bright outside. Arnold had told Rena and Karen Stannard that in view of the amount he had had to drink, he would prefer to walk back to the Drover's Rest — it was only about two miles down the lane and the night air would clear his head. Karen Stannard was happy enough to agree, and he watched the lights dwindle down the drive ahead of him as he strolled through the gardens towards the gateway on to the main road.

In the moonlight he could make out the old ruins he had noted on the way to Haggburn Hall, earlier that day. He wondered what they were. It was possible they could have been outlying farm buildings, or maybe the decayed remains of the original house before the existing hall was built on a new site. Curious, he wandered away from the main drive and stood looking at the massive stones that lay strewn in front of the ruins. The moonlight was sharp on the cut stone; the ruins were ghostly, picked out against the black backdrop of the woods some twenty yards beyond.

As he stood contemplating, he thought he detected a movement in the darkness of the trees. He narrowed his eyes, startled, and his blood quickened as he realized someone was moving quietly out of the woods, walking towards him. He stood still, irresolute, aware of the sudden, unreasoning surge of adrenalin in his veins. Then he recognized the thickset bulk of the man approaching him.

'Not going back by car, Mr Landon?' George Mahoney asked curiously.

Arnold laughed, sheepishly, as the excitement in his blood died. 'Nice night for a walk,' he explained. 'Is that what you've been doing, too?'

Mahoney came closer, glancing about him. 'Oh, on a bright night like this I like to take a stroll around the grounds occasionally. We've had a bit of trouble of recent months. There's been someone shooting in the woods.'

'Poachers?'

'Nothing much to poach around here. Mrs Delaney doesn't believe in raising grouse or pheasant. So there's not a lot to hunt — it'll be some townie, I would guess, who doesn't know any different. There's someone down at the village — Hush . . . there now.'

They were both silent for a few minutes. Arnold thought he detected some sounds in the trees, but it could have been anything — a badger, maybe, or some nocturnal rodent. Suddenly, above their heads, an owl hooted mournfully, and both men laughed.

'I'll walk down to the main gate with you, Mr Landon. I live in a cottage just across the road from there.'

'How long have you worked for Mrs Delaney?' Arnold asked as they strolled along.

'It's about seven years, now,' Mahoney replied. 'I answered an advertisement; she interviewed me, and that was it. It's not a bad job.'

'You worked in Ireland before that?'

Mahoney laughed. 'No. Mrs Delaney makes remarks about my Irishness because it amuses her, but I've never actually been to Ireland. I worked in Canada most of my life — forestry, then the Army there.' He paused. 'So

83

what did you think of this evening, Mr Landon? A strange bunch?'

'I think Mrs Delaney enjoyed herself,' Arnold replied guardedly.

'She always does . . . I get invited to dine there quite often. I think she enjoys my — detachment.'

'How do you mean?' Arnold asked.

Mahoney shrugged, pushing his hands into his trouser pockets. 'Well, I'm different, you see. I'm not so closely involved with her as the others are, and I've no axe to grind. The Newtons, they're related to her, Rick is her brother's son. He looks after her investments — he's an accountant but he's not in practice. Works only for Mrs Delaney. She's very much aware that he's waiting for her to die. He expects to inherit her estate. I've a feeling he may be disappointed.' He glanced around him at the trees, dark against the moonlit sky. 'His wife tries to control him, because she's looking forward to the inheritance, but he can get stupid in drink. Like tonight.'

'He upset his wife this evening . . .' Arnold hesitated. 'He was clearly interested in Karen Stannard. I thought he was a bit . . . obvious, in front of his wife, trying to arrange to meet Karen tomorrow evening, at the stables.'

Mahoney grunted. 'Gabriella won't let anything happen there. She's a possessive woman; she's got a Latin temperament — and temper. She'll sort him out, believe me. And Miss Stannard too, if she doesn't back off.'

Arnold shook his head. The thought of a confrontation between Karen Stannard and Gabriella Newton was interesting, but Mahoney didn't know the deputy director as he did. Arnold knew which of the two women he'd put money on. 'What about Vartek?'

Mahoney laughed mirthlessly. 'A fool. I don't know where Mrs Delaney came across him, but he amused her, and she invited him to stay for a while. That pretentious name — he refuses to divulge his real name because he says he is now in touch with the other world, where the names we are given in baptism are meaningless. It's all claptrap and mumbo jumbo.'

'So what's his objective?' Arnold asked.

'He thinks he's going to persuade Mrs Delaney to put a lot of money into a scheme he has — wants to call it the Delaney Foundation, in her honour. The idea is to conduct research into longevity and reincarnation, life of the soul after death. Administered by him, of course, and under his control. He thinks a well-heeled old woman like her, not too far off from the grim reaper herself, will be an easy touch. He's wrong. It amuses her to dangle him, listen to his nonsense, have a giggle at his next-world fantasies.' He shook his head. 'She'll never give him the money. She's playing him on the end of a line.'

'And does she play you on a line?'

'Me?' The surprise in Mahoney's voice seemed genuine. 'Hell, no. I'm just an employee — paid well, I admit. No, I'm here and I watch it all with a certain detachment, as I said. Watch the games being played: Vartek, the Newtons — and Mrs Delaney, too. She asks me what I think, from time to time.' He glanced at Arnold, searchingly. 'She's no fool, Mr Landon.'

Arnold recalled the mischief in her eyes. 'I gained that impression.'

The main gate was looming up ahead of them, solid and black under the shadow of the trees that lined the drive. 'It's all like a bit of a comedy being played out at the hall,' Mahoney said quietly.

Arnold glanced at him, smiling. 'And you see yourself as a kind of Greek Chorus?'

Mahoney laughed again. 'I suppose you could say that. The detached observer, uninvolved in the action, commenting on the follies of the players. It's a good enough description . . . Well, here we are, Mr Landon. I'll leave you now. And I look forward to seeing you at the hall tomorrow night.'

'So she was serious about our staying here at the hall?'

'Indeed. It will be additional entertainment for her. And don't be fooled by her getting drunk. She was serious — and she'll remember!'

CHAPTER THREE

1

When Arnold returned to the office the following Wednesday, gossip was surging around the departments. He had not seen the newspapers himself, but it seemed that Councillor Mulberry had raised the stakes somewhat over the weekend. He had come out with a statement that in his view severe spending restrictions should be placed on all departments because of serious deficiencies exposed in the targets and budgets agreed between officers and councillors.

The headlines in the local newspaper were bold: 'Inquiry Chief Slams Overspending Mandarins'. It was the first time Arnold had ever seen the senior officers in the authority designated as 'mandarins', but the meaning was dear enough, and the newspapers were scenting a good story. They were behind Mulberry, and his stock was rising. One editorial spoke of him as a crusader against local authority corruption 'well-known, well-rooted, and ripe for extirpation.' They were getting the bit between their teeth.

The inquiry itself had continued its deliberations but had taken no new evidence because of the holiday. On the Wednesday morning it convened again and to Arnold's surprise he heard that Brent-Ellis had been recalled to give evidence. Jerry Picton was quick to theorize, once again.

'Obvious, isn't it?' he sneered. 'They missed a trick first time around. They were concentrating on the Cossman leak as far as our department was concerned. Now, after taking evidence from the legal boys, they realize they should have cross-examined the director on financial matters as well.' He winked at Arnold. 'At least you'll be in the clear there, bonny lad. You've never had the chance to put sticky fingers in the till, have you?'

That evening Arnold felt unsettled and decided to ring Jane. She had given him her hotel phone number in New York, so he left it until late before ringing in the hope that he might catch her there at the end of her working day. He was lucky.

'Hi. How are you?'

'Arnold! I'm delighted to hear you. I've only this minute got in, and I'm off to dinner in a couple of hours, so your call is timely.'

'You're being well treated, then?'

'Wined and dined, feted and fantasized over. It's been an incredible experience — I'm treated like a film star. How are things with you?'

'Busy, of course.' They chatted inconsequentially for a while, and then she asked him how the dig was going. He explained that he had left Ravenstone because of the invitation to the dig at Haggburn, but added that the four days he had spent at the site had not been particularly productive. There was a considerable amount of careful sifting to be done. They were, however, hoping to open up some new burial sites in the next week.

'So, Rena Williams is up there with you — and Karen Stannard. Surrounded by your women, hey?'

There was a certain crispness in the comment that he thought best to ignore. Instead he entertained her with a description of the dinner party held by the idiosyncratic Mrs Delaney. She was amused.

'I'd have said eccentric, rather than idiosyncratic! Did you see much more of her after that dinner?'

'Oddly enough, no. We had an imperious call to stay at the hall, but in fact we didn't see Mrs Delaney again for a couple of days, even though we were staying as her guests. It seems she was "indisposed". It was a bit awkward, really, since there were certain tensions among the group . . .'

Had Jane been with him, Arnold would have given her the full details, but clearly it would have taken too long on the phone. The tensions that had manifested themselves that first evening at Haggburn Hall had developed further: Rick Newton had continued openly to pay court to Karen Stannard and Gabriella Newton had made no secret of her anger regarding what she saw as a developing relationship. On the third evening, when they had congregated at the hall for dinner — to receive a message that on this occasion Mrs Delaney would be gracing them with her presence — there had been a confrontation between Karen Stannard and Gabriella Newton. Arnold had been making his way to the dining room to join the others when he had heard raised voices in the library. He had not caught much of the conversation, but it was enough to reveal who the protagonists were. He heard Gabriella Newton snarl, 'I know exactly what you're playing at, and I'm warning you to stay away from him.'

Karen Stannard's tones had been cool and controlled. 'I assure you, Mrs Newton, that I have not the slightest interest in your husband. If he chooses to make a fool of himself, that's his problem — and yours. You really should attempt to control him. He's your husband, I agree, and you're welcome to him!'

'Then why don't you say it to him? You're just a damned gold-digger!' Gabriella Newton raged. 'You lead him on — you make assignations with him—'

'Mrs Newton, you're out of your tiny mind if you think I'd be seen dead with your husband. I've no interest in him whatsoever. And I've heard quite enough on this subject . . .'

Arnold had left them to it. But it was noticeable that evening that Newton did not have to make the running. Karen Stannard sat next to him, opposite Arnold, and she deliberately set out to make Gabriella angry. She flirted outrageously with Newton, their heads close together in semi-hushed conversation; she laughed merrily at his jokes; and she leaned towards him while she spoke, her shoulder — bare in a low-cut evening dress touching his. For her, it was a delicious revenge for the scene in the library, and perhaps a demonstration of her power. If she really wanted Newton, she seemed to be saying, she could have him. For Gabriella Newton, it was torture. For Arnold and the others, it was an embarrassment.

Mrs Delaney was hugely diverted by the performance. She was in better form that evening: her drinking did not proceed at the rate she'd demonstrated at the first dinner party and consequently her speech did not become slurred. But from time to time, Arnold noted, she still switched off her hearing aid and seemed to take no interest in the proceedings. Gabriella Newton took advantage of the timing to make some pertinent and salty remarks concerning her husband. It led to Fred Harkness taking an early leave of the company — he still had his tent to escape to. Arnold and Rena Williams were forced to remain until Mrs Delaney, beginning to sag in her chair, finally dismissed the company. On their way to their respective rooms, Rena and Arnold agreed that Karen was playing with fire, and really was behaving badly.

'So, there's been fun and games, then,' Jane commented when he gave a sketchy account of life at Haggburn Hall. 'And I'm not there to get all the details!'

'I wish you were,' Arnold said carefully.

'Do you, Arnold?' There was a short silence. 'I've been thinking rather a lot, in the dark hours, about us. We've been good friends, haven't we?'

'We have.' He smiled. 'Somewhat prickly from time to time.'

'I don't want to lose that friendship.'

'Is there any reason why you should?'

'I don't know. Things don't seem to be quite the same since our relationship changed. Maybe it wasn't the best idea to go to bed together.'

'I haven't heard you complain up to now.'

'You know what I mean,' she said sharply, unwilling to descend to banter. 'I'm being serious, Arnold. Things were fine before . . . they still are, really, but I'm getting to feel that I'm demanding too much of you now. You've been somewhat reluctant to . . . talk to me, about . . . well, making commitments, and I suppose that's upset me. One half of me says leave it alone, we're still friends even though we've become lovers; the other half argues that things just can't stand still, can't go on as they are. We took a step together, but it's as though that's as far as it goes, for you. There's a sort of wall, a personal barrier . . . I'm confused, Arnold; maybe I'm simply being a woman! But this . . . escape to the States, it's making me think, making me review situations . . .'

'And have you reached a solution?' Arnold asked gently. She sighed audibly. 'I don't know. All I do know is that life's hectic here, I've no time to turn around, so when I do think of you it's after I've retired for the night, when my mind is still whirling; I'm overtired, and I can't think straight . . .'

When the conversation was over, Arnold was as unsettled as he had been when it started. There had been no catharsis for him in talking to Jane. He seemed suddenly to be surrounded with problems: ill-defined, hazy, vague in their outlines. He felt on edge, but did not really know why. The situation in the department and the Mulberry inquiry were on his mind, and Karen Stannard's behaviour at Haggburn Hall was curiously irritating to him. As for his relationship with Jane . . .

Eyes half-closed, he sat down in a deep armchair with a glass of brandy and soda. He thought back over what she had said and was forced to admit she was right. Their becoming lovers had perhaps been an inevitability, resulting from the closeness of their friendship, but it had brought its problems, too. Different levels of expectation; maybe a desire to move on, to progress to a deeper commitment than merely loving friendship. The fault probably lay with him, and it was something he could not explain to himself, let alone to her. And certainly not over the telephone.

She had not told him when she was likely to return. Indeed, she'd hinted that she might be in New York working with the scriptwriters rather longer than she had anticipated. It was two hours — and several brandies later — before Arnold got to bed.

He arrived at the office a little late the following morning. He was not in the best of moods: his tongue was furred and a dull, steady thumping in his skull informed him he should not have over-indulged the night before. In addition, he was still somewhat unsettled about the conversation with Jane over the phone. At some stage, he knew, he would have to attempt to rationalize the situation, identify just where the relationship was going. But not yet, he thought gloomily. He had too many things on his mind.

He was not the only one who was upset that morning.

Arnold had barely settled behind his desk when there was a tap on the door. It opened, and Miss Sansom walked in. He stared at her in surprise. Her Teutonic jowls were sagging; her bent iron mouth had lost its strength and drooped at the edges; her eyes were red-rimmed and angry, but the anger was rooted in desperation. She was not the forceful personality she usually was. And she had come to him.

She had never before entered his office.

'I thought you'd better have these,' she said. Her voice had lost its savage, barking undertones. She glared at him, but there was no heat, no conviction in the glance. It was as though the world she knew had been taken away from her and she found herself on unfamiliar territory. It was remarkable: away from her power base she was an ordinary, middle-aged, bad-tempered but essentially uncertain woman. Her domineering attitude had gone. She seemed, Arnold considered, lessened.

'What are these?' Arnold asked, accepting the papers she clutched in her hand.

'Correspondence. It's been waiting for a few days — while Mr Brent-Ellis was away, ill. And there are some committee notes that I've prepared — they'll need approving.

There's some schedules there too. I think you'll have to check them. Usually, it's Miss Stannard who does that. But she's not here. And now, Mr Brent-Ellis—'

He thought for a moment that she was going to cry. Hastily, he said, 'I'm sure Mr Brent-Ellis will get over his influenza pretty soon. Are these papers really so urgent? Can't they await his return?'

She straightened and some of her old fire returned. In a stiff, resentful tone, she said, 'I'm sure I don't know when he'll be coming back. I'm not a person the powers that be consult on these matters. I'm not privy to discussions and I'm not prepared to take the responsibility if the department goes to the dogs. They're on your desk, Mr Landon. You'd better deal with them as you see fit.'

It was the longest speech he had ever heard her make. He stared at her, not knowing what to say as she turned on her heel and marched out of the door. In the corridor outside he heard a scuffling sound, and a brief altercation. A few moments later, Jerry Picton stuck his head round the door. 'The Gauleiter — in your room! Hey, bonny lad, how are the mighty fallen!'

Arnold sighed. 'What do you want?' he growled ungraciously.

'Taking the opportunity to offer you congratulations.'

'Having Miss Sansom come to me, rather than me go to her, is not what I see as a reason for congratulations. The woman—'

Picton flapped a hand, waving him to silence. 'Hell, no, that's a result, not the main event itself. Haven't you heard? Don't you know why she had to come to you? Didn't you wonder why she's so upset? I mean, she nearly walked over me in the corridor a moment ago, but that wasn't her normal savagery other days she'd have kicked me as well as trample me against the wall. And with deliberation. This time, it was because she just didn't see me! Tears in her eyes! I tell you, the woman's distraught.'

'Why?' Arnold asked. 'Brent-Ellis only has influenza. There's no need for hysterics.'

Jerry Picton leered with greening teeth. His weasel features were twitching with excitement. 'So, you really haven't heard. Fraulein Obergruppenführer Sansom is mighty upset, bonny lad, because her dear director, the darling of her eye, the font and source of all her imagined power, is not recovering from the flu. He appeared before Mulberry on Wednesday. And he was actually in the office early this morning . . .' He paused, portentously. 'Clearing his desk!'

Arnold sat up. 'What the hell are you talking about?'

Picton was almost dancing with delight at being able to give Arnold the news. 'He's gone the way of all flesh, man — the way Ms Standoffish Stannard has gone. The powers that be have decided. Brent-Ellis is suspended!'

'That can't be right!'

'I'm telling you. I picked it up as our dear departing director was leaving the building. It was tail-between-legs stuff. He slunk out like he'd been hit with a sledgehammer.' He giggled unpleasantly. 'If you can slink after you've been flattened.'

'On what grounds would he be suspended?' Arnold wondered. 'I mean, Karen Stannard was suspended because of the suspicions regarding the departmental leak to a television presenter, but there's never been the suggestion that Brent-Ellis . . .'

'But you must have heard that Mulberry has extended the scope of the inquiry. That's why Brent-Ellis was called back in. And something has come out of that to make them suspend him. So, the king is dead . . .' He grinned wolfishly. 'Long live the king.'

'What's that supposed to mean?' Arnold growled, confused and irritable.

'Why do you think the SS marched in here this morning? Bringing those papers to you shows that she at least knew the implications of the suspension of both Stannard and Brent-Ellis. You're elected, bonny lad! Congratulations. Just as long as you remember who was the first to congratulate you!'

Arnold sat as though stunned for some minutes after Picton had gone. He felt unable to grasp all the implications. He was amazed that the authority had seen fit to suspend the two senior officers in the department, at the same time. The Mulberry inquiry was taking its duties seriously, of that there was no doubt, but it smacked of prejudgement, to suspend people before the verdict of the committee, by way of its report, was in. As for the job itself, it was not something Arnold was seeking. He had no desire to become head — even in an acting capacity — of the department. He was not an ambitious man, and he certainly was not prepared to undertake the kind of politicking with councillors that senior officers were forced to do. He liked his job; enjoyed the freedom it gave him to go out on the moors and highlands; delighted in the opportunity it gave him to indulge his own interests. He was not happy at the thought of being desk-bound, pandering to the whims of local politicians, and attending endless committee meetings.

The phone rang on his desk. He picked it up. It was Miss Sansom. There was a new note to her voice, the kind of tone she used when speaking to Simon Brent-Ellis.

'Mr Landon? Mr Powell Frinton would like to see you in his office, as soon as convenient.'

Arnold felt a coldness in his chest. So here it was, the formal statement of appointment. Unhappily, he said, 'I'll be there in a couple of minutes, Miss Sansom.'

He replaced the phone, walked over to the window and stood staring out towards the hills. He felt a great reluctance washing over him. Karen Stannard and Brent-Ellis suspended — it meant that if he was put in control of the department and they did not return, he would stand a good chance of being confirmed in office. Unless he made a pig's ear of the job. He didn't want to demonstrate incompetence — but neither did he really want the job. Yet it seemed the die was cast.

Slowly, he made his way to the office of the chief executive. It was situated at the far end of the building, away from the other senior officers' accommodation and close to the committee rooms used by the councillors. It was also close to the hospitality room — the Chairman's Parlour — where late-night drinking sessions were reputed to occur. It was rumoured that Powell Frinton attended but partook of nothing stronger than mineral water. He was a cold, ascetic individual; careful, legalistic and humourless. But he was not the kind of person who would ever be under a Mulberry indictment.

His room was tastefully furnished, as befitted the chief officer of the authority, but somewhat spartan in appearance. Powell Frinton was seated behind his desk, its surface was clean-swept. He gestured towards the seat facing him and placed thin fingertips together as he inspected Arnold. His eyes were cold, his mouth narrow. Arnold knew the chief executive did not approve of him. Powell Frinton felt he *was* something of a wild card among the career-oriented administrators in the authority. And he did not approve of Arnold's interests; in his view local authority officers should not have outside interests.

'Thank you for coming, Mr Landon . . .' He paused. He was not at ease with small talk. 'We live in uncertain times.'

'It seems so, Chief Executive.'

Powell Frinton blinked. There was something saurian about the slowness of the movement. 'Uncertainty breeds rumour. And you will no doubt be aware that there are various rumours circulating within the authority, largely as a result of the . . . ah . . . Mulberry inquiry.'

'I try to ignore rumours.'

'Most wise. But there are also facts . . . such as the suspension of Miss Stannard. That will have increased your workload, Mr Landon.'

'To a certain extent. Nothing I can't cope with . . . in the short term.'

Powell Frinton grimaced. 'Quite. Well, events move on. The committee has been taking further evidence . . . as a result of which there was an extraordinary meeting of the council yesterday evening.' He sniffed, pinched his nostrils thoughtfully between finger and thumb. 'The consequence of that meeting was that I was instructed to take certain steps that further affect your department.' He paused, frowning at Arnold as he chose his words with legalistic care. 'Miss Stannard was suspended pending further enquiries into the unfortunate leak which prompted Cossman International's suit, naming the authority. Since then, certain . . . allegations have come to light concerning departmental finances. I don't need to go into details, because they are allegations only, but they concern the claiming of certain . . . expenses. However, to make it brief, the consequence is that Mr Brent-Ellis has also been suspended, *sine die*, and I was instructed to inform him of that fact. I did so, by telephone last night, and we had a brief interview this morning. He is suspended until the committee reports in due course.'

Arnold was silent for a few moments. Mulberry was clearly gaining in power. He must have pushed hard for the full council to meet and endorse recommendations that were presumably his. Powell Frinton waited, expecting Arnold to say something; when he did not, the chief executive went on.

'It creates a problem, of course, having the two senior officers in a department under suspension. The matter of a replacement was raised by me at the council meeting. It was discussed there. The suggestion was therefore made that the simplest solution would be to ask you to hold the reins . . .'

The basilisk eyes were fixed on Arnold, unblinkingly. 'I feel it would be wrong if I were not to tell you that I opposed that solution. The reasons I gave are, I believe, sound. And it is only right and correct that I should apprise you of those reasons.'

He inspected his immaculate fingernails with apparent distaste. 'You were to a certain extent involved in the Cossman business — it was your report that was leaked. So there is still a degree of uncertainty about the part you played in those events — at least as far as some of us are concerned. Secondly, you have no experience of the kind of teamwork undertaken by the senior officers as a management group. I think it would be inappropriate to expect you to fit in easily. And finally, you are a man of a certain . . . irregularity of interest. You have been known to cause certain embarrassments to the department.' He breathed in deeply, twisting his mouth as he did so. 'Consequently, the council took the view that they would *not* be asking you to take over the management of the department in the absence of the director and deputy director.'

Arnold was silent for a little while. At last he nodded, slowly. 'May I ask who will be taking over?'

'It's been decided we should put into place an individual who already has experience of the senior management team. A short-term contract will be offered to Mr Elliott Scarisbrick. You will, no doubt, be aware of him and his previous work.'

Arnold knew the man. He had held the position of Director of the Department of Leisure for some years, before his early retirement last summer. His reputation was that of a self-seeking bombast. He had courted the councillors avidly and had been held in some regard by them for his open drinks cabinet, the occasional parties he held at the large house he had bought with his wife's money, and his outgoing, booming, hail-fellow-well-met personality. He had not been held in high regard by the administrators who worked in his department as they had discovered, to their cost, that when difficulties arose, he usually found someone else to blame, unless it was a favourable outcome, in which case he took the credit. And this was the man they were bringing back to run the department on a short-term contract. His friendliness with individual councillors had obviously paid off.

Arnold considered the matter. Powell Frinton regarded him with cold eyes, awaiting his comments. At last Arnold asked, 'May I speak freely, Chief Executive?'

Powell Frinton licked narrow lips. His eyes were wary. 'Of course, Mr Landon.'

'You spoke of rumours. I've heard some of them. And one of them was that I was going to be asked to run the department. Indeed, I think there's a general assumption that I was going to be so asked. That's why Miss Sansom, for instance, dropped a pile of papers on my desk this morning.'

'I'm aware that such a rumour could well have been circulating.'

'Now let's be clear about this, Mr Powell Frinton. Whatever you think of my capabilities, I like my job — and in my view I do a good job. Be that as it may, the rumour of my . . . elevation was not welcome to me. I have no desire to sit in the director's seat. My present job suits me, and although I came here expecting you to ask me to take over, I came reluctantly. I would have suggested you look for someone else. True, had you said the decision was made, I would have done my best to run the department as it should be run. But I wouldn't have enjoyed it.' He regarded Powell Frinton steadily. 'But you didn't ask me to take over. You told me Scarisbrick will do the job. So I'm relieved. I didn't want the job; I don't have it.'

Powell Frinton smiled thinly; there was no real amusement in the smile. 'In which case, there's no problem.'

'I didn't say *that*,' Arnold replied. 'I'm relieved that you haven't offered me the job, but that doesn't mean I approve of what's going on.'

'Your approval is not a requirement, Mr Landon,' Powell Frinton responded acidly.

'I'm not suggesting it is. But you've given me permission to speak plainly, so I'll take the opportunity to tell you what I feel. I'm aware there are problems in the authority. I'm aware that Councillor Mulberry is probing, looking into those problems with his committee. But it seems to me that things are going too far, too quickly. Allegations are being made, rumours flying around the departments, morale is sagging — and then not one, but two officers are suspended from the department in which I work. Now it seems to me that the council is wrong to take such action when the committee is still hearing witnesses; no facts have been proved, there has been no opportunity for charges to be heard and possibly rebutted. Stannard and Brent-Ellis have been treated unfairly.'

Powell Frinton raised a cynical, arched eyebrow. 'I've always had the impression that you held your director . . . not in high regard, shall I say? And your relationship with Miss Stannard has been clearly of a somewhat . . . fractious nature, I understand.'

'I'm talking about principle,' Arnold replied. 'Not personalities.'

Powell Frinton regarded him steadily. 'I hear what you say. But the council has now made a decision.'

'And I too have made a decision,' Arnold announced.

The wariness was back in the eyes of the chief executive. 'What might that decision be, Mr Landon?'

'I have some leave due to me. Two weeks. I wish to make a request that I be allowed to take those two weeks now. Immediately.'

Powell Frinton frowned. He was puzzled. 'This would place the department in some difficulty — perhaps an impossible position. Losing two senior officers on suspension, another allowed to go on leave — at a time when Mr Scarisbrick, who knows nothing about the work of the department, is about to take over. I think to take leave at this juncture might be seen as demonstrating, on your part, a lack of loyalty towards the other staff in the department.'

'As the failure of the chief executive to strenuously resist the suspension of senior colleagues might be seen as disloyalty to those colleagues, and others in jeopardy?' Arnold replied steadily.

The chief executive was silent for a little while. He fixed Arnold with his cold eyes, his thoughts were unreadable. 'You don't know that I didn't . . . strenuously resist, Mr Landon.'

'True. But Stannard and Brent-Ellis *were* suspended. And you're still here.'

The silence grew around them. Powell Frinton picked up a pencil and carefully revolved it between his hands as he continued to stare at Arnold, thoughtfully. He pursed thin, contemplative lips, a lawyer considering the options. At last he said in a cold tone, 'Your request for leave might be seen as a matter of . . . pique, at not being offered the job.'

'I'm not concerned with what rumours may fly around the authority. Pique? You know otherwise.'

'Yes . . .' Powell Frinton took a deep breath. 'So you say. And you do have an entitlement . . . I suppose this is your way of making a protest, Mr Landon, at what you see as an injustice? You want the council to become aware that work in the department will probably grind to a standstill, because of your absence on leave?'

'No. Because two senior officers have been suspended without a proper hearing.'

Powell Frinton threw down the pencil. It rolled across the desk and dropped to the carpet. He ignored it. His gimlet eyes bored into Arnold's. 'Perhaps you have a point. Perhaps it's necessary that the council should take cognizance of the effect their actions might have, if they continue to accept Mr Mulberry's recommendations. Perhaps they should be made aware of the fall in morale in the departments. And you are, of course, entitled to take your leave . . . provided the interests of the department are not affected. And in this case . . .' He permitted himself a thin smile, edged with malice. 'I suspect the interests of the department might actually be in a roundabout way . . .'

He stood up. There was an odd glint in his eyes, and a hint of grudging respect in his tone. 'All right, Mr Landon. You've made your point. You can have your two weeks' leave. I'll sign the necessary authorization this afternoon. If you call in at my secretary's desk at three it will be ready for you. And when the inevitable screaming starts from the council — as it will when committees and files and written advice don't match up — we'll all know where the responsibility lies, won't we?'

The interview was clearly over. There was no more to be said.

Arnold nodded his thanks, and rose. The chief executive was still standing behind the desk, watching him, when he reached the door. Arnold opened it, stepped through, and was closing it behind him when he caught the gleam in Powell Frinton's eye.

'Enjoy your leave,' the chief executive said drily.

2

Arnold left for Haggburn Hall in the early morning.

He had not slept well for the second night running. He was still on edge, his mind churning with thoughts of Jane, and the problems in the department, and he decided eventually that he might as well make an early start and head up to the fells where he could clear his head, and maybe get a better perspective on things that were bothering him. He was still a little surprised at the temerity with which he had faced Powell Frinton — and the chief executive's capitulation. He was also surprised at his own defending of two people he disliked: Karen Stannard and Simon Brent-Ellis. But as he'd said to Powell Frinton, it was a matter of principle.

He contented himself with an orange juice before he set off; consequently, when he came over the shoulder of the fell and saw the village of Haggburn below him, he realized he was hungry. It would be a good idea to stop off at the Drover's Rest for breakfast before he made his way onto the site of the dig.

He parked in the main street and entered the hotel. The breakfast room was only half full and he had no difficulty finding a table. He placed his order for bacon and eggs and it arrived quickly. He rarely took much for breakfast at home, but the drive had sharpened his appetite. He ate with relish, and was waiting for a fresh cup of coffee, having finished the first small pot, when he became aware that someone was standing at his table. He glanced up; it was the pale-faced man he had met briefly in the bar the previous weekend.

'Good morning,' the man said.

Arnold desperately searched for the name, and after a moment it came to him: Steve Quaid. 'Morning, Mr Quaid.'

'You didn't stay long here at the hotel, then.'

'At the hotel? No. I . . . I was offered other accommodation.'

The almost non-existent eyebrows twitched and there was a sneer on Quaid's lips. 'Yeah, I gather you were invited to stay up at Haggburn Hall. What do you think of her?'

'Who?'

'Mrs Delaney. The crazy old cow who owns the place.'

Arnold was irritated. He stared at the slim, fair-haired young man coldly. 'It was she who invited me — and my colleagues to stay. She's very hospitable.'

'Your colleagues as well! So that's why I haven't seen that stuck-up piece around the last few days. I fancied her . . . even if her nose is up in the air. I know what *she* needs. But that Mrs Delaney, she's something else, I hear. She's around the twist, hospitable or not! It must be a real laugh, evenings up there!'

The coffee arrived and Arnold turned away. Quaid stood there for a moment, as though he wanted to carry on the conversation, but perhaps the set of Arnold's mouth told him his presence was unwelcome. 'See you around,' he muttered, and left the room.

Arnold sipped his coffee. He frowned, wondering how Quaid had come into contact with Mrs Delaney. He seemed to be aware of the peculiarity of evening sessions at Haggburn Hall, — but that might have been a matter of common gossip in Haggburn village itself. Arnold shrugged the thought away. His brief meetings with Steve Quaid left him with no desire to extend the acquaintance. There was a surliness, an unpleasantness about the man that Arnold disliked.

When he came out of the hotel some ten minutes later having discovered that he had come away from home without his shaving tackle — he walked along to the chemist shop in the high street to buy a packet of disposable razors and some shaving foam. He had completed his purchases and was walking back towards his car when he caught sight of a familiar face from the Haggburn dig.

'Morning, Fred!' he called out.

Fred Harkness turned and saw Arnold. He ran a hand over his bald head, smiled and crossed the road to join him. His weather-beaten features were creased with pleasure. 'Arnold . . . are you on the way up to the site? I hadn't realized you'd be back so soon, and during the week as well. We thought maybe at the weekend . . .'

'I'm taking some leave,' Arnold explained. 'So I'll be available to help out for the next couple of weeks, if that's OK with you.'

Fred Harkness beamed. 'Delighted to have you. We'll be opening up another couple of burial sites this week, if the weather holds, so we're keeping our fingers crossed. Have you had any more thoughts on the cult figurines?'

Arnold shrugged. 'I've no further information, but I did have a conversation with the archivist at Newcastle Library and he's let me have some photocopied sheets relating to ancient cults in the northern areas, along with a few map references, but I haven't had time to go into detail with them yet. I thought I'd discuss the possibilities with you and Rena while I'm up here.'

'Grand. I look forward to that. Maybe we can crack the puzzle, hey? I've just come into the village this morning because I'm running short of a few basic supplies — I see you've been shopping, too. Anyway, I'll see you up—' He stopped suddenly, his glance sliding past Arnold. His brow furrowed, and his mouth became thin and hard. 'Sorry about this, Arnold, will you excuse me for a moment? I'll see you up at the dig, later.'

'Surely.' Arnold stepped aside as Harkness strode, stiff-legged, shoulders hunched aggressively, to re-cross the road. Arnold made his way to his car, parked some fifty metres away. As he was unlocking the door, he looked back down the street and could see Fred Harkness standing near the vegetable display counter outside a grocery shop. He looked angry and he was talking to someone, prodding a finger in the man's chest. Then, as the man stepped back, Arnold recognized him.

It was Steve Quaid.

The two men were clearly in the middle of a heated altercation. Quaid was dressed in a windcheater and jeans, and over his left arm he carried a broken shotgun. His narrow features were twisted, his fair hair falling over his forehead as he argued with Fred Harkness. The older, heavier man was still threatening with his finger, prodding away as Quaid fell back, his features suffused with anger. As Arnold watched, Quaid snapped the barrel of the shotgun back into place and held the weapon upright, muzzle pointing to the sky. He thrust at Harkness with the side of the shotgun butt, aggressively, pushing him away.

Harkness almost went berserk. He grabbed at Quaid's collar and swung the younger, lighter man sideways, so that he collided with the vegetable display. Several loose potatoes fell and rolled along the pavement, into the gutter. As the two men wrestled — Harkness with one hand on Quaid's jacket and the other on the shotgun — a middle-aged woman emerging from the shop itself, cowered in fear. Quaid and Harkness swayed and stamped, Quaid desperately trying to release himself from the grip on his collar. The woman shouted something at them, angrily, and Harkness seemed to come to his senses. He released his grip on both collar and shotgun, and Quaid stepped back, glaring at him, the shotgun lowered now.

The woman hurried away. Words were still being exchanged between the two men, but some of the aggression had gone. Harkness was back to finger-wagging, as if he were warning Quaid about something. The sneer was back on Quaid's pale, washed-out features. He turned, began to walk away, throwing some comment over his shoulder. Harkness stood in the shop doorway, staring at his retreating back for several seconds and then stumped into the shop. As Arnold got into his car and turned on the ignition, he saw Harkness come out of the shop again, somewhat sheepishly. He began to pick up the potatoes that had been disturbed from the display, placing them in a paper bag. He glanced around a couple of times, as if to check that Quaid was not in sight.

As Arnold drove past, Harkness was re-entering the shop; Arnold thought it best not to draw his attention by sounding his horn and waving. He guessed Harkness would be embarrassed if he knew that Arnold had witnessed the altercation.

Rena Williams and Karen Stannard were working at the site when Arnold arrived. They were in the hut; he tapped on the door and entered. Rena Williams opened her eyes wide in surprise, and smiled. 'Arnold! What are you doing here?'

'I've taken some leave.'

'So you can work up here with us — that's great, isn't it, Karen?'

Karen Stannard's eyes were of an indeterminate colour this morning, maybe green, maybe hazel, but her glare was as hostile as ever as her eyes met Arnold's. She parted her lips, touched them thoughtfully with her tongue. Her tone was edged with sarcasm. 'Leave . . . I wonder that the department can manage without you.'

He smiled and shrugged, ignoring the jibe. 'What's happening here?'

Rena Williams turned to the table and leaned over it. 'We've not been able to open up the next grave site yet but we have turned up some more bits and pieces. We've come across a silver pendant, here: you see the three ornamental arms, and the suspension loop around the coin? Fred Harkness has identified the coin as Roman.'

'And if you look at the pendant closely,' Karen Stannard added, drawing nearer so that she was standing just behind Arnold, 'you can see it bears a roughly executed chi-rho symbol outlined by small circular punch marks.' She was staring at Arnold as she spoke, and her gaze was keen, weighing him up carefully. He was very much aware of the light scent of her perfume.

Arnold leaned over the coin, examining it. 'So what do you make of it?' he asked.

Rena Williams humphed quietly. She brushed a loose lock of hair back from her eyes. With a certain triumph in her tone, she said, 'Well, it looks to me that we have confirmation of the long usage to which the site has been put. We have Saxon graves; we have some evidence of the Mórrigan cult; and now we have a late Roman artefact. We know that the Romans were not about imposing religions on their conquests, and I think what we see here is a late emergence of Christianity at a site which has already been, shall we say, consecrated to other religions and cults in previous generations. Christianity was certainly an uneasy bedfellow in Ireland with the Mórrigan, but there's no doubt that co-existence occurred. Peasant superstition would often cling to the old religion while paying lip service to the new. And it seems the same situation applied here. It's going to be interesting now to open up the next few grave sites — I think we'll confirm the multi-usage, and we might find some clear evidence as to just how long the Shape-Shifter was worshipped here.'

'Or at the least, placated, if not worshipped,' Karen Stannard added. She was still staring at Arnold, a faint frown on her features.

A little after eleven, Fred Harkness appeared at the hut and joined them in their discussion of the artefacts. At noon they went out to survey the site again, discussing how best to start work on the next grave sites, and when they broke for lunch — Harkness had bought a selection of sandwiches in the village — Arnold had a clear idea of what they would be doing for the rest of the week, and had been assigned to work with a couple of the young students on one particular burial possibility.

They were seated on camp stools, eating their sandwiches a little apart from the women, when Fred Harkness said, in a slightly embarrassed tone, 'I'm sorry I left you so abruptly in the village. And I suppose you saw what happened.'

Arnold nodded. He glanced at Harkness; the man appeared shamefaced. 'So what was it all about?'

Harkness shrugged. 'I just lost my temper, really. That little bastard . . . he gave me a mouthful when I spoke to him, and I guess I saw red. It's that bloody gun, you see.'

'How do you mean?'

Fred Harkness grimaced, and gestured towards the woods flanking the top end of the site, above the outcrop of rocks. 'He's been up there a couple of times, the careless bastard. I bet he's got no licence for that bloody shotgun, either. I've no idea what he's been shooting at up there, but I've got students in my care, and he's been blazing away within fifty metres of them. I don't reckon he's any expert with the gun, either. I got hold of him a few weeks ago and warned him off, but he was back again last week. I couldn't catch him — he slipped away when he saw me coming. So when I saw him in the village I went up to him . . . and lost my temper, when he argued with me. It's a free world, he said. I couldn't stop him walking, or shooting, if it wasn't my land . . . I'd like to break his damned neck!'

Arnold frowned. 'How long has Quaid been around here?'

'Quaid? Is that his name?' Harkness shrugged, carelessly. 'Several weeks.'

'A long holiday, then. Strange . . . I'm sure he told me he was just here for a couple of weeks, and bored with the place at that. Maybe I misheard.'

'Is that what he says . . . he's on holiday?' Harkness shook his head. 'I wouldn't know about that. But holiday or not, I've told him if I catch him near the site again with that bloody gun, I'll wrap it round his weaselly neck!'

And Arnold gained the impression Fred Harkness wasn't fooling.

Arnold worked on the opening of the next burial site with his two students during the afternoon, stripping the topsoil, beginning the long, patient task of sifting soil through a rough then a fine mesh to make sure that nothing that might be of interest was missed. In the mid-afternoon, when he called a halt for a tea break Karen Stannard strolled across towards him. Her hair was tousled, framing her face, and her skin was slightly flushed, touched by the breeze that came down from the fell. She was wearing an open-necked shirt that accentuated her figure; her jeans were moulded to her legs. But her attitude was still hostile.

'You're close-mouthed, Landon.'

'What's there to talk about?'

'Don't play silly games with me,' she said quietly. 'Let's have the story.'

'What story?'

'I'm not stupid, Landon. You being here means that something's going on back in Morpeth. With my suspension, the department will be short-handed at senior officer level. You'll have had to cover for me, because Brent-Ellis won't pick up the extra work. He wouldn't be able to do without you. So how come he allowed you to take leave?'

Arnold was silent for a moment. 'It wasn't his decision to make.'

She frowned. 'I don't understand. If it wasn't his decision, who gave you permission?'

'Powell Frinton.'

'What's the chief executive doing, interfering in Brent-Ellis's departmental business? And didn't Brent-Ellis oppose your taking leave at this time?' She glared at him in frustration. 'What the hell's going on, Landon?'

Arnold looked up at her. He hesitated. 'Brent-Ellis has been suspended.'

There was a long silence. She chewed at her lower lip as she struggled to absorb the news and its implications. Then she exploded with an incredulous laugh. 'They've found him out at last!' When he made no response a wariness came back into her eyes; she frowned as another thought came to her. 'Is this Mulberry again?'

Arnold nodded, and stood up. He looked around the site; clouds were gathering above the fell and the wind was

111

cooler. There was a hint of rain in the air, so it might be as well to get tarpaulins stretched over the sites that were currently being opened. He glanced at Karen Stannard, her eyes were as grey as the clouds as she stared at him, calculatingly. But she wasn't getting the answers she sought. 'I don't understand what's going on,' she said slowly. 'Both Brent-Ellis and I have been suspended. And you choose to take leave at this precise time. Moreover, the chief executive allows it. What are you playing at, Landon?'

Arnold shrugged. 'The two weeks' leave was due to me. And the dig's at an interesting stage.'

She barely heard him. Her eyes were on him but they were unseeing; it was as if she were looking inward, searching deeply for the answer to a conundrum, suspicious of motive and wary of something she could not understand. When she spoke at last, her voice was soft, almost gentle in its questioning, and yet there was veiled steel in her tone. 'Two weeks' leave . . . I don't understand.'

He looked at her, doggedly.

There was confusion in her eyes, an unwilling doubt in her own fixed certainties. The doubt was reflected in her voice. 'Why would you do this, Landon . . . ?'

* * *

He felt a perverse inclination to enlighten her in no way whatsoever. Perhaps it was his petty way of getting back at her for all the slights she had visited upon him; perhaps it was because he was still not certain in his own mind of his motivation, or the wisdom of his actions. But for the rest of the afternoon he was aware that she was watching him, perplexed, disturbed.

He admitted to himself that he rather enjoyed her puzzlement, which seemed to be having an effect on her behaviour towards him. She had been surly throughout last weekend, except when she had been provoking Gabriella Newton by her flirtation with the woman's husband and had had little to say to Arnold. Now, she seemed to be wary; not unpleasant to him, but careful, weighing him up as though she mistrusted his intentions, and yet was grudgingly granting him a certain respect.

Towards the end of the afternoon the threat of rain became a reality, the sky darkened, the wind rose and the rain began to sweep across the field in a steady, thickening downpour. Under Fred Harkness's direction they dragged out tarpaulins and pegged them down to cover the newly opened sites, but as they did so the wind tugged at the edges of the sheets, and they were forced to further weight them down with stones. It was almost six before they finished and made their way to Haggburn Hall. Mrs Delaney had guessed at their situation and had arranged for hot drinks to be available as they entered her home. There were times when she could be the perfect hostess.

It was not quite the same situation that evening. She was in an effervescent, mischievous mood. She teased Vartek about his claimed connections with the spirit world until he began to glower his displeasure, well before the main course was served. She needled Gabriella, making pointed references to Karen, who, surprisingly, seemed to have discarded her flirtatious behaviour and was rather reserved and withdrawn, having little to say for herself. Several times Arnold caught her glance. Once she held his eyes almost challengingly for several seconds, until he was forced to look away. He gained the impression that Mrs Delaney had observed the interchange and was amused.

She soon began to slur her words, and once again she was guilty of a number of malapropisms. Rick Newton matched her drinking and became openly scornful, the more so because since he seemed to have lost the attention of Karen Stannard he felt it necessary to be more boisterous in his speech. When, inevitably, Mrs Delaney grew tired and switched off her hearing aid, he became openly scornful, in spite of warnings from his wife.

'My father was her younger brother, you know, and there wasn't much love lost between them. The fact is, she was a bit of a scandal to the family. They were solid working class and they knew what was right. Or so he told me. Vita, now, she was different. She didn't want the millwork in Lancashire . . . Didn't realize she was a Lancashire lass, did you? Poshed up her accent, you see. After she took to the stage in the forties. Well, took to dancing, anyway. It was in the war. She'd have ended up as a tart, no doubt, except that the Yanks were in town . . .'

Mrs Delaney stirred in her chair and moaned slightly; her mouth dropped open and a slight snoring sound was emitted from her scarlet-outlined mouth.

'So she escaped,' Newton continued, his eyes contemptuous and his tone surprisingly bitter. 'Jack Delaney married her after they'd lived together for a while in the States. And he was loaded. Five years later he was dead of a heart attack. She copped the lot: chorus-line floozie to wealthy widow in one fell swoop. And ever since she's lorded it about and ignored her origins. She came back to England, bought Haggburn Hall, made wise investments, and there she is . . . drunk every night, incapable of coherent speech, surrounded by hangers-on like Vartek, there.'

The distinguished-looking object of his comment merely stared at Newton with loathing. He made no reply, but after a few moments he rose with deliberate dignity and walked out of the room. Rena Williams herself rose and glared at the half-inebriated Rick Newton. 'You seem to do a fair bit of hanging on yourself.'

'Me?' he sneered. 'I'm an employee — not like you lot, taking any handouts she gives! I make sure she's got the money to do all this' — he waved his hand to take in the room — 'and if it wasn't for me working as her accountant, where the hell would she be? But it's slave labour . . . slave labour . . .'

Vita Delaney jerked in her chair, and her eyes opened. They were bleary, and she seemed unable to grasp where she was for a moment. She blinked, and shook herself, reached for her brandy glass, and drained it. She switched on her hearing aid, fumbling at her breast. 'Ahhh. Did I drop off? I was having such a lovely dream. I was shopping . . . I'd been to Harrods, and then . . .' She wrinkled her nose, seemed confused as she sought for a name. 'Ah, yes, then I went on to Denimbum's.'

Rick Newton groaned openly. 'Debenham's,' he said with contempt.

* * *

The rain grew in intensity overnight. Arnold woke at four in the morning to the sound of the wind moaning in the eaves, and the rain pattering on the window. Finding it difficult to go back to sleep, he lay in a half-dozing state where his mind remained active while his body was relaxed. He thought again about Karen Stannard and her reserved demeanour during dinner with Mrs Delaney; even Rena Williams had commented upon it to Arnold, wondering whether Karen was not feeling well.

She had certainly not been her sharp, flirtatious self. He guessed it was because of her uncertainty about what had happened at the department — or about his reaction to her and Brent-Ellis's suspension.

It was still raining at ten o'clock in the morning. Rena and Karen decided they could do some work in the hut, sorting out the cataloguing of the artefacts, and helping Fred Harkness with any other tasks that might be necessary to prevent the rain from flooding the site. Arnold decided he would be better employed going through the papers he had been given by the librarian at Newcastle and Rena agreed; she added that it might be useful if he were to browse the shelves in Mrs Delaney's library. 'It's a fairly catholic collection of materials, and there's some antiquarian stuff there. I suspect it was bought by Mrs Delaney when she took the house — the library doesn't seem to have been used very much. And she's already told me that we can use it if we wish.'

Arnold agreed, so while the women went off in the car to the site, he stayed back in the library, first of all reading the papers he had been given and later in the morning making a search of the shelves. He was disturbed finally by Mrs Delaney's butler. 'You'll excuse me, Mr Landon, but Mrs Delaney is aware that you're in the house this morning. She suggests you might wish to partake of a little lunch — I've arranged for it to be laid. And she asks whether you would like to join her for afternoon tea, at about four o'clock.'

Arnold was agreeable to both suggestions.

The lunch comprised some cold cuts of beef and pork, and a small decanter of white wine. He enjoyed it, but was soon back at work in the library because he had found a collection of Edwards's *Antiquities of Northumberland* and a series of volumes with which he was not familiar, entitled *A History of Notable Events in the Borders and the Debatable Lands*. He spent most of the afternoon reading and making notes, and it was with a start that he realized it was almost fifteen minutes past four. He laid aside the books and made his way to the drawing room, where he found Mrs Delaney in subdued afternoon dress, carefully coiffured, taking tea with the man who called himself Vartek.

'Mr Landon.' She smiled a welcome. 'I was beginning to think you were going to ignore us.'

'My apologies. I became engrossed in some volumes in your library.'

'How interesting! It's nice to know that we're able to be of some assistance to you. You must tell me all about it. Tea?'

'Please.' He glanced at Vartek, who seemed vaguely disgruntled. 'I hope I'm not interrupting anything.'

Vita Delaney gave a little fluttering laugh. 'Of course not! Vartek and I were having an intellectual discussion. You might find it interesting. Vartek has been telling me all about reincarnation. Please continue, Vartek, I'm sure Mr Landon will find it fascinating.'

There was a short silence. At last, unwillingly, Vartek mumbled, 'I was just telling Mrs Delaney of the research that has been done, and remains to be done, in the field of the human soul, and its capacity for regeneration through the ages.'

'You see?' Vita Delaney interrupted. 'Didn't I tell you it would be fascinating? Please go on, Vartek.'

Grudgingly, avoiding Arnold's eye, he continued. 'To talk of reincarnation is merely a form of shorthand, in my view. It is not the body that returns; it is the soul that comes back on spirit wings, wings that beat around us and can be seen in the beliefs that men have held for centuries, for millennia . . .'

'Tell Mr Landon of the evidence you point to,' Vita Delaney said innocently, as she poured a cup of tea for Arnold.

Vartek shuffled in his seat. He was uncomfortable. 'It's all around us. Mistletoe, oak, long white beards and flowing robes — these are trappings by which we've been misled for generations past. The hoary old country legends, Robin of the Wood, sacred groves, magical branches, sacrifices and offerings, all these are merely confusing side issues, cloaks and veils which have in the modern world resulted in disbelief, enabling people to scoff at them and, in consequence, at the realities, also. There have always been priests with their cults, who have developed the mysteries to enslave gullible minds. But I believe there is an essential, eternal truth, and that is the soul.'

He glanced at Arnold, who kept his head down. Vartek began to warm to his task, his tones becoming more confident. 'It is difficult for us, with our post-mediaeval minds, to comprehend the strength and profundity of ancient beliefs and superstitions which pervaded all aspects of everyday life to a powerful extent. Religion in those far-off times was dominated by a veneration of the natural; the ideology included particular respect for trees and birds, greenery and animals, and all watery places. Fertility rituals and totemism involved identifiable elements . . . and all these elements, all these different cults in different ages, different millennia, yet involve an essential base, a basic truth. The transmigration of the human soul—'

'Sugar, Arnold?'

'No, thank you.' Arnold was barely able to hold back a smile as he saw the mischief bubbling in Vita Delaney's eyes. She passed his cup to him.

'Vartek feels he is on the verge of a great breakthrough; he believes he can trace the origins of the human soul through a study of the cults that have developed over the last thousand years. He wants to build a temple to research, to find the true meaning of life, in the transmigratory element that exists after death. Isn't that the case, Vartek, dear?'

'You paraphrase it somewhat,' Vartek muttered, uncertain of his audience now that Arnold was there. 'But I believe—'

'It would cost five hundred thousand pounds,' Mrs Delaney announced.

Vartek began to shuffle his feet; colour crept into his cheeks. 'I've never actually placed a figure on what would be required in terms of finance, Mrs Delaney, and—'

'Oh, I'm basing it on what you've told me, and what my nephew Rick suggests it would cost in reality: bricks, mortar, manuscripts . . . Some would say it was cheap at the price, wouldn't you agree, Arnold?'

Arnold hesitated. 'It depends on what you'd be getting for your money,' he suggested.

She beamed at him, fluttering a handkerchief in her left hand. 'Oh, I'd get my name on it. The Vita Delaney Foundation. Or something like that. It would be guaranteed, wouldn't it, Vartek?'

The man looked uneasy. He smoothed down the white wings of his hair and twisted his neck in his collar. He was uncomfortable at Arnold's presence, but he was also aware of the mockery in Vita Delaney's tone. 'The research, and the building project — nothing can be achieved without expense—'

'I'm sure, Vartek, I'm sure. And we must go into that in more detail, soon.' She leaned forward and patted him encouragingly on the hand. 'But I'm also sure you've got some work to do, before we talk again tomorrow. Finish your tea and then perhaps you wouldn't mind leaving me with Mr Landon. I think he and I have things to talk about.'

Vartek was not averse to taking his leave. He finished his tea quickly, rose, made a formal little bow and left the room with long, purposeful strides that somehow only served to emphasize his general discomfiture. Vita Delaney smiled at Arnold with a self-satisfied air. She sipped her tea and nodded.

'There. Now isn't this cosy?'

3

'You unnerved poor Mr Vartek.'

'It was more your doing than mine,' Arnold countered.

Vita Delaney laughed. 'Perhaps there's some truth in that.'

'Why do you tolerate him? He's an obvious phoney.'

She raised an eyebrow and regarded him with a certain amusement. 'You're very direct, Arnold.' She shook her head. 'I'm an old woman. He amuses me. I like to have people around me; some for the intellectual stimulation they might provide, others who enable me to enjoy myself. I listen to their self-serving flattery, pander to their belief that I am just a foolish old woman.'

'You're sharper than they think.'

'I believe that is the case,' she agreed with a slight smile.

'And much more manipulative than they suspect.'

'Now what makes you believe that?'

He leaned back in his chair and smiled at her. She was at ease in his presence. She had shed some of the apparent frailty she assumed, and her mannerisms had also disappeared. He was now seeing the real Mrs Delaney. It was time her bluff was called. 'Are you *really* hard of hearing?'

There was a short silence. 'What do you think?'

'I think there's very little wrong with your hearing. It's a ploy . . . an act.'

'I used to be an actress,' she giggled suddenly, glancing at him sideways. 'But that was a long time ago.' She watched him for a little while, contemplatively. 'I've enjoyed our little dinner parties. An interesting group of people. Vartek, of course, is here because he wants me to give him money, but on long boring afternoons he can be quite interesting to listen to, with his half-cocked theories and half-baked ideas. He's trying to con me — I've come across better in my time.'

'I'm sure you have.'

'And then there's your little group: Fred Harkness I see as a somewhat short-tempered, bluff kind of individual; honest enough, and committed to the work he delights in. I suspect one of these days his temper may get the better of him . . . I hear he's had trouble with some young whippersnapper up in the woods. Rena Williams, now . . . a strong exterior, but there are hidden fires, damped down with uncertainties. Do you know what they are?'

'I'm not certain what you're getting at.'

Vita Delaney shrugged. 'It's no matter. Woman's stuff, really. I think she is maturing, beginning to believe that work shouldn't be everything. Soon she'll reach some kind of crisis, I suspect.'

'And Karen Stannard?'

She smiled a feline smile. 'I like her. I see a great deal of me in her. A strong-minded woman, clear in her goals and objectives, and tough enough to fight for them. I understand she's in some difficulty at the moment, though I don't know what the details are. A confident, extremely beautiful woman who'll be the match for most men in this world . . .' She was silent for a while, observing him. 'Then there's you, of course.'

'You can sum me up, too?'

'Not easily.' She cocked her head on one side, inquisitively. 'But before I try, you must tell me. I'm curious. When did you first suspect I don't need a hearing aid?'

Arnold shrugged. 'It wasn't just the hearing aid. It was the performance. I was startled the first time we met, at your dinner party, when you seemed to be . . . getting under the weather, and you used the word *shogun* instead of *slogan*.' He smiled wryly. 'I thought it was a slurring, the effect of alcohol. But later, I began to believe you could handle your liquor rather better than the rest of us have been led to believe.'

She sighed dramatically. 'It's the result, I'm afraid, of an over-imaginative personality, a sojourn in the States, and a husband who adored Jim Beam whisky. I gained, shall we say, a certain tolerance . . . ?'

'Yes, well, I still wasn't sure . . . but the performance was repeated. And it followed a pattern — you'd drink, you'd get tired, you'd make foolish mistakes with your words, then you would switch off your hearing aid and have a little sleep. Eventually, I realized you were doing it deliberately: you wanted us to believe you were a senile old woman who couldn't hold her drink and you did the hearing-aid trick so you could listen to what comments were made while we all thought you were no longer with us.'

'What a witch you must think I am.'

'No. Manipulative, yes.'

'But when exactly did you realize it was just a performance?'

Arnold laughed. He shook his head. 'I'm afraid it was only last night that I became certain. *Denimbum's* . . . I mean, that really was going somewhat over the top!'

She giggled wickedly, an old lady happy at outsmarting people of another generation. 'Well, yes, I suppose I did go a bit too far there. But I couldn't resist it. I thought *transfertights* was pretty good too. And it's such fun to see your faces . . . and of course to hear what Ricky really thinks about me.'

Arnold was silent. She regarded him quietly for a while, then she tapped him gently on the arm. 'You needn't be embarrassed. Ricky's my nephew and he's greedy — even greedier than Gabriella. She tries to keep him in check, because she's looking to the future — she's desperately afraid I'll leave him nothing but he can't handle drink. I pay him a good salary and he hopes to inherit my wealth. But it's not enough. He's been trying to swindle me . . . However, he's family. And so is she, really, that's why I bought her a couple of horses. She's crazy about horses. And Rick treats her badly — he can be very dismissive of her . . .' She paused, reflectively. 'He will be disappointed one day, even though I'll look after him, financially — in a manner he doesn't really deserve. But it will not be enough for him, or Gabriella.'

'Have you no other relations?'

She shook her head. A certain sadness crept into her eyes. 'No, I never had children of my own. You see, I left my home in Lancashire in 1942 and, as Ricky told you all, became a tart, dancing on the stage. I guess he wasn't far wrong . . . Still, that was how I met Joe Delaney. He was a major in the US Army. We fell for each other like a ton of bricks. He took me back to the States, and we lived together — though I knew he was already married.' She paused, as her mind drifted back to the past, and her eyes became shadowed with memories. 'He had a hell of a life with his first wife. She was violent. She ended up in an asylum — alcoholic, crazy. I would have taken in the children, but Joe would have none of it. He wanted to cut free — and I think he was like a child, really; he wanted it to be just us. We were very much in love . . . I suppose it was a hedonistic kind of existence. Anyway, the children — a boy and a girl — they went to live with a sister of his first wife, I believe. Carnforth, I think she was called . . . I wonder how they made their way in life, at the end . . .'

'You came back to England when your husband died?'

'That's right. I didn't know it when I met Joe, but his family was seriously wealthy. Engineering, a stake in a small oilfield — there was a lot of money. His own father never liked Joe's first wife and that was a real problem, not least because when Joe died suddenly — cancer — his father was still alive. He comforted me in my loss, then died himself just eight months after his son. But with Joe gone, the old man left everything to me. I was badly shaken at the time

. . . I came back to England, bought Haggburn Hall, and after a while I was able to forget. Poor Joe . . . we had only a relatively short time together . . .'

There was a brief silence. Arnold said, 'I'm sorry, I shouldn't be so inquisitive—'

'No, not at all. It's good to talk about it again, after all these years. I have George Mahoney — you know, my estate manager — come in sometimes. He lived in Canada for many years and we have a good old chat about what things used to be like. The last year he's been of great assistance to me; I've treated him as a confidant, but I've never been able to talk to him about family matters. Except Rick, of course.' She fixed him with a curious glance. 'I wonder how it is I'm at ease talking to you, about Joe, and the past.'

'Because I'm a stranger.'

'That may be . . . Anyway, you said you'd been working in the library. What exactly were you looking for? Is it to do with the dig in the field?'

Arnold explained how he had come to be at the Haggburn dig. He told her of the finding of the icons at Ravenstone, and of Karen Stannard's phone call to tell Rena Williams that a similar artefact had been found at Haggburn. 'It poses a problem, you see. When we came across the icon at Ravenstone it was puzzling: a Saxon grave containing an icon linked to an Irish cult of some antiquity. I suppose it was explicable, in the sense we know there was considerable movement across the Irish Sea in ancient times, but nevertheless it was a challenge. Then, when we learned there was another icon here, it became more interesting, posing the question whether the cult could have been widespread up here, in Northumberland.'

'And the books in my library might help?'

'I haven't finished my trawl yet. But I'm beginning to develop a theory.'

'As ridiculous as Vartek's?'

Arnold laughed. 'I hope not!'

'And what is this cult you're talking about?'

He told her of the great winged, female war deity of Irish legend, called the Mórrigan by some, the Shape-Shifter by others. She was violent and treacherous, and she interfered with the doings of men. She was able to take any shape she pleased — wolf, boar, stag, raven — but in the iconography she tended to be depicted as a woman with the head of a bull. She lent her aid to men in battle and then betrayed them; she promised victory and gave death; she bathed in blood and spread her raven's wings across the battlefields of the Celtic world. She was revered and worshipped and feared — and the terror of her name spread dismay and despair throughout the land. She came on the cold, ancient winds and no man knew in what shape she would come, and in what form she would return. She was the Mórrigan, who had destroyed the hero Cuchulain.

Vita Delaney shivered involuntarily. 'You have a feeling for the cold past, Mr Landon.' She considered him for a moment or two. '"The Shape-Shifter", a strange name, but a descriptive one. You think Vartek is a shape-shifter?'

'How do you mean?'

'I don't know. I have a feeling about him. He likes to make out he's a man of mystery, and in a sense he is. He goes only by the name of Vartek, and however much I tease him, he won't tell me his real name. And sometimes, in spite of myself, I feel uneasy in his presence. I suspect he has a past.'

Arnold smiled. 'Don't we all?'

She nodded. 'I read him well enough, really. But there is something . . . As for you — I didn't get around to telling you what I read in you.'

'Now's your chance, Mrs Delaney,' Arnold said lightly.

She leaned forward, elbows on the table, hands cupped beneath her chin. Her eyes were sparkling as though she were a child enjoying an exciting game. She seemed to have shed years, and Arnold caught a hint of what she must have been like when she first attracted Joe Delaney, over fifty years ago.

'How can I begin?' she said. 'You're tolerably good-looking, but unmarried. You lack ambition, I suspect, and you're not prepared to scramble over other people to get to what you do want. You've a steady, analytical mind, perceptive without being arrogant, self-analytical without being introspective. You leave strangers with an immediate impression of being someone they could write off, but that's only with people who are so self-important and arrogant themselves that they don't see what's behind the rather . . . self-effacing mask you wear. I don't quite know why you give an overt under-valuation of yourself — I suspect it's because there's a certain need for privacy in you. You like people, but you can do without their company; you have a fascination for the past, and the fells, and a passion for your work. You're untrained, professionally, but you've made a reputation for yourself by—'

'I have a feeling,' Arnold interrupted drily, 'you're performing again. You've been talking to someone who knows me.'

She laughed. 'You don't believe I have the gift of second sight?'

'I told you — I think you're manipulative rather than an out-and-out witch.'

'Well, Rena Williams was a certain help.' She glanced at him mischievously. 'So have you and Karen Stannard been lovers?'

The abruptness of the question startled him. For a few moments he was unable to reply, then he gave a nervous laugh. 'What on earth makes you ask that?'

'It's a simple question, from a curious old woman.'

Arnold shook his head. 'You're way off beam. I believe . . .' He hesitated, reluctant to retail Jerry Picton's gossip, but he felt on the defensive. 'I understand her inclinations lie in another direction.'

'Is that so?' Vita Delaney pursed her lips, her keen glance still fixed on Arnold. 'It's possible . . . but it doesn't explain the way she looks at you sometimes.'

Arnold laughed. 'The way she looks at me? That's pure hatred! You need to be aware, Mrs Delaney, of the fact that Karen Stannard and I are in a state of almost constant hostility.'

'That's what I mean,' the old woman said, leaning back in her chair with a self-satisfied air. 'It's all about sparks.'

'Sparks?'

'Electricity. Storms and misunderstandings; competition and arguments — and denials. A refusal to acknowledge something when it's there all the time. You have feelings of respect for her?'

'As a professional, yes, but—'

'She holds you in high regard.'

Arnold shook his head. 'I find that hard to believe—'

'It's an old woman's summation, based upon a knowledge of life, and observations derived of long experience. But you find the thought disturbing. Forgive me. I should not interfere.' Vita Delaney gave him a secretive smile. 'Maybe I've talked too much. Maybe I've misread a situation. Let's leave it there. We'll wait and see, hey? Wait and see . . .'

* * *

Over the next few days, once the rain had eased, they were able to get down to serious work, uncovering the new grave sites. Rena Williams had propounded a theory that the field as a whole had probably constituted a settlement, and during the Iron Age a hillfort. There was some evidence to support the theory in the site's location high above the village of Haggburn and in the ridge that ran around the perimeter of the field. It was common practice in such situations to inter individual human bones, as opposed to articulated limbs or incomplete skeletons, within the settlement itself, and they had discovered skull fragments and long bones, mainly from the right side of the body. The evidence suggested that the bones had been manipulated, probably after the initial process of decay, and carefully selected bones had been stored or hidden for ritual purposes in occupation sites prior to their individual burial at a later date. Rena Williams attempted to sum up.

'Evidence from this site, and others elsewhere like Danebury and Hod Hill, leads me to believe that the burials were not interred at random. Rather, it was practice to cluster them at chosen sites within fixed locations inside the zone of occupation. We've already uncovered a horseshoe-shaped ditch which I suspect was a ritual enclosure. We may well find evidence of shamanistic rituals in the grave sites within the horseshoe.'

Fred Harkness had split them into three teams, and they had commenced the opening up of the burial sites.

It was not long before evidence began to be unearthed which supported Rena's contention. Small ornaments came to light: copper-alloy brooches, a shale bracelet, pins, rings, glass beads and some scattered horse fittings. And finally, in Rena's grave site a crouched body burial, quickly followed by that of another — female — lying in a similar crouched position, resting on the right side.

They held several conferences as the work went on. 'It seems to me,' Rena concluded, 'that what we have here is a family cluster. It's unlikely we're going to find a high-ranking burial — you know, the so-called wheel chariot burials — because the horseshoe ditch isn't large enough. And I don't think we're going to come across anything like Arnold's famous *Kvernbitr* discovery.' She smiled at the stir of excitement among the young students, who had heard of the discovery of the Viking sword a couple of years ago.

'So you don't think,' Harkness asked thoughtfully, 'that we're dealing here with anything like the Maiden Castle war cemetery: they were crouched burials, on their right sides, with scattered grave goods.'

'The site just isn't extensive enough, under this rock outcrop,' Rena Williams insisted. 'I'm not suggesting we won't find a high-ranking burial, but the chance is slim.'

'And no chance of sacrificial burials?' Karen Stannard asked.

'I'm not saying that. My present view is that it's a family cluster, but since there are suggestions of shamanistic activity — not least in the discovery of the Mórrigan icon — it may well be we'll come across burials of outcasts, criminals, religious heretics, who knows? But we have to remember, there won't be a great deal to find. Most people in those ages received a burial rite invisible to us: long-term exposure of the body or cremation followed by a scattering of ashes on land or water. Those were the rites in accordance with the spiritual world-view of the Celtic societies we're likely to find here — centred on the powers of nature and the elements.'

'And the Mórrigan,' Arnold murmured.

He was not working in the same group as Karen Stannard, but they tended to meet at lunch times when the party exchanged information over sandwiches and coffee and at dinner, where in spite of being caught out by Arnold, Mrs Delaney continued to indulge in her performances. Her comments about Karen Stannard had struck home, naturally, and he found himself watching her from time to time, puzzled, essentially certain that Mrs Delaney had got it wrong, but wondering, nevertheless. The old lady had said that Karen Stannard held him in high regard. In professional terms, that was just possible — even though she seemed to resent his expertise from time to time. But in personal terms . . . in that, he was sure the old lady was wrong.

He obtained confirmation later in the week. He was working in the library in the early evening, before dinner, when she entered. He looked up and nodded. Her mouth was set in a grim line. Her tone was sharp. 'What's got into you?' she demanded.

'I don't understand,' he replied, startled.

'You've been staring at me.'

'I don't think I have,' he lied.

'I don't like it. There's something going on,' she insisted, nettled by his denial. 'Every time I look up at dinner I catch you staring. You know something. Is it to do with Mulberry?

Have you heard any more about my suspension? Because believe me, when I get back—'

'I've heard nothing at all. And if I've been staring at you, it's absent-mindedness, daydreaming — I've got things on my mind.'

'Such as?' she sneered.

'These volumes and maps . . .' he replied desperately, uncomfortable under her anger, 'I have a feeling I'm moving towards some kind of thesis about the Mórrigan cult, but it's still not clear in my mind . . .'

'Oh. I see,' She sniffed uncertainly, and after a certain hesitation came to stand just behind him, leaning over his shoulder, her professional interest overcoming her annoyance. 'What are you looking into?'

He was very conscious, again, of her perfume, and the softness of her breast touching his shoulder. 'Er . . . I've got these antiquarian volumes. In this series they touch upon a range of legends and myths about the north. And there's quite a lot about the Viking raids.'

'But we're talking about an Irish cult figure.' She seemed to have forgotten her anger.

'Yes, but there are one or two hints in old manuscript sources — unfortunately I haven't turned up originals, only eighteenth-century commentaries upon them — which would suggest there's a tradition of a war lord coming out of the west and conquering the river valleys in this area. It's a verbal tradition, I suspect, which will have been an embroidered story over the generations . . . and I've been looking at these maps, also.'

'Let me see.' She was half leaning over him now, her gaze scanning the map spread out on the table. He wished seriously that Vita Delaney had never given him her views on the subject of Karen Stannard.

They looked at the commentaries in the antiquarian volumes and the maps Arnold had brought with him, and he showed her the references he had been given by the librarian at Newcastle. They discussed some of the possibilities, a certain heat returning to their relationship as they disagreed with each other over some of the issues. It was almost an hour later when Karen Stannard, her cheeks flushed by the debate, glanced at her watch and swore. He liked that about her at least: she could swear uninhibitedly when the occasion demanded. 'It's almost dinner time — and I need to take a shower!'

He was going to make no comment about that, with the scent of her perfume still in his nostrils.

She moved away from him, then as she reached the door she hesitated and turned back to look at him steadily. 'There's something else I feel I should say. I was somewhat . . . taken aback when you arrived here, saying you were on leave. It threw me. I still don't understand what motivated you, taking that action when Brent-Ellis and I were suspended. But there is . . .'

She struggled for the words, and even when she found them, she seemed reluctant to say them. 'There is one interpretation that could be put on your action. If . . . if what you're doing was done . . . if in some way, it was a kind of protest . . .' She glared at him, angry with him and herself. 'Well, it's appreciated, you understand? Not that I think . . .' She was flailing, mentally.

He helped her out. 'It was just that the leave was due to me.'

She didn't believe him, and she hated to feel that she was in any way indebted to him. It was apparent in every line of her body as she swept out of the library to get changed for dinner.

That subdued anger, with him and with herself, might have accounted for her behaviour that evening. For most of the week she had been relatively reserved at dinner, but now she was back at her worst, openly flirting with Rick Newton, whispering with him and giggling uncharacteristically at his quips, leaning against him while she talked, deliberately taunting the fuming Gabriella by her conduct. George Mahoney was also sitting next to her, and from time to time Arnold caught his glance. The estate manager raised his eyebrows and smiled wryly. Arnold got the impression he considered the whole thing could end in an explosion.

And Vita Delaney behaved herself. She put on no performance, but she watched Karen Stannard and Rick Newton, and occasionally she glanced at Arnold with a mischievous glint in her eyes. He had no doubt that she had a theory to account for what was going on. He suspected it would be twisted to involve him.

The evening ended sourly. Gabriella Newton suddenly rose as coffee was being served and announced icily that she had a headache and would be going to bed. Vita Delaney raised no objection. Once she was gone, Karen Stannard's mood changed, or possibly it was something that Rick Newton had said to her. However, she turned away from him and began to discuss site matters with Rena Williams, sitting next to Arnold. Mrs Delaney presided with an enigmatic smile and once or twice she cocked a questioning eyebrow in Arnold's direction. It seemed to be saying, 'You talk about performances. So, what about Karen Stannard, then?'

He was not prepared to rise to the unspoken bait. Vita Delaney had completely misread the signals. There was nothing between him and Karen Stannard. And any sparks were purely professional competitiveness running along a conduit of personal dislike.

But when he finally got to sleep that night, his dreams were confused.

He woke at about six in the morning. It was already light.

He had left his window open, and he could hear sounds outside: confused shouting, running feet. There was some kind of panic on, and he pulled on his clothes quickly. Unshaven, unshowered, he went down the stairs and into the yard. Three employees of Mrs Delaney were standing huddled in a group, they seemed animated but somewhat frightened.

'What's going on?'

'It's the stables, Mr Landon. They've found something down there.'

Arnold crossed the yard and headed for the stables. He saw a small, tight knot of people gathered there. George Mahoney was pushing them back, trying to break up the group. Arnold heard him say something about the police. As he approached, Mahoney saw him and shook his head. 'Bad business, Landon.'

'What's happened?'

'Someone's been killed.'

'What?' The straggle of employees was breaking up, drifting white-faced back towards the hall behind one man who had run ahead to get to the telephone. Arnold caught sight of the figure on the ground in front of the stable door. From within the stable came the sound of one of Gabriella Newton's hunters stamping nervously in the darkness.

'Looks like he's had his skull crushed,' George Mahoney said in a flat voice.

'By the horse?'

'Stable door's not open. I don't think he's been inside.'

'Do you know who it is?' Arnold asked.

Mahoney shook his head. 'It's not anyone from the hall, that's for sure.'

Arnold squatted on his heels beside the body, suddenly curious. He had a feeling there was something familiar about the blood-matted fair hair, the slimness of the body. He peered more closely, then was aware of a cold feeling in his stomach. He stood up.

Mahoney watched him stonily. 'You recognize him?'

Arnold nodded. 'I've spoken to him, down at Haggburn village. He's been staying at the Drover's Rest for some weeks past now.' He took a deep, restless breath. 'His name's Steven Quaid.'

133

CHAPTER FOUR

1

In the confines of his office at headquarters, Detective Chief Inspector Culpeper stretched and yawned prodigiously. He had taken his wife to a dinner dance in North Shields the previous evening where the wine had flowed and good companionship had been noisy in its approbation of the occasion. It happened once a year, and it was one of the curiosities of the annual calendar.

They had all been there: the Lord Lieutenant, the Chief Constable from Northumberland and Tyneside, senior police officers from both forces, local dignitaries, a scattering of councillors and three MPs. The function was held at the same hotel every year, the host a self-made millionaire who owned a chain of hotels at various locations in Northumberland and the Borders.

And when they all gathered to enjoy their host's hospitality, there was no discussion of his background even though they all knew how he had made his money in the early days: illegal gambling on Tyneside.

For now he was a local hero, a successful hotelier, a provider of jobs, holding a seat on various charities, recipient of an OBE, shaker of hands with royalty. So they all trooped to North Shields each year at his invitation and policemen were cheek by jowl with villains too big to be touched, and everyone turned a blind eye and everyone had a good time. It was a cynical acceptance of the realities of life, Culpeper concluded, and he was as bad as any of them. There had been champagne, fine wine, a feast startling in its size and enterprise, and the best of the local comedians to round off the evening before the dancing started. His wife Margaret had loved it, as she always did.

It was a lot better than Seahouses, she'd confided in him. But she said that every year.

Too much wine, not enough sleep, and a vague feeling of presbyterian guilt lay heavily on his mind as the food lay heavily in his stomach. The combination made him reluctant to face the paperwork that sat waiting on his desk. He stared at it gloomily and sighed. There was this pile of paper and there was Farnsby. Not a great deal to choose between them: both were disagreeable obligations, tasks he had to face. Perhaps it was better to sit and listen to Farnsby, rather than crouch poring over files with a hammer tapping away in his head. Reluctantly, he rose and walked down the corridor. He found Farnsby chatting to a young female police constable. Farnsby had had trouble in his marriage; maybe he was becoming a ladies' man again. Culpeper scowled.

'Work, bonny lad, not play. My room in five minutes.'

He got himself a plastic cup of water and returned to his room. Farnsby tapped on the door a little while later and entered clutching a file under his arm. 'Was it a good night, sir?'

'It's always a good night.' He finished the water, relieving some of the dehydration, and glowered at Farnsby: as far as the police were concerned, the North Shields occasion was open to those who had attained the rank of chief inspector and above to whom invitations were sent out automatically. He wondered how long it would be before young Farnsby got an invitation. Not long, if the Chief had his way, he thought sourly.

'Right, we'd better get up to date, bonny lad,' he growled. 'I've been monitoring our friend Mulberry's activities, like the Chief suggested, and it seems he's really going to town. I've made some discreet inquiries among senior councillors in the authority — the ones I've had contact with over the years, known since they were young pit-lads, some of them — and to say that they're hopping mad is an understatement. Mulberry's getting under their skin.'

Farnsby nodded. 'So I understand. I had lunch with the Director of Finance at Morpeth the other day—' He broke off, as he became aware of Culpeper's disgruntlement.

'I have a suspicion it's that bugger who's responsible for setting us on this witch-hunt,' Culpeper snarled. 'Had a word in the Chief's ear, I don't doubt . . .'

'I wouldn't know about that,' Farnsby replied, nervously. 'Look, DCI, I'm as uneasy about this as you are. It smacks too much of political pressure for me — I see no reason why we should be doing the dirty work for people who are suffering under an internal inquiry from one of their own kind. But we're under orders to do it . . . so I contacted him—'

'You've met him socially before, I suppose?'

Farnsby flushed. 'We happen to be members of the same club.'

'Bloody hell!' Culpeper despaired. There was a long silence.

At last, Farnsby asked, somewhat stiffly, if he should go on.

Culpeper flapped a world-weary hand. 'Might as well. As you say, we've got to keep the Chief happy.'

'Well, in the course of conversation he told me that his own department had not yet been called to give evidence, but he had been in touch with his fellow directors, naturally, and there was considerable disquiet amongst them and other senior officers. Moreover, it seems the nervousness has spread to the councillors themselves — even some of those who toe the same party line as Mulberry. They think he's going too far, and too fast, but now he's got the bit between his teeth he's going to be difficult to stop.'

'They let the lion out of the cage, Farnsby; if they get bitten themselves, that's their problem.'

'That may be so, sir, but Mulberry seems hell-bent on keeping up the pressure. And there's evidence in the wards that his stock is rising — all this is going to do his popular standing no harm whatsoever.'

'As we've all predicted.'

Farnsby nodded. He glanced at the file he was holding in his hands. 'Anyway, the departments are now being investigated for financial irregularities. The Director of the Department of Museums and Antiquities has already been suspended—'

Culpeper grunted and twitched his eyebrows. 'I'd heard. That makes two of them, then.'

'That's right — though it seems the allegations against them are different. With Brent-Ellis it's something to do with expenses claimed for attending a conference when he was actually on the golf course.'

'He's always on the bloody golf course,' Culpeper commented drily.

'Anyway, he's suspended pending further inquiries, but I'm told that it's all a bit of a put-up job. There are no real financial irregularities, and the whole thing could well fizzle out after the election. On the other hand . . .'

'They're nervous.'

'Morale shot to pieces. And then—' Farnsby hesitated — 'there's the Chief's suggestion that we should look into Mulberry's own business interests.'

Culpeper yawned again, and felt a stab of pain in his stomach. Wind. He grimaced: too much garlic on that damned lamb last night. 'I've already done that. While you've been trawling around these scared rabbits of senior officers in the authority, I've called up all the files on council matters I can get my hands on. Mulberry really is Mr Clean. He's got his fingers in no pies whatsoever. He's made no declarations of interest at council or committee meetings because he's got no damned interests to declare. So it's not a line worth proceeding with, bonny lad.'

'No,' Farnsby replied carefully. 'I agree. Except I've been advised to look closely at his business interests *before* he became a councillor.'

Culpeper scowled. 'Are you suggesting he was up to something nefarious before he took up good works?'

'It was suggested to me, sir.'

'*What* was suggested to you?' Culpeper snapped. The pain in his stomach came again, to be followed by a long gurgling sound.

'It was suggested that I have a conversation with certain people in the Social Services Department in Newcastle.' Farnsby hesitated. 'You see, Mulberry came under their jurisdiction, so to speak, for several years.'

'Obviously. He ran a string of nursing homes for the elderly. That's how he made enough money to be able to sell out, pack in, and become a committed, humble servant of the people.'

Farnsby ignored the sarcasm. He nodded soberly. 'That's correct, sir. And those homes were inspected by the Social Services Department and always got a clean bill of health. However, what is not generally known is that Mulberry also owned two other establishments — one at Rothbury, and another up at Spittal.'

'For the elderly?'

'No, sir. For young offenders.'

Culpeper quelled the churning in his gut. He leaned forward in his chair. 'Now wait a minute. You mean he was also involved in looking after young tearaways?'

'There was a problem — still is — in relation to young people who've been put into local authority care. Secure accommodation is at a premium, and the system hasn't been able to cope for years. Deals were struck with the private sector, and it seems that at some stage Mulberry saw the financial advantage of jumping on to that bandwagon. He bought up some suitable premises, undertook the necessary conversions, appointed appropriately qualified staff and took in a number of young people in local authority care. Not the real rough stuff . . . mainly young people at risk.'

'I'm not sure I know where this is going,' Culpeper said, becoming more and more aware of the discomforting, swishing ache in his stomach.

Farnsby opened the file he was holding. He glanced at it, stroking at his lower lip thoughtfully. 'There's no chapter and verse here, sir, but I've made notes of several conversations I've had with the Social Services people. It seems there was a certain . . . disquiet around the house at one stage.'

'Get on with it, man. Stop pussyfooting around,' Culpeper snarled, wriggling in his seat.

'Mulberry was approached by a consortium some six or seven years ago. He agreed a sale of all his nursing homes. It made him a wealthy man. So he could afford to give up business and simply work as a councillor, seeking approbation and — one imagines in due course, honours. But I'm told there might have been a little hiccup which could have stopped the sale, shortly before it went through.'

'Hiccup?'

'Scandal. There were rumours of certain . . . problems in the Spittal home.'

'What kind of problems?'

'Sexual abuse of young people in care.'

Culpeper groaned. 'You're not going to tell me nothing was done about them. We're not going to be pulled into the frame, are we?'

'It's not quite like that, DCI,' Farnsby replied earnestly. 'The fact is that the rumours started, and Social Services were approached. There were two cases . . . two individuals that are named here in this file, in my notes. But the allegations were never pursued because after the initial investigation started, all under wraps of course, the plug was suddenly pulled.'

The pain was getting more intense, Culpeper's stomach cramping unpleasantly. 'The investigation was cancelled?'

'It had to be. The complainants withdrew their allegations. I've got their names in my notes. It looks to me as though they might—'

It was no good. Culpeper could stand it no longer. 'Hold on,' he said, rising from his chair. 'I'm going to have to pay a call. Got to let the dog see the rabbit. I'm busting a gut here. Stay there. I'll be back . . .'

He hobbled from the room and hurried down the corridor. It was almost ten minutes before he returned.

'Hell's flames,' he said as he re-entered his office. 'That's the last time I'll indulge myself with lamb and bloody garlic!'

'Problems after last night, DCI?'

Too late, Culpeper realized that Farnsby was standing to attention. He turned his head, looked past the door. The Chief Constable was standing with his back to the window. He was holding the file that Farnsby had been discussing with Culpeper.

'Ah, sir, I wasn't aware that you wanted to see me. I'd have come—'

'No. It's good for me to get out of my own office from time to time. A prowl does no one any harm. Keeps people on their toes, knowing the Old Man is around the corridors. It's what I always felt as a young officer.'

Culpeper glanced at Farnsby, then he looked at the file in the Chief Constable's hands. 'We were just discussing the progress of the Mulberry investigation; the one you asked us to instigate.'

'I gather you've not got very far,' the Chief Constable said smoothly. 'Until, that is, young Farnsby here came up with an interesting line of inquiry. What do you think of it, DCI?'

Young bloody Farnsby. 'I haven't had time to . . . evaluate it yet, sir.'

'Inspector?' The Chief Constable was looking at Farnsby. The young man's eyes darted towards Culpeper, noted the gathering fury in his brow, and swallowed. 'Sir, it's a little early to say. I was reporting to the DCI, and he's had no time—'

'But *you* have, Farnsby,' the Chief Constable interrupted crisply. 'So tell us both, now.'

Farnsby took a deep breath, avoiding Culpeper's jaundiced gaze. 'It's unsupported, sir, and it's not evidence. But rumour would have it that an investigation was about to be started by Social Services into the running of one of the Mulberry homes for young offenders. The investigation was suddenly called off when the complainants withdrew their allegations. It's possible that if the Social Services people had had a smaller workload they would have tried to persist with the investigation, but in the circumstances—'

'It went no further,' the Chief Constable supplied. 'So why do you think the allegations were withdrawn?'

'I don't know, sir. But . . . well, Mulberry was about to sell the homes as part of his deal with the consortium. It's just possible a little pressure was applied . . . or maybe some money changed hands. The names in the file — well, they might be difficult to trace now, because it seems they left the area shortly afterwards — but I think, if you wish us to proceed, it's quite possible that—'

'No,' the Chief Constable interrupted. His tone was quiet. He was silent as he glanced through the contents of the file. 'No, I don't want you to proceed.'

'But if there's any truth in—'

'I'll take over this file myself, for the time being, Farnsby,' the Chief Constable said smoothly. 'There may well be wider considerations in this whole business that will need taking into account. It could be a delicate matter, so for the time being I'll hang on to it and make some . . . inquiries of my own. Besides, there are now some more important matters on your plate.' Culpeper was glaring at Farnsby, so the Chief Constable's last words failed to register with him immediately. After a moment he came to himself and looked at the Chief. 'Sir?'

'More important matters to deal with,' the Chief Constable repeated. 'They've found a body up at Haggburn Hall. The call came in early this morning. At the moment there's a detective sergeant dealing with it, but I feel it needs someone with more seniority and experience to handle it, don't you?' He turned and began to walk towards the door. 'You and Farnsby had better get on to it right away. The reports suggest it was murder. More up your street, hey? Meanwhile, I'll keep hold of this file and check out a few things.'

He made no attempt to close the door behind him. Culpeper waited until his measured steps had retreated down the corridor; when they could no longer be heard he approached the door, raised his foot and kicked it violently, so that it crashed shut. He turned on a still wincing Detective Inspector Farnsby.

'You arsehole!'

'DCI—'

'What the hell did you give him that bloody file for? Why did you even start discussing it at all, when I wasn't here?'

'I had no choice, sir! He asked where you were. I told him. Then he asked me what I was doing, how we were getting on with the Mulberry inquiry. I had to tell him. I had to explain—'

'Explain, hell! Are you still wet behind the ears? Have you got any sense in that so-called educated skull of yours? You don't give the brass more than you have to! If I'd have been here I'd have told him inquiries were proceeding. I'd have told him we were getting on top of things. I'd have mollified him while treating him as if he were the bloody press — not given him the whole thing in a nutshell!'

'But I don't see the harm, sir!' Farnsby replied smartly, nettled and reddening as he faced the angry Culpeper. 'We've got to hand it over now anyway, with a murder inquiry on our hands.'

'That's not the flaming point! When he came in we didn't know we were going to be switched to a murder inquiry. And if you hadn't blurted out what we've got, he might have left the thing with us anyway! He's never been a man to lighten workloads, for God's sake!'

Farnsby drew himself up. His eyes were bitter, angry at receiving a dressing-down he felt was unjustified. 'I don't know why you're getting so aerated, sir. You didn't want to take on this task in the first place. You said it was too political; that we shouldn't be muck-raking for the friends of the Chief Constable!'

'But we *did* take it on; we *did* have it shoved down our gullets — and that's precisely why we should have held on to it now! Are you too stupid to see what'll happen next? If there's any truth in the allegations that've been made, it may well be they'll be embarrassing not just to Mulberry but to the Great and the Good, as well. Do you think the Chief Constable isn't going to weigh up the balance? Do you think he might not want to have a quiet word with someone, and have the whole matter quietly dropped, again? Get his own result, of course . . . warn Mulberry off. But we don't know what that desired result might be, do we? If we'd had more time to look at it all, to maybe patch some flesh on to the allegations . . . but now — I'll bet you fifty quid, Farnsby, we'll hear no more of the allegations against the Mulberry homes!'

Farnsby licked his lips. There was a stubbornness in his eyes that suggested he was not convinced, and that he felt he had had no choice other than to hand over the file.

'You've got a loose mouth, Farnsby,' Culpeper said disgustedly. He walked across the room to the hooks on the wall and took down his topcoat. He shrugged it on to his shoulders with a resigned air. 'Ah, the hell with it. Haggburn Hall . . . I'd better get up there right away. Jump to the orders of our revered Chief Constable.'

'I'll meet you downstairs, sir,' Farnsby said hurriedly. 'It'll just take me—'

'No,' Culpeper growled. 'You're staying here. I've got other plans for you, my lad.'

Farnsby stared at him. 'The Chief Constable—'

'Bugger the Chief Constable. There's a sergeant already up there at Haggburn, and I'm on my way. You'll stay here and play office boy. Get a scene-of-crime unit together, and layout an incident room. But there's something else you've got to do at the same time.'

Farnsby looked puzzled. 'Sir?'

Culpeper thrust his face close to Farnsby's, his eyes bulging with suppressed anger. 'You can begin to learn from your mistakes. You've given that file to the Chief. It might never see the light of day again. So I want insurance. You interviewed those people in Social Services; you made notes in that bloody file. You're now going to sit down and write out those notes all over again, as far as you can remember. Names, dates, events, the lot.'

'But I—'

'I don't want you butting me buts. I want as near as dammit a replica of the file you've handed over to the Chief, so that if the balloon goes up at any time, at least we'll know what the hell is going on! And if he does sit on it, and it comes to light later, we're not going to be made the scape-goats. We'll have our own copy, to show that we at least took action, until we were stopped!'

'Sir, I'm not sure—'

'Whether you're sure or not is irrelevant. It's your fault we got into this position. So do as you're ordered. Names, dates, the lot,' Culpeper insisted, and dragged open the door he had earlier kicked shut. He glared at Farnsby: the detective inspector seemed about to rebel, make an argument. Then the light of battle died in his eyes under Culpeper's formida-ble presence. Stiff-backed, Farnsby marched out of the door and down the corridor.

Culpeper marched along behind him and down the stairs, out to the car park and his waiting driver.

'Arsehole,' Culpeper repeated in a quiet, satisfied tone.

2

The plump, short, matronly figure of the nurse preceded Culpeper into the drawing room of Haggburn Hall. She gestured towards one of the deep armchairs placed near the stone fireplace carved with the arms of the original owners of the hall. 'If you'd like to take a seat, sir, I'll tell Mrs Delaney that you're here to see her.' She hesitated, wrinkling her good-natured features in a doubtful frown. 'I'm afraid she's not too well today. The news about this . . . this dead man down at the stables, and all the activity since, it's upset her. So I think it would be wise if you didn't spend too long with her. She's very frail, you know.'

Culpeper nodded sympathetically. He could guess how Mrs Delaney must be feeling: the discovery of a corpse on her premises would have been upsetting enough; the knowledge that it was being treated as a murder was worse. Add to that the coming and goings of the scene-of-crime unit, forensic pathologists, constables combing the area near the stables, questioning of the stable hand who had first found the body — it would all have been enough to upset anyone. And if she were old and frail . . .

Culpeper prowled around the room. He admired the eighteenth-century portraits in their gilt frames, appreciated

147

the view from the tall windows across the meadow, noted the ride where the horses would be exercised, and contrasted it all with the modest house in which he and Margaret lived.

It was a far cry, he thought, but Haggburn Hall was not unusual. There was quite a number of such stately homes scattered throughout Northumberland: the county had a high proportion of landed gentry, with large estates. Some mortgaged up to the hilt, but he doubted whether that was the situation here at Haggburn Hall.

Hearing a noise behind him, he turned to see the nurse pushing a wheelchair into the room: it held a small, frail woman in her mid-seventies. 'Detective Chief Inspector Culpeper, I am led to believe.'

Her voice was shaky. There was a greyness about her mouth, and a darkness round her eyes that told him she really was ill, possibly badly affected by the events of the last twelve hours. He walked forward to meet her. 'I'm Vita Delaney,' she said.

There remained a certain brightness in her eyes which he admired. As the nurse withdrew, he took the chair and wheeled her closer to the fireplace and then at her request took a seat facing her.

'So,' she said in a low, constrained voice, 'what is it you want of me?'

He felt sorry for her. She was very shaky; there was an involuntary tremble in her bony hands as she gripped the arms of the wheelchair. 'I won't keep you long, Mrs Delaney. Just a couple of questions, and then I'll leave you in peace.'

'Fire away.' It was a spirited attempt at levity. Her cheeks were ashen.

'You know about the body found early this morning at the stables. Is there anything you can tell me about it?'

'Nothing, Chief Inspector.'

'The dead man has been identified as one Steven Quaid. Did you know him?'

'I've never heard of him.'

'Can you think of any reason why he should have been on your property?'

She hesitated fractionally, then shook her head. 'I know nothing of him. I have no idea what he might have been doing at Haggburn Hall.'

Culpeper probed a little more, gently, aware of her frailty, checking whether she could shed any light on Quaid's presence there, whether any of her staff might have had contact with the dead man, but she denied knowing anything at all about the situation. 'And your guests?' he asked. 'Did you ever hear them mention him, or was there any hint that might lead you to believe—'

'I've already told you,' she said with a hint of asperity. 'I know nothing. As for my guests, you'll need to talk to them. I wouldn't know whether they were acquainted with this dead man, or not. And I'm sorry, but I fear you must excuse me . . . I really am very tired . . .'

'Of course, Mrs Delaney, of course.' Culpeper rose and then, with a certain embarrassment, he said, 'I wonder whether I could ask you a favour, Mrs Delaney? I need to conduct interviews, urgently, with the people who have been staying at the hall, or working at the archaeological site. Would it be possible to interview them here? It would save time, and perhaps render it unnecessary for them to come to Morpeth.'

'If you talk to my nurse,' Mrs Delaney said faintly, half-closing her eyes, 'she'll make the necessary arrangements. Now, if you can excuse me . . .'

Culpeper rang for the nurse. She came in quickly; while she wheeled the old lady out of the room, Culpeper stayed on, feeling somewhat uncomfortable. At last the nurse returned. 'Mrs Delaney has explained to me your requirements. I think it would be best if you could use the library, Mr Culpeper. Will it be for long?'

'I can't say, at this stage — maybe a couple of days.' He hesitated. 'Mrs Delaney seems to be very ill.'

The nurse seemed close to tears. She nodded. 'This has been quite a shock — it's knocked her sideways. Of course, her system isn't up to taking this, at her age . . .' She gestured towards the door. 'Perhaps you'd like to see the library, to decide whether it's suitable for your purposes.'

'I'm sure it will be,' Culpeper replied soberly, following the nurse into the hallway. It echoed to their footsteps, and he gazed up towards the grand, curving, oak-balustraded stairs. 'Mrs Delaney . . . what exactly is wrong with her?'

The nurse sniffed worriedly. 'Apart from old age, you mean? She has heart disease. She's kept it from her family and guests, though I think her nephew has guessed, and maybe Mr Mahoney, too . . . Mr Newton, of course, he finds out most things that go on in this house.' She grimaced, aware of the hint of malice which had entered her tone. 'But this has all been a great shock to her. She's deteriorated in a matter of hours — you wouldn't believe. The doctor is calling this afternoon. And she also wants to see her solicitor . . .'

* * *

Detective Inspector Farnsby arrived the following morning, at about eleven. Culpeper was sitting in the library, checking over the notes he had made of the interviews conducted the previous day. He gave the younger man a sour glance as he entered the room. 'Chores all complete?' he asked.

Farnsby's tone was stiff with resentment. 'I've re-created the Mulberry file for you, sir. I think most of what I found out is there. I've brought it with me, in case you wanted to check it through.'

Culpeper shook his head, ignoring the proffered file. 'One thing at a time, bonny lad. Let's keep our minds fixed on what we've got here. This is our priority, the Chief Constable said. We'll get back to your Mulberry file later. Did you call in at the Drover's Rest like I suggested?'

Farnsby nodded. 'I stopped off there on the way up to the hall. I had a long chat with the landlord this morning.

He reckons that the dead man — Quaid — claimed to be an actor, resting up. He's been staying at the Drover's for about five weeks now and didn't seem to get out and about much. The landlord also said he had the feeling Quaid was waiting for something, or someone. Never went far from the hotel. He went shooting, it seems, on odd days and evenings, but never came back with anything. The landlord guessed he wasn't too hot with a shotgun and didn't seem the hunting type.' Farnsby paused, scratched his cheek thoughtfully. 'In fact, he said he was like a lot of actors he'd come across in the course of his business.'

'What did he mean by that?'

Farnsby shrugged. 'I think he was trying to say that, in his opinion, Quaid was a bit . . . limp-wristed.'

Culpeper stared at him sourly for a moment. 'That's not the first politically incorrect description you've given me, Farnsby. As an educated man you ought to be ashamed of yourself. After all, we're all brothers under the skin.'

The detective inspector met his gaze without flinching. 'I was quoting the landlord, sir. I gathered that he meant Quaid was somewhat effeminate, a bit prissy. Not exactly a — man's man,' Culpeper grunted. 'Anything else?'

Farnsby hesitated. 'Well, there was something else, but whether it's important or not, I don't know. After a couple of weeks, the landlord got a bit . . . wary. He'd taken a phone booking from Quaid, with no time limit stated. And Quaid was running up a bill, so the landlord suggested it would be a good idea if Quaid let him have an imprint of his credit card or settled his bill up to date. He wanted some kind of assurance that Quaid was a viable proposition, so to speak, financially. Anyway, Quaid paid up.'

'So?'

'Well, he didn't produce a credit card . . . or a cheque backed with a card. He paid cash.' He shrugged. 'And he did the same again, last week.'

'And that's an odd thing to do?'

'The landlord seemed to think so.'

'Hmmm.' Culpeper shook his head. 'Sergeant Leslie arranged for Quaid's possessions to be taken to Morpeth. They'll be going through them there. We'd better check how much cash our friend was carrying.' He eyed Farnsby speculatively. 'Talking of friends, I interviewed one yesterday.'

'Who was that, sir?'

'Arnold Landon. You know, the guy who's always turning up at archaeological digs around the county.'

'How is *he* involved?'

Culpeper shrugged. 'I'm not sure he is, really. But it was Landon who identified the body. It seems he came across Quaid at the Drover's Rest, briefly. And he did know about Quaid's shooting exploits. In fact, he led me to a certain line of inquiry . . .'

Culpeper had spent most of the previous day questioning the employees at Haggburn Hall. No one claimed to have known Quaid, though two of them admitted they had seen him at Haggburn village, in the bar of the Drover's Rest. But they had not spoken to him, nor did they know his name. 'It seems that Haggburn Hall employees tend not to fit too well into the general life of the village. Although they're local to Northumberland, they're self-contained at the hall and have little commerce with what one of them described as "the natives".'

But what Landon had had to say led to Culpeper calling for Fred Harkness, the site manager at the field dig, to come to see him in the sober quietness of the library. He had looked the big, broad-shouldered man over, noted the strength of his upper arms, the air of wary belligerence, and he had come straight to the point.

'So you knew Steve Quaid.'

'Aye. We'd met,' Harkness had growled.

'Before he came to Haggburn?'

'No.'

'So he wasn't hanging around this area because he knew you?'

'I've no idea why he was in the area. All I knew was that he was a damned nuisance.'

'You didn't like him?'

'I told you. He was a damned nuisance.'

'Why did you quarrel with him?'

'Who told you that?' Harkness blustered unconvincingly. 'I didn't have any problem with the man. It's just that . . .'

Culpeper raised an eyebrow. 'Yes?'

Fred Harkness grunted and ran a nervous hand over his bald head. 'Well, he was dangerous. He was wandering around Haggburn property with a damned shotgun! It was nothing to do with me really — I mean, there's no shoot at Haggburn, no grouse or pheasant or any game like that, other than the odd bird. I believe Mrs Delaney didn't believe in it — raising game for the gun, I mean. But this bloody townie was armed with a shotgun, and I'm damned sure he didn't really know how to use it. It was like a toy with him, and he was incompetent. I caught him a couple of times, in the woods near the dig. He was blasting off indiscriminately! I warned him that there were people within range, working at the dig, and he just told me to piss off.'

'And?' Culpeper prompted, as Harkness fell silent.

'I caught him a second time, and then I went for him. Verbally, I mean,' he added hastily as Culpeper raised his head. 'But he just sneered at me, walked away, gave me a mouthful. That was it, really. Little bastard . . .' Harkness frowned suddenly; aware he was speaking of the dead.

'And what about the quarrel in Haggburn High Street?' Culpeper asked smoothly.

Harkness swallowed hard. He stared at Culpeper, anxiety staining his eyes. 'Am I being suspected of bashing his head in, or something? I was up at the dig, waiting for the lads to turn up — they'd gone across to Rothbury for a night out and didn't get back until sunrise. I had no reason to smash Quaid's head in.'

'Didn't you threaten something like that in Haggburn High Street?' Culpeper persisted.

'It wasn't like that! I just came across him in the street, and he was carrying that bloody gun, and I said to him I hoped he wasn't going up near the site because there were students up there, people I was responsible for, and he gave me another mouthful and—' He shook his head in frustration, as the words spilled out. 'It was the same thing . . . that bloody shooting. He swore at me, I told him I'd . . . sort him out if he came near those woods; he raised the gun, and — I guess we both lost our rag. I grabbed the gun, we tussled . . . but it was all handbag stuff really. I mean, we both lost our tempers, but it wasn't *serious*. It was just the two of us . . . well, you know what I mean . . .'

* * *

After Culpeper had given an account of the interview to Farnsby, the detective inspector pursed his lips. 'So he admits to knowing Quaid, and that there was bad blood between the two of them. They had quarrelled, both up in the woods, and more publicly in Haggburn High Street — where Landon was a witness to the argument.'

'That's about the size of it.'

'So, is he in the frame, this Fred Harkness?'

'He's not *out* of it,' Culpeper replied, 'because at least he knew Quaid — no one else seems to admit to that, except Landon. Neither of them admit they have any knowledge as to why Quaid was hanging around Haggburn village, and why he should turn up at the hall. Anyway . . .' Culpeper consulted his notes, 'I've got other people to see, before we wind up the preliminaries here. You'd better hang on with me now — I'm expecting a certain Mr George Mahoney next. But the housekeeper did promise me some coffee and biscuits around about now. Who knows? She might even provide a cup for you.'

She did. She had been told of Farnsby's presence in the library and when the tray was brought in there was a large silver pot full of coffee and two cups.

'I'm sorry I can't offer you a cup, Mr Mahoney,' Culpeper said brightly when the estate manager arrived and took a seat on the other side of the long, polished oak table. 'I should have taken the precaution of advising the housekeeper—'

'It's of no consequence,' Mahoney replied easily. 'I've never managed to become enamoured of English coffee. I spent most of my time in Canada — it ruined me for English coffee.'

'I see. What were you doing in Canada?'

'I did my growing up there.' Mahoney explained that he had been in the Canadian Army for some years; prior to that he had drifted from job to job, working in forestry for a while, and then, footloose, had come eventually to England, looking for a job. Culpeper observed him as he spoke: the man had an open, intelligent face, somewhat weather-beaten from an outdoor life, but Culpeper thought his eyes were odd. They were rarely still, flickering quick glances nervously around the room. Of course, it could have been merely the tension that arose from being questioned by the police after a violent death had occurred. But Culpeper felt the man had something on his mind.

'So, it was you who found the dead body,' Culpeper prompted.

'No.' Mahoney's voice was firm and steady. 'The body was found by the stable hand, Rogers. I was up and about early, as usual — I only live a short distance away at the cottage near the entrance to the hall. I was on my way up to the hall when I heard Rogers shouting. I was next on the scene. But I didn't find him.'

'And did you recognize him?' Farnsby asked quietly.

'How could I? I'd never seen him before.'

Culpeper sniffed, glancing in surly fashion at Farnsby. 'You mean you'd never seen him to speak to? Or never seen him at all?'

'I'd never seen him at all.'

'That surprises me,' Culpeper drawled. 'I mean . . . you're the estate manager. I guess you're out and about the estate a fair bit. We've been led to believe that this Quaid character was on the property more than a few times . . . with a shotgun. You didn't know that?'

There was a short silence. Mahoney frowned. 'I knew someone was coming into the woods. I'd heard a shotgun fired several times. In fact, one evening I was talking to Mr Landon and I told him I thought there was someone prowling in the trees that night. But I never saw who it was. And I never met, or saw, this man Quaid. It was Mr Landon who recognized him, not me.'

'So I understand,' Culpeper growled. 'Did he have a shotgun with him?'

Mahoney's features were blank. He shook his head. 'We didn't touch the body. Rogers and I, we just looked at it, then people started coming, in response to the shouts. It was all a bit confused. It was a shock . . . but I saw no shotgun.'

'So maybe he wasn't out hunting, the night he died? Maybe he was coming up to see someone?'

'I wouldn't know.'

'So it wasn't you?'

'Certainly not.'

'Maybe Mrs Delaney?' Culpeper queried gently.

There was a short silence as Mahoney gazed steadily at Culpeper. The shadow in his glance could have been calculation, or it could have been a controlling of the need to say something. At last, Mahoney asked, 'Why would you think that?'

Culpeper shrugged. 'I don't know. She tells me she didn't know Quaid, but . . . I got the impression Mrs Delaney has sort of . . . collapsed, you know what I mean? She's been very upset by this . . . situation.'

Mahoney's tongue slipped from between his lips, undecided; it slid across the dryness, flickering. He took a deep breath. 'Mrs Delaney is an old woman. She is not a well woman. I think this . . . killing will have been a tremendous shock to her. I saw her yesterday afternoon, and I was taken aback. I mean, she's changed so much, deteriorated so badly . . . and in a matter of hours. The previous evening, she was fine, in control, her usual self. But if she says she didn't know Quaid, I would believe her. And I've no reason to suspect she would have known the dead man.'

Culpeper tapped a pencil against his fingers. He leaned back in his chair, watching Mahoney thoughtfully. 'You know Mrs Delaney well?'

'She's been my employer for some years,' Mahoney replied calmly. 'And, I think, she's become . . . a friend.'

'Is that so?'

Mahoney coloured slightly, and was quiet for a while. Farnsby opened his mouth to ask something but was warned by Culpeper's sharp glance. The quiet grew heavy around them, but the two policemen made no attempt to break the silence.

Mahoney was uncomfortable. At last he spoke. 'She began to confide in me, some two years ago. I think she liked my commitment to the job; she started inviting me to dinner, began to treat me as a friend as well as an employee. And she talked to me. I know, for instance, that she has a heart condition . . .' He waited, struggling, in the lengthening silence. 'Coming up here to dine with Mrs Delaney I also got to know . . . other things, about the hall. I learned about the tensions . . . her nephew, for instance, and his wife. Rick Newton expects to inherit from Mrs Delaney, but is impatient.' Snappishly, he added, 'I suspect he won't be unhappy at her sudden deterioration. And his wife . . . she's been well looked after by Mrs Delaney — the hunters in the stable were bought for her — but she's never been satisfied. There's tension between her and her husband, and that was exacerbated recently . . .'

'You don't like the Newtons,' Culpeper said quietly.

'They're parasites,' Mahoney rasped.

Culpeper played with his pencil, thoughtfully. 'The situation was recently exacerbated, you said.'

Mahoney seemed reluctant to go on. He shrugged. 'The people from the dig — Mr Landon, Dr Williams, Fred Harkness, and Karen Stannard — they were dinner guests here. With the exception of Harkness, they also stayed here, along with Vartek. And Rick Newton, well, he drinks heavily, and he lost control.'

'In what way?'

'I think he's become infatuated with Karen Stannard. He made his admiration obvious. In front of his wife.' He paused, uncertainly, wrinkling his brow. 'In fact, the other night at dinner, I was sitting next to her and she was . . . I suppose flirting with Newton. I heard him press her, he wanted her to agree to a meeting. I was amazed, I'm sure his wife heard what he was saying—'

'Did Miss Stannard agree to meet him?' Culpeper asked, curiously.

Mahoney stared at him for a few seconds, a wooden expression on his features. 'You'd better ask her about that . . . I don't know what this has to do with the investigation into Quaid's death.'

'*You're* doing the talking, Mr Mahoney,' Culpeper remarked cheerfully. 'And it's useful, perhaps, as background . . . So if Quaid wasn't up here to see Mrs Delaney, just who do you think he might have been coming to visit?'

'I've no idea,' Mahoney replied doggedly. 'It certainly wasn't Mrs Delaney, in my view, and it definitely wasn't me. The Newtons — and that charlatan Vartek — will have to speak for themselves.'

Culpeper smiled. 'Charlatan . . . There's not many people at Haggburn Hall you like, is there, Mr Mahoney?'

The estate manager's glance was direct, and truthful. 'I recognize when people try to take advantage of an old, dying woman. And that's what I dislike.'

When Mahoney had gone, Culpeper finished the coffee in the pot. He seemed thoughtful. After a while, he said, 'Farnsby, you'd better learn to keep your mouth shut. If I'm conducting an interview, I don't expect you to butt in unless I give you a lead, you understand? Or unless we work out lines of inquiry beforehand.' When Farnsby made no reply, he went on, 'However, bonny lad, what did you make of all that?'

'Mahoney?' Farnsby wrinkled his nose. 'Seems committed to the old lady, as much as anything. Seems genuine. But he got very nervous—'

Culpeper chuckled mirthlessly. 'There was something on his mind — I wondered about it earlier. Yes, odd ain't it? Sometimes you get to learn more when you *don't* ask questions, than when you do. The tension of silence gets to them. Anyway, he's given us something to get on with.'

'The Newtons?'

Culpeper nodded. 'And Vartek.'

* * *

The man was sweating.

He was wearing an expensive, light sweater and his tanned features were composed, his elegant white hair carefully smoothed back, shining in the afternoon sunlight. His hands were folded in his lap; Culpeper had noted the slim, beautifully groomed fingers. Vartek's whole appearance was one of studied casualness, at ease with his surroundings. But he was sweating.

Culpeper had relented. He had suggested that Farnsby take over the interviewing of Vartek. It enabled the DCI to sit slightly to one side, observing the man in the chair. He heard Farnsby take Vartek through the obvious questions: no, he did not know Quaid; he had never met him, for he rarely visited the village. He had heard no shooting in the woods. He had no idea who Quaid might have been coming to see at Haggburn Hall. He had no information whatsoever to impart that might be of assistance to the investigation.

He grew edgy when Farnsby asked him about the reasons for his own presence at Haggburn Hall. At first he was vague, but then he admitted that he was there at the invitation of Mrs Delaney, whom he was trying to persuade to invest in an enterprise close to his heart. He was even more reluctant to describe the nature of that enterprise, but finally outlined his scheme to develop a property for research into the occult, life after death, reincarnation of the soul.

'Surely, a misnomer, Mr Vartek? Incarnation and soul are mutually exclusive concepts. The soul cannot be carnate.

The word relates to the flesh, the body. But the soul is spiritual in concept . . .'

Stick to the point, Culpeper thought sourly. Bloody graduate coppers!

But as Vartek struggled to explain himself and his presence at Haggburn Hall, Culpeper came to the thought that Mahoney was right: the man was a charlatan, a con man. He'd take looking into further.

'So,' Farnsby summed up, 'you didn't know Quaid, never met him, have no idea what he was doing here — in fact, you can't help us at all.'

'That's right.' Vartek lifted a slim finger to his left eyebrow and flicked away a bead of sweat.

Farnsby smiled. 'Well, there's one thing you can help us with, at least.'

'Yes?'

'What's your real name?'

Vartek blinked. 'I am called Vartek. I—'

'Your real name, sir.' Farnsby leaned forward, seriously. 'The one you were given at birth, if you please.'

Good lad, thought Culpeper. There was steel in Farnsby's tone. Good lad, put the boot in.

'I don't see that this is at all necessary,' Vartek blustered. 'My name—'

'Is necessary to us,' Farnsby interrupted coldly. 'I surely don't need to remind you that this is a murder investigation. We need to look into the background of everyone here at the hall. Clearly, Vartek is an assumed name, maybe necessary to your . . . profession. But you must understand we need to carry out a check — on everyone here at Haggburn Hall. So, if you please . . .'

There was a long silence. Vartek licked his lips. 'It's another life. I've left it behind me.'

Farnsby raised an eyebrow, and waited, staring at the man.

Culpeper thought for a moment that Vartek was going to hold out, but there was defeat in his eyes. He shrugged, at last. 'Daniel Nicholson.'

Farnsby made great play of noting it down. He did the same with the man's previous occupation and address, information which he dragged out with some difficulty.

Farnsby leaned back in his chair and looked at the notes he had taken. 'So you were a solicitor's clerk, with a firm in Nottingham. What made you leave that occupation?'

The man who called himself Vartek licked his lips. 'I . . . I felt a calling . . . to other things.'

Farnsby nodded. 'Solicitor's clerk. Suitable background for establishing a foundation in the name of Mrs Delaney. All right, Mr . . . er . . .' He consulted his notes deliberately. 'Nicholson. That'll be all for now.'

Culpeper nodded. This man needs looking to, he thought as Vartek sweated his way out of the room.

3

Although work continued at the site of the dig, the effects of the investigation were obvious. It had little impact on the students, who were normally boisterous and were still inclined to horseplay, but Fred Harkness was uncommunicative and kept very much to himself. He had spoken little about his interview with Culpeper, but it was clear to Arnold that he was a worried man.

Arnold's own questioning by Culpeper had been mild enough. There was little that Arnold could tell him, but he gained the impression that Culpeper was concerned that neither Harkness nor anyone from the site who had been staying at the hall seemed to have an alibi for the time at which Quaid had died.

'You say you were in bed,' Culpeper had said, 'and I get the same story from everyone. Dr Williams had gone to bed; Karen Stannard had retired for the night; Fred Harkness had left the hall for his tent in the field; George Mahoney had gone back to his cottage. But none of you can produce corroboration . . . it's a pity there weren't a couple of affairs going on — that way we could eliminate some of you at least from the investigation.'

Arnold had thought the comment in bad taste.

'The one exception, of course,' Culpeper had continued, 'is the Newtons. They say they'd gone to bed together. What impression do you have of them, Landon?'

Arnold shrugged. 'I suppose, like all married couples, they have their problems.'

'So I hear. Bit of snarling going on, I gather. Maybe over Karen Stannard?'

Arnold was reluctant to feed the suggestion. 'Rick Newton tended to drink heavily. When he was drunk, he got a bit . . . obvious.'

'And his wife didn't like it?'

'I suppose not.'

'Do you think the Newtons still sleep together?' Culpeper squinted at Arnold. 'Because if they don't, they could be lying about being together at the time Steve Quaid was killed.'

Arnold had looked at him levelly, with hostile eyes. 'I have no information whatsoever about the sleeping arrangements of Mr and Mrs Newton,' he replied.

But at the site, Karen Stannard was also subdued. Arnold was working on the burial site assigned to him, with two students, when finally she came over to talk. There was a slight frown on her face. 'Do you think I could have a word?' she asked.

Arnold glanced at the students. 'Let's take a break for coffee,' he suggested.

Karen Stannard walked with Arnold towards the hut. They stepped inside; the hut was empty and Arnold picked up the Thermos flask and unscrewed the top. She was silent, leaning against the wall just inside the door. He was very conscious of her presence. During the last few days he had become much more aware of her as a woman. He had always seen her as attractive, but the hostility between them had been a barrier; subtly, in some manner, the situation seemed to have changed for him. It was Vita Delaney's fault, he told himself.

When he gave Karen Stannard a mug of coffee he avoided her eyes as though fearful that she might read what lay in his mind. She took it silently. When he did finally look at her he realized her eyes were fixed on him. They seemed to be green this morning, shaded with caution.

She shifted her stance against the wall, uneasily. 'Who do you think this man Quaid was coming up to see?'

'I've no idea. No one seems to have known him . . . or admits to having known him.' He looked at her curiously. 'You actually saw him, at the Drover's Rest.'

'He made no impression on me.' She was silent for a while. 'I had a sort of . . . odd interview with Culpeper. I told him I didn't know Quaid, but the questions Culpeper addressed to me weren't really about Quaid. He seemed more interested in the dinner party that night.' She glowered at him. 'What have you been saying?'

'Me? About what?' Arnold asked in surprise.

Her lips were set grimly. After a moment she said, 'I seemed to detect certain . . . implications in the questions Culpeper asked me. He wanted to know about Rick Newton and his wife. He asked me what "relations" between us were like.'

'And what was your answer?' Arnold asked, in spite of himself.

A certain anger sparkled in her glance. 'What the hell are you getting at? What did you say to Culpeper? You were in there before me.'

Arnold sighed. 'Your name barely came up. I certainly made no comment on your behaviour. Though I suppose I could have done.'

'Are you suggesting—'

'Now look here,' Arnold interrupted fiercely. 'I don't know why the hell you seem to assume anything that happens around you, which you don't like, is somehow my responsibility. You seem to have some kind of chip on your shoulder, and I'm fed up with you laying into me with your damned suspicions. You seem to think all your difficulties are down to me. If you've got a problem, keep it to yourself — but in any case, stop blaming me for situations which you yourself were responsible for! I've no intention of continuing as your whipping boy!'

164

She was not used to his speaking to her in this manner. She flared at him. 'And just what do you mean by that? What situation are you referring to?'

'I'm referring to the ridiculous way you've been behaving with Newton. It's no surprise to me that someone will have mentioned it to Culpeper. All I can tell you is that it wasn't me! God knows why I should protect you from your own follies—'

'*Protect* me? I don't need your protection, Landon,' she snapped icily.

He took a deep, calming breath. 'No. I know you don't. You're not the kind of woman who would ever want to be beholden to anyone.'

For a moment he thought she was going to say something to break the almost palpable tension that lay between them, but then she cupped her hands round the mug and turned away. He watched her walk back across the field until she stood a little way off, looking towards the areas of stripped turf where the dig was continuing. Her back was stiff, and yet he gained the odd impression that she would be seeing nothing, and was struggling with something within herself. He sighed. He'd never understand women.

And particularly not Karen Stannard.

The morning wore on. Arnold scraped away at the burial site with the students but very little came to light from the sifting. He heard the occasional shout from Rena Williams's group as they came across the odd shard or horse-buckle, and Karen Stannard's group found a few Roman coins when they returned to their work after lunch. But it was almost three in the afternoon before Arnold struck lucky. It was a thigh bone, protruding from earth still sodden from the recent rain which had drained under the protective tarpaulin. He drew his group together and painstakingly scraped away at the edges of the protrusion. Fred Harkness came over at his call.

'Another skeleton?' he asked.

'I don't think so. I can't see signs of any other bones. And just there . . . you see? It's a piece of metal, badly corroded. I suspect what we've got here is not a body burial but a ritual site. We may well find a scattering of offerings.'

'You want assistance from the others?'

'I don't think so. If we keep to our own groups, we're more likely to find some kind of pattern. Have there been any more figurines?'

'Not down our way. Okay, I'll leave you to it, Arnold.'

They worked on steadily. It was backbreaking, crouching, kneeling over the site, scratching away at the earth, sifting material, looking for the slightest signs of metal, or pottery, or bone, or precious stones. Finally, Arnold stood upright, stretching to ease his aching back; his kneecaps were sore, and when he caught sight of the stocky figure marching up the field he was relieved, because George Mahoney seemed to be heading for him. He would be glad of the break.

'Arnold. How are things going?' Mahoney called out as he approached.

'Slowly.'

'Nothing much new emerged, then?'

'Not a lot.' Arnold glanced curiously at him. 'Haven't seen you up here before. What brings you now?'

George Mahoney was silent for a few moments. He stared blankly at the students still working nearby. He seemed troubled; his mouth was tight and there was a sagging to his cheeks that made him look older than his fifty years. It was as though certainties had deserted him, and resolve was crumbling. 'Mrs Delaney wants to see you.'

'Me?' Arnold was surprised. 'Now? What about?'

'I don't know.' Mahoney's glance slipped to Arnold; there was a stolid blankness about him that puzzled Arnold. 'I was with her after lunch. We talked . . . She asked me to come up to fetch you.' He paused for a moment, then he said abruptly, 'She's going downhill fast.'

'Has the doctor been to see her?'

'He's been. He wanted to transfer her to hospital. She'll have none of it.' He gave a slight, enigmatic smile. 'She always was a stubborn, egocentric, selfish woman, I guess. And she says she wants to die in her own bed.'

Arnold frowned. He looked at the grime on his hands; the dirt had worked its way through his gloves. 'I suppose I can wash up at the hall. I'll come right away.'

Mahoney waited while Arnold went across to Harkness to explain what was happening. The two men then walked down the field together, through the woods, along the track that provided a short cut to Haggburn Hall.

'Is Culpeper still at the hall?' Arnold asked.

Mahoney nodded. 'He's still interviewing in the library. I think Rick Newton has been with him most of the morning. Though I suspect he's about finished. I'll be glad to see the back of him. It's all so damned disruptive. And none of us can do much to help. Except maybe that bastard Vartek.'

'Why him?'

Mahoney shrugged. 'I don't know. It's just that I've never really trusted him.' He shook his head resignedly. He seemed to want to change the subject. 'Anyway . . . what about your theories regarding the site? The Mórrigan thing.'

'Nothing more has come to light. Though I've been looking at old maps, and reading various commentaries — legends, old stories. I'm beginning to see some light, maybe. Still a theory, of course . . .' He hesitated, aware that Mahoney was troubled. 'You're very concerned about Mrs Delaney. But I've had the impression she's bright, a fighter—'

'I doubt you'll recognize her, for what she was,' Mahoney replied abruptly. 'She's sinking. This investigation seems to have knocked her about completely. I'm fairly certain she doesn't have long to live.'

* * *

When he saw Mrs Delaney, Arnold was shocked by the change in her, Mahoney had been right — she was sinking fast.

She was lying in her own bed; the curtains were half drawn so the light was not bright in the room and she lay propped up on white, embroidered pillows, in a pale blue bed jacket. Her hands lay on the coverlet: the fingers seemed thin and bony, the veins on her wrists blue traces under an almost transparent skin. Much of the light had gone from her eyes and her cheeks were hollow, the skin drawn and grey about her mouth. But she managed a grim smile when she saw him.

'Arnold. I don't really like gentlemen callers to see me in this state.'

'And what state is that?'

'Drugged to the piebalds.'

'Eyeballs,' he corrected, smiling. 'Some things never change. Now, really, how are you feeling?'

'Resigned.'

'You should be in hospital.'

'The hell with that!' she replied with a flash of the old spirit. 'Let the bloody nurses come to me, rather than me to them. I can afford it. And I like my own bed, even if it has been lonely for years. Anyway, what a stupid question. How am I? It's obvious, surely, I'm dying.'

'I wouldn't say—'

'You don't have to say, Arnold. *I'm* saying it.' She smiled weakly. 'I'm not complaining. I've had a good innings — or a lively one, at any rate. And I've known for some months that I don't have much time left to annoy people in this world.'

'I would have said entertain rather than annoy.'

'Well,' she admitted, 'maybe a bit of both . . . The fact is, my friend, I've known I have heart disease for some time. My doctor, of course, gave me wise advice — about alcohol, smoking, excitement, all that sort of thing. But what's the point of living without booze and excitement? The cigars I could always take or leave. They were just a prop really. Like the hearing aid.' Her eyes gleamed wickedly. 'And I *could* turn on a performance, couldn't I?'

Arnold smiled. 'I can endorse that.'

She shifted painfully in the bed and began to cough. It was a harsh sound, grating, unpleasant. Arnold offered her a sip of water. The way she drank it made him suspect it was not simply water. She grinned at him. 'Yeah, it's primed, but don't tell that miserable sod of a doctor. Anyway, I wanted to see you.'

'I'm sorry to see you like this.'

'No matter.' She fixed him with a clear gaze, as a certain determination settled upon her. 'The fact is, Arnold, when you're in a situation like this — when you're aware that there's not much time left — you start going over your past life, dwelling on your mistakes as well as your triumphs. And the need to put things right becomes more important. You and I had a long chat the other day . . . and we talked, I talked, about matters that are dead and buried. About Joe, about his wife . . . I haven't spoken about those things to anyone else. I wonder, why you? . . . Maybe I fancied you.'

'Well,' he teased, responding to the weak attempt at archness, 'maybe another time, another place . . .'

'Another time, certainly. Like half a century.' She managed a giggle. 'No, the chat with you . . . it brought me back to the old days, and I've not been able to get rid of . . . certain thoughts. I've come to the conclusion that I don't want to meet my Maker without trying to put right some wrongs that I've done. Or maybe omissions is a better word.'

'Such as?'

'I think you can guess. I told you a story. You made no comment, but I had a feeling there was an element of disapproval in your eyes when I finished the story.'

'I'm not sure I know what you're talking about.'

'I believe you do.' She was silent for a while. 'I told you how I fell in love with Joe. I told you about living with him in the States; how we got married and had a marvellous few years before first he, and then his father died. And I ended up with . . . well with what Joe would have called the caboodle. He had a vulgar streak, you know, oddly enough . . . I loved it.'

Arnold watched her quietly. She was drifting, her mind slipping back over the past, dwelling on memories that were happy, and perhaps moments that were regretted, opportunities not seized. She turned her head and looked at him again; she blinked, and he knew there were tears in her eyes. 'I was self-centred,' she said, 'and I was distraught. And after that, well, somehow I never faced up to the fact of my selfish behaviour. There was the money, and the estate, and time slipped by — Arnold, I didn't do right by them.'

'Joe's children, you mean?'

'That's right.' A tear trickled down her wasted cheek; there was regret and pain in her eyes. He reached out and grasped her hand.

'I told you Joe had divorced his wife to marry me, and that she had died an alcoholic, in an asylum. There were two children — a boy and a girl — and I should have done something about them, done something *for* them. But after their mother died, they were taken in by an aunt, and then Joe had gone, and his father followed soon after, and it was all too much for me. My heart was breaking, I couldn't handle things, and I came back to England. With the money. And I never made contact with them . . . never did a damn thing for those kids. Now I think it's time I faced up to those old responsibilities . . . even if it's all a bit late.'

'I understand what you mean,' Arnold replied gently.

She gripped his hand, fiercely. 'The trouble is, it wouldn't be easy — there could be problems.' She watched him carefully, her eyes swimming. 'I don't think I can trust my own family to do what I want.'

'How do you mean?'

'I've made a will. It contains a number of legacies—'

'Are you sure you want to tell me all this?' Arnold asked, troubled suddenly.

'I want to. I've made a number of legacies — various people, staff, that sort of thing. And there's one very large legacy for George Mahoney. He's become more than an employee to me, he's become a friend. And that's made an enemy for him — my nephew Ricky.' She clucked her tongue, impatiently. 'Apart from the legacies, the residue is to go to Ricky, so he'll get the bulk of the estate even though he doesn't deserve it. At one time I asked George to run a quiet check on Ricky, and sure enough, the little bastard was milking the estate. George wanted me to do something about it . . . I didn't. The way I looked at it, it was peanuts and maybe Ricky . . . he was only getting in advance what would have come to him anyway. But Ricky has always been greedy, and he hates Mahoney because he's terrified that if anyone were to get close to me, he could lose out in my will. He never understood, it couldn't be that way, because he's family . . .'

She was silent for a little while, her breathing laboured.

'Are you sure you're up to this?' Arnold asked.

'It's now or never, my friend,' she gasped. She took a deep breath. 'So that's the problem, you see. In my old age, when there's not much time left, I've suddenly developed a conscience. Talking with you about the past made me dwell upon it, made me realize that while I've been prepared to look after Ricky — for all his failings — and that damned greedy wife of his, I've pushed to the back of my mind the obligations that have always been there. Joe's children. I've done nothing for them, all these years. It's time I did. Time I accepted my weakness and selfishness and . . . greed, all those years. So I'm going to do something about it. I've asked to see my solicitor; he's downstairs at the moment. He'll come up when I call. Then I'll write a codicil to my will.'

'You want me to call him now?'

'Not yet. I have to talk to you first. I need to explain — and then ask you a favour. You see, I intend changing my will, to take account of Joe's children. I intend to arrange for payment of the legacies and then leave the residue to be split. At the moment Ricky gets everything; I want to change that so it will be split equally between Joe's children and Ricky.'

Newton certainly would not like that, Arnold thought.

'But there's a problem,' Vita Delaney continued. 'Those kids were last heard of with their aunt in New York. And

Ricky is named as executor to my will. I'm afraid that once I'm gone, he and Gabriella will do their level best to screw things up. There'll be trouble enough over the legacy to George Mahoney, because Ricky hates him, but I'm afraid there'll be even more trouble over the split in the residue. Ricky won't follow through; he won't look for them; he'll slow things down — he'll do his level best to keep the estate all for himself. I don't want that, Arnold. I want to do what's right.'

Arnold was silent for a while. He understood her anxieties, thought she was probably right in her summing up of the likelihood of trouble after her death. There was no love lost between Mahoney and Newton. 'You said you wanted a favour of me.'

She took a deep breath. There was a light rattling sound in her throat. She looked frightened suddenly, and vulnerable, much of the sparkle and fight gone from her. But the grip of her fingers on his wrist was strong.

'I found I was able to talk to you, Arnold, in a way I haven't talked to anyone for years. Our acquaintance has been brief, but I know people, I trust my judgement, and I know there's a fundamental decency about you. You're honest, you're loyal . . . you're blind too, sometimes, I think . . . but basically you're a man to rely on, and trust. And that's why I want your assistance.'

'What is it you want, Mrs Delaney?'

'I'll make arrangements for you to be paid expenses, as much as you need. My solicitor will sort that out.'

'Expenses?' Arnold frowned. 'To do what?'

'I want you to trace Joe's children. I want you to tell them about my will. I want you to make sure that they get what's coming to them.' She paused, gripping his hand tightly. 'I want you to make sure that everything comes out right.'

'Mrs Delaney—'

'Arnold, I want you to be the executor to my will.'

CHAPTER FIVE

1

Standing at the library window, Culpeper had seen Arnold Landon arrive at the hall, walking down the drive with George Mahoney. He wondered what had brought him from the site, before the others. He watched idly as Mahoney left Landon at the front entrance to the hall and turned to make his way back down the drive. Then as he heard the door open behind him he turned.

'Mr Newton . . . Mrs Newton. I'm grateful for your time.'

Rick Newton was pale; his mouth was grim and unsettled, and a certain wildness in his eyes suggested that he was on the verge of anger. His protest was immediate. 'You've already seen each of us. You've already questioned us. There's no way we can help you. We've told you that. What do you want to see us again for?'

Culpeper wondered if they had been quarrelling. He ignored Newton's blustering tone and pulled forward a chair for Gabriella Newton. Her dark eyes were veiled, but she held herself stiffly, a constraint in her bearing as if she were holding her emotions on a tight rein.

'I've seen you separately, of course,' Culpeper said easily. 'I just thought it might be useful if I were to see you together.'

'Why?'

Culpeper shrugged. 'Confirmation, I suppose. Tie up a few loose ends. You'll forgive me, I'm sure. It won't take long.'

'What is it you want to know?' Gabriella Newton said harshly.

Culpeper made a show of consulting the notes in front of him as he sat down behind the polished table. Rick Newton was prowling the room, pacing nervously as though this was the last place on earth where he wanted to be.

'Well,' said Culpeper, 'it seems your separate stories hang well together. Neither of you knew Quaid, there was no connection with him. When the dinner party broke up, you went to your room . . .' He hesitated, pushed out his lower lip as if taken by a sudden thought. 'Actually, I understood from comments made by the staff that you occupy a sort of suite in the hall . . . with separate bedrooms.'

Newton stopped his pacing. 'So?'

Culpeper shrugged. 'So, theoretically it would be possible, once you'd gone upstairs to your separate sleeping accommodation, for one of you to have returned downstairs for some reason.'

'Now why would either of us wish to do that?' Rick Newton snarled.

'You tell me.'

'There's nothing to tell.' Gabriella Newton intervened in a grating tone. 'It's true we have separate bedrooms — Rick snores, you know, and it disturbs my sleep — but on this occasion, we used the same bedroom. Mine.'

'Why would you do that, on this particular night?' Culpeper asked, in wide-eyed innocence.

'Can't you guess?' she snapped.

Culpeper smiled indulgently. 'Maybe to have an argument?'

'What are you driving at?' Rick Newton demanded.

Culpeper sighed. 'It's come to my attention that there was a certain amount of unpleasantness at the dinner party that evening. Not for the first time, I'm told, you'd been drinking heavily, Mr Newton. And paying rather too much attention to one of the other guests — Miss Stannard, to be precise.' He smiled vaguely at Gabriella Newton. 'How did you react to that, Mrs Newton?'

'As any other wife would,' she replied coolly. 'I wasn't pleased.'

'I'm told you were very angry.'

'And I can guess who told you,' Rick Newton snapped viciously. 'It's that bloody schemer Mahoney! He's always out to cause trouble for me. He's ingratiated himself with my aunt, and right from the start he's tried to stir things up. But he'll get his come-uppance, believe me—'

'Rick . . .' Gabriella Newton warned. He subsided into a frustrated silence.

Culpeper looked from one to the other, eyebrows raised. 'So is that it? You've nothing to add?'

Gabriella considered the matter for a moment and then managed a tight little smile. 'You're quite right, of course. I wasn't pleased at Rick's behaviour.' A slight edge crept into her measured tones. 'But it's not a new experience for me — Rick gets somewhat . . . carried away, when he gets drunk. But, yes, I was angry. And there was a quarrel. In fact, that was why Rick was in my bedroom. We had a flaming row there. I told him in no uncertain terms what I thought of his behaviour — humiliating me in front of the other guests.' Her dark eyes seemed to glow with a subdued anger. 'Miss Stannard egged him on — I'd had words with her already, as she probably told you. But then . . .' Gabriella Newton paused, eyeing Culpeper steadily. 'You know how it is. Anger, strong emotions . . . it sort of turned into something else. Reconciliation. We made it up, the quarrel. In the best way possible.' She raised one eyebrow, provocatively. 'I'm sure you know what I mean, Mr Culpeper.'

She was lying, of course. Culpeper was aware of the tension that still lay between man and wife. It had been apparent in their body language when they entered the room. But there was nothing he could do about it if they swore that they had been together at the time Steve Quaid died . . .

Rick Newton came forward, put one hand on the table. 'I'm not clear just why you're prying into our personal affairs, anyway. What's this got to do with Quaid? We've told you we never met him. Now you know we were together, in the bedroom, when he died. Perhaps you can explain—'

'Background, Mr Newton, just background,' Culpeper insisted cheerfully, hiding his annoyance. He wished there was a way in which he could break their story. Maybe there was something he was missing. 'And you're quite right . . . if you two were together when Quaid died — and you didn't know him anyway — that's the end of it. I will be troubling you to make a statement, in due course, but for the time being I think we can leave it there. I'm grateful for your cooperation.'

Gabriella Newton rose immediately. Her husband, however, showed no inclination to take his leave; standing his ground, he asked angrily, 'And what about Mahoney?'

'I beg your pardon?'

'It was he that put you up to this, wasn't it? He's always trying to promote mischief. It'll be Mahoney who told you Gabriella and I were at odds that night—'

'There were others at the dinner, sir,' Culpeper said easily. 'I've heard from several sources—'

'But it'll be Mahoney who started it,' Newton insisted. 'I'll get that bastard. I've been doing some checking . . . I'll get something on him yet—'

'Rick!' Gabriella Newton's tone was sharp. She was glaring at her husband. 'I don't think we need to take up any more of Mr Culpeper's time. He's got a murder to investigate — and he'll be keen to get back to his headquarters.'

Culpeper nodded slowly. Pity. He liked dealing with people who had short fuses. They could easily be led into indiscretions. Unlike Mrs Newton. Spanish she might be, but her Latin temper was completely under control. She had an endgame she was playing for, and nothing was going to be allowed to disturb that and certainly not her husband's looseness of tongue.

After they had left the room, Culpeper sighed and stretched his arms above his head. He looked around him, at the high shelves lined with expensive-looking books, the tall windows that permitted long shafts of sunlight into the room and views down the drive and across the meadows at the south side. It was a far cry from his cramped office, and the scene-of-crime room back at Ponteland. And there wasn't the same kind of service at headquarters — tea and biscuits provided by the housekeeper.

He began to gather up his papers. He felt vaguely depressed. He'd spent a long three days, interviewing the employees and relations of Mrs Delaney, the old lady herself, and each of her guests: Harkness, Vartek, Landon, Stannard, Rena Williams. It didn't seem to have got him very far. Fine, he'd started up some hares with what was clearly a problem lying between the estate manager, George Mahoney, and the Newtons, and had managed to expose the scar tissue in the Newtons' marriage, but he had a feeling it was all a sideshow, really. He still had no idea what Steve Quaid had been doing at Haggburn Hall, why he had come up here at all, and who had smashed in the back of his head with a murder weapon that had yet to be found.

Culpeper sighed. He put his papers into his briefcase, took one last look around the room in case he had left something behind — his wife always accused him of being careless in such matters — and then he stepped into the hallway.

Arnold Landon was coming down the stairs; above him, a small bald man in a pinstripe suit was walking along the landing towards Mrs Delaney's room. It was not anyone Culpeper had seen before.

'Who's that?' Culpeper asked, as Landon stepped down into the hallway.

'Mrs Delaney's solicitor.'

He seemed troubled about something. Culpeper stared at him. 'How is Mrs Delaney?'

Landon shrugged, began to turn away. 'She's tough . . . who knows, she might pull through yet. But she's very ill.' He glanced back at Culpeper, changing the topic. 'You about finished here now?'

'For the time being.' Landon was heading for the entrance and Culpeper swung into step beside him. 'The rest of it can be dealt with at headquarters. No need to disrupt the even tenor of life at Haggburn Hall further.'

'Even tenor?' Landon grunted. 'Hardly that.'

As they stepped out in the weak sunshine of late after-noon Culpeper muttered, 'I gather you like her — the old lady?'

'That's right.' Landon squinted up into the sun. 'It's been a brief acquaintance, but . . . a rewarding one. She didn't deserve all this . . . hassle.'

'Maybe so.' Culpeper hesitated. 'You going back to your digging?'

Landon shook his head. 'No. I've left my address book in the car. I've got a phone call to make. And then . . . well, I think we'll all be packing up here. We can hardly stay on at the hall when Mrs Delaney is so ill. Rena, Karen Stannard and I, we'll all go back to the Drover's Rest.'

'Where you first met Steven Quaid,' Culpeper mused. 'Funny that, in a way. I mean, you and Harkness — you're the only ones who admit to having even seen the guy. It's as though he was almost invisible to the rest of them — the regulars, the ones who actually live here. Vartek, Mahoney, the Newtons — none of them have ever seen him, they say.' He paused, aware that something seemed to have disturbed Landon. 'You alright?'

Landon nodded.

'What do you think happened here, Landon?' Culpeper asked quietly. 'Who do you think clobbered Steve Quaid?'

'I've no idea.'

'No theories at all?'

'None.'

179

'So how would it be if I ran one past you,' Culpeper suggested, after a moment. 'Just as a thought. These dinner parties — they've been odd affairs.'

'If you say so,' Landon replied noncommittally.

'I just get the feeling,' Culpeper continued thoughtfully, 'that the last one was a sort of . . . culmination. Brought things to a head, you might say.'

'In what way?'

'From what I gather, Gabriella Newton got a bit wound up. You know, what with her husband playing up to Karen Stannard and all that.'

'So?'

There was a curiously defensive note in Landon's voice as he turned to stare at Culpeper. The policeman smiled, deprecatingly. 'Well, I don't know, it's just a thought. Maybe a bit of lateral thinking is useful at times. We've been proceeding with the standard hypothesis, that Quaid was killed by someone who knew him. But that's not necessarily the case, is it?'

'I don't know what you mean. What are you suggesting?'

'I don't know,' Culpeper said easily. 'It's just something that came to me this afternoon, after talking to the Newtons. They told me that they spent the night together — went upstairs after dinner, had a row about Karen Stannard, and spent the rest of the night making it up. But . . . they *would* want to say that, wouldn't they? I mean, if Newton roughed up Quaid, it wouldn't suit Gabriella's book to have that come out. I mean, I understand Newton is Mrs Delaney's nearest heir and stands to make a lot of money when she dies. He's Gabriella's meal ticket — and Gabriella wouldn't want to jeopardize his inheritance. So she's got good reason to protect him, say he was in her room when in fact he wasn't.'

'But you've no evidence to suggest—'

'And in a sense, you could also put the boot on the other foot, couldn't you? It would suit Newton to go along with his wife's story, because that puts him out of the frame — and he'll not want to be the subject of a police investigation. After all, I've heard rumours that he's got sticky fingers . . .'

'I'm afraid you're losing me with your theorizing, Mr Culpeper,' Landon said coldly.

Culpeper shrugged. 'Ah, well, I'm just a simple copper thinking out loud. So let me try to clarify my own thoughts about the matter. I mean, there was an unhealthy atmosphere at the dinner party. It wasn't the first time that Newton had been chatting up your delectable colleague, Miss Stannard. And I'm told — I won't divulge my source, of course — I'm told that she didn't seem . . . ah, unreceptive.'

Landon's mouth was oddly stiff. 'I can't really believe that it was anything other than a game to Miss Stannard.'

'Be that as it may, it didn't look like a nice game to Gabriella Newton. I think you'd agree with that. Anyway, this little dicky-bird source of mine tells me that towards the end of the evening Newton was pressing Karen Stannard to agree to a meeting. Clandestine stuff.'

Arnold Landon shrugged. 'He'd been trying that on ever since he met her.'

'Well, maybe Gabriella took it seriously; maybe she thought it was fixed up, that evening.' He paused, looking at Arnold owlishly. 'Now, what do you think she might have done in such a case?'

'I've no idea.'

'Well let's just assume husband Rick wasn't in his room — and wasn't in Gabriella's. Or even that he was in his room and the little wife wanted to teach someone else a lesson. She could have stepped lightly down the stairs, got herself away to the stables, hidden in the darkness, and then when someone came stepping past — wham!' Culpeper took a pipe from his pocket, tapped it, stuck it into his mouth. Arnold Landon was staring at him as if he were crazy. 'It would have been a mistake, of course,' Culpeper went on. 'She would have been intending to hammer Karen Stannard, or even her faithless dog of a husband — if he had left his room. Instead of which she clouted the unfortunate, nocturnally wandering, Mr Quaid.'

'That's preposterous!' Landon exclaimed. 'You can't really believe that story would hold water.'

'No, I suppose not,' Culpeper replied cheerfully. 'It is a bit far-fetched, isn't it? But you never know what a wronged woman will do. And there's one other problem it doesn't solve . . .'

'What's that?'

'It doesn't tell us what the hell Steven Quaid was doing up at Haggburn Hall, and who the hell he was hoping to meet.'

* * *

After Culpeper had driven away, on his way back to Ponteland, Arnold went up to his room at the hall. He felt disturbed by Culpeper's theorizing. The suggestion he had made was, in Arnold's view, absurd, but it reminded him of the part played by Karen Stannard in the events of the evening, and it left an unpleasant taste in his mouth. He took out his address book and rang Jane in New York.

The hotel told him she wasn't expected back for another two hours. Arnold began to pack.

They had discussed the matter earlier in the day. Rena, Karen Stannard and he had decided to go back to the Drover's Rest. Fred Harkness would stay on in his tent at the dig. From now on there would be no dinners at Haggburn Hall to look forward to.

The packing took little time. Arnold carried his bag down to his car, said goodbye to the housekeeper and thanked her for what she had done for them all. She was upset, her eyes red-rimmed; it was clear that Mrs Delaney had won the respect of her employees. 'Do you think she'll recover, Mr Landon?'

It would be dishonest to suggest she would. 'She seems to be very ill.'

His reply brought forth a flood of tears.

He returned to his car and started the engine; he was about to drive away when he saw Mrs Delaney's solicitor leaving the hall. The lawyer raised his hand. Arnold turned off the ignition and waited.

The solicitor walked across the driveway to the car; he had a precise, clipped manner of speech. 'Mr Landon. Glad I caught you. Save too many journeys. Mrs Delaney's spoken to you?'

'About her will? Yes.'

'And you agree to act as executor?'

Arnold hesitated, then nodded. 'I suppose so. I promised.'

'Good. There will be some papers for you to sign. A consent form. It's as well. I'll get it along to you tomorrow. You'll be here?'

'No. The Drover's Rest.'

'Good. We don't want to leave it too long, do we?'

The implications in his tone left Arnold with a leaden feeling in his chest.

He booked in at the Drover's Rest again and Rena and Karen Stannard joined him for dinner at the hotel. It was a subdued occasion. No one seemed inclined towards small talk, and after a brief nightcap in the bar they soon retired to their separate rooms.

Arnold finally managed to get through to Jane late that evening. She seemed somewhat constrained. He got the impression there was someone else in the room. When he asked her, she explained that her agent was there — they were still discussing some business.

'Then I won't keep you too long,' Arnold said. 'I have a favour to ask.'

'Ask away.'

He explained to her briefly about Mrs Delaney's condition, and the request she had made of him. Jane sounded puzzled. 'So how can I help?'

'It just occurred to me that, in the circumstances, rather than I should start ringing up various agencies, engaging tracing operators and so on, you might . . . since you're there in New York . . .'

'Of course. Anything I can do to help.'

'Mrs Delaney's husband had two children by his first marriage. I've got the details regarding Joe Delaney, date of birth and death and so on, and the date of his first marriage. If I fax them through to you, I wonder whether you'd be able to find time to make some preliminary inquiries.'

'What exactly do you want?'

'I need to trace the children. The first Mrs Delaney's maiden name was Carnforth. She had a sister. I don't know whether the sister ever got married or not, but she was entrusted with the raising of the boy and the girl. And if you can do this, expense is no problem. Mrs Delaney's estate is a large one. If you can find these people, they are likely to end up with quite a large amount of money. Do you think you could take this on?'

She was silent for a moment. Then she said, 'If I can't find the time personally, I'm sure I can find a New York agency who will take it on for a fee. Leave it to me, Arnold . . .'

2

Culpeper disliked the smell of formaldehyde, so normally he tried to stay away from the forensic laboratories in Newcastle. On this occasion he made an exception; he was beginning to feel frustrated at the lack of progress on the Quaid killing, and since he was driving past the laboratories he decided to call in to add weight to the police liaison officer's attempts to get some early answers from the staff.

Dr Demos was disinclined to give early answers. A small, pudgy man, bald-headed except for spring-away tufts of brown hair above his ears, he was of Maltese extraction, with a pale olive complexion and brown eyes which looked enormous behind his thick glasses, giving him a somewhat owlish look. 'You don't understand the difficulties, Mr Culpeper,' he moaned. 'We have had cutbacks again this year. The crime rate seems to be rising continually. We get knifings, car accidents, paint-matchings, murders — the list is endless and I am always supposed to give priority, come up with quick answers, deliver verdicts, when I am in no position to do so. Find me some more staff, my friend, and I will give you speed.'

Culpeper was not Demos's friend. He scowled. 'I appreciate that you're under pressure. We all are. But this is a murder inquiry; the longer it goes on the less likely we are to find the culprit. Speed is essential. And I'm not asking for a verdict. All I want are a few simple answers, and at this stage I'll be satisfied if you could give me a rough idea — accuracy can come later when all your tests are complete.'

Demos spread his hands wide and assumed an air of injury. 'But if I say something, you people will pretend later that it is the Gospel truth. What am I to do?'

'Just answer me some questions,' Culpeper snapped. 'Guesstimates will do.'

Demos shook his head mournfully. 'Provided you are prepared to agree that you must not hold me to these . . . guesstimates, as you put it.'

'All right,' Culpeper breathed out slowly. 'Let's start with what killed him.'

Demos shrugged. 'Something heavy, blunt. It is possible it was a stone. My guesstimate is that he was struck from behind, just one blow, but it was enough to drive shards of bone into his brain. The left—'

'One blow,' Culpeper interrupted hastily, not desiring to have the gory details. 'One blow only, enough to kill him. So, it's likely that it was a man rather than a woman?'

'Not necessarily so,' Demos considered, frowning. 'In this case one blow was enough because the dead man, he had what I believe is called in common parlance, an eggshell skull. One blow was enough — from a man or a woman. The force involved, beyond a certain point, was irrelevant — the thickness of the skull and the consequent likelihood of fatal injury was the essential element.'

'Time of death?'

Demos pursed his lips. 'From the calculations made at the scene and our later investigations, we would conclude that he died before midnight that evening. It's difficult to be precise, of course, though we will come up with a range—'

'Midnight.' Culpeper nodded. 'Is there anything else of significance about the body, that you can tell me?'

'There was no sign of a struggle — no detritus under the nails, no damage to body or clothing to indicate that he put up a fight. It seems he was taken by surprise, from behind. One blow only. But then, he was not a strong man.'

'Anything about his clothing?'

Demos shrugged and regarded Culpeper owlishly. 'We've looked at what he was wearing, and what was brought in to us from his room at the hotel. There are certain oddities. I think your sergeant, Stevenson, he will confirm that there seemed to be nothing by way of identity among his belongings — no credit cards, no addresses, no personal papers. He was a man without roots, it seems to me. And there was the other thing, of course . . .'

'What was that?' Culpeper asked suspiciously.

Demos wrinkled his nose. 'After I had seen some of his wardrobe, I did take another look at the body, but the evidence was inconclusive. However, from the nature of certain articles of . . . rather exotic underwear obtained from his hotel room, I would draw the conclusion that your Mr Quaid had, shall we say, homosexual tendencies. It is not a forensic view, of course, but one I give as a man of the world. I think Mr Quaid perhaps made a living, if that is what you can call it, as a rent boy.'

* * *

Farnsby was not at headquarters when Culpeper returned to Ponteland. The DCI sat behind his desk and shifted some of the papers that had accumulated there during the last few days. He was in no mood to deal with day-to-day matters.

He got himself a cup of tea and sat reflectively in his room.

He stared at the notes in front of him, the names scribbled on the top sheet. His mind drifted around the possibilities, and the questions. He was still staring blankly at the sheet when there was a tap on the door. It was Farnsby. Somewhat reluctantly, Culpeper waved him in.

'Anything new on Quaid?'

'Not really, sir. We've been through Quaid's belongings and—'

'Dr Demos told me,' Culpeper interrupted. 'A distinct lack of personalized items. And we know he paid cash at the hotel no credit cards, no identification.' Culpeper sighed. 'It's all so bloody vague and inconclusive. Take Fred Harkness. We know he'd had a quarrel with Quaid, up at the site of the dig, in the woods, and in the village. And he claims to have returned to his tent after dinner at the hall — but of course there's no one around to corroborate that since the students were on some sort of binge that night.'

'Doesn't seem a terribly strong motive for murder, though, sir. On the other hand—'

'Then there's Rick Newton, Mrs Delaney's nephew. Both he and his wife give each other an alibi, deny any knowledge of Quaid, and don't seem to have any motive for killing him.'

'There is a—'

'Karen Stannard possibly plays some part in the proceedings,' Culpeper mused. 'I was proposing a theory, just to see how Landon reacted to it, though it doesn't hold much water with me. I was thinking maybe Quaid was killed by mistake, you know? Perhaps Gabriella Newton killed him, thinking it was either her husband — with whom she'd quarrelled — or Miss Stannard herself. These Latin temperaments, you know, they can lead to blind rage . . .'

'I got the impression Mrs Newton keeps her temper under close control, except maybe when she lays into her husband. But I need to tell you—'

'George Mahoney, of course,' Culpeper interrupted, 'he's another piece in the jigsaw. He's as controlled as Mrs Newton. All the stories suggest that he's at daggers drawn with Rick Newton, that they dislike each other. Newton thinks he's trying to get an inside track with Mrs Delaney, but you never get much reaction from Mahoney. He reckons he didn't know Quaid, and there seems to be nothing to connect them . . .'

'He did give us some idea of what he was thinking . . . his dislike for Newton,' Farnsby pointed out. 'It was he who told us of the way Newton had been chatting up Karen Stannard, of the assignation that was set up . . .'

'Which Miss Stannard insists was never a serious option as far as she was concerned.'

'That's right, but there's something more important—'

'So I don't know where the hell we're going, other than round in circles—'

'Chief Inspector,' Farnsby interrupted firmly. 'There is one thing of some importance that I've been trying to bring to your attention.'

'Well, spit it out, bonny lad,' Culpeper snapped. 'What's stopping you?'

Farnsby's eyes betrayed a certain irritation. 'I've been trying . . . Well, anyway, we've been running checks while you were still up at Haggburn Hall. There's one thing that doesn't check out. The man who calls himself Vartek.'

'Yes?'

'When he was questioned, we pressed him for his real name. He gave it to us only with reluctance. Nicholson, he said. Daniel Nicholson.' Farnsby gave a little grimace. 'The information he gave us seems to be less than accurate. We checked on the solicitor's firm in Nottingham, the address, the name.'

'And . . . ?'

'There's no record of a Daniel Nicholson at the firm. Vartek lied to us. He didn't give us his real name.'

'Is that right?' Culpeper pulled a face. 'Now why would he do that? He must have known we would check.'

'Panic? Didn't think quickly enough?' Farnsby shrugged. 'Anyway, I think we ought to have another go at him, sir. Clearly, there's rabbit away somewhere.'

'I think you're right. I tell you what, Farnsby—'

The telephone on Culpeper's desk rang. He picked up the receiver. 'Culpeper,' he growled.

'There's a lady at reception who wants to talk to Mr Farnsby, sir.'

'About what? He's here with me and we're in conference.'

'Yes, sir, I'd tried his room first. The lady declines to state her business, but says she's got some information for him.'

'What's her name?'

'Sharman.'

Culpeper covered the mouthpiece with his left hand. 'A woman called Sharman. She's got something for you.'

Farnsby's eyes widened. 'Ah, yes, she's from Social Services. It'll be the Mulberry thing. Perhaps I should go down to see her and—'

'No, no,' Culpeper replied irritably, 'let her bring it up here, whatever it is. You can deal quickly with her, and then we'll get on. I could do with a break, anyway.'

He was away in the washroom for a short while; when he returned to his room there was a young woman seated in the chair Farnsby had occupied while the DI himself was perched on the edge of Culpeper's desk. Farnsby removed the smile from his face and his haunch from the desk when Culpeper came into the room. 'This is Eileen Sharman, sir.'

'I'm a social worker, in the department at Morpeth,' she explained as she rose to shake hands with Culpeper. She had frizzy brown hair, a nervous mouth and nice eyes. A good figure, Culpeper noted, but dressed rather dowdily. For some reason an image of Karen Stannard came to his mind; a matter of contrasts, he thought.

'You wanted to see young Farnsby, here. I'm sorry to rush you,' Culpeper apologized, 'but we are involved in another inquiry and—'

'I won't keep you long,' Eileen Sharman interrupted in a voice firmer than Culpeper had expected. 'It's just that Mr Farnsby had been making inquiries at our department and . . . well . . . I was involved in the matter he was asking about. The allegations made about the home up at Spittal, some six years back. I know you were given the basic information but . . . I should explain it was I who took the original statements, and got to know the complainants very well, and . . . well, I was more than a little upset when the allegations were never pursued. The charges were withdrawn, you see.'

'So we understood,' Farnsby said quietly.

She turned her brown eyes on him. There was a spark of resentment in them. 'I spent a long time on those boys. I wasn't allowed to see them again, after they withdrew the complaints. I believe they were subjected to some sort of pressure.'

'Or they were paid a sum of money, maybe?'

'There are all kinds of ways to describe pressure,' Eileen Sharman said primly. 'Anyway, if you're reopening the inquiry—'

'That's not necessarily the case,' Culpeper interrupted quickly. 'We're just pursuing a certain line—'

'Whatever.' Miss Sharman pursed her lips. 'I just thought that if you were looking at the events of six years ago, you might like to have a look at my case notes, the ones I compiled at the time. They're in this folder here. I'm reluctant to leave them, of course, and it's not departmental policy, but I feel so angry about it, even after all this time . . . and you are the police . . .'

She hesitated, glancing at Farnsby, who smiled reassuringly. He was always good with women, Culpeper thought with a surly grimace. Smooth.

Farnsby took the folder from her and placed it on Culpeper's desk. 'We're very grateful, Eileen. We'll look into it.' He turned to Culpeper. 'I'll just see Miss Sharman to the stairs,' he said.

'That's fine, I can make my own way from there,' she replied with a nervous smile. She nodded, shook hands with Culpeper, and then followed Farnsby to the door. He walked along the corridor with her. Casually, while waiting for Farnsby's return, Culpeper picked up the folder and opened it. It consisted of a series of sheets clipped together; the handwriting was microscopically neat, so that he had to squint to read it properly. He was getting old; his wife had insisted that he get some glasses. He grunted. He would leave it to Farnsby to plough through the notes, make his own transcript, a summary of what might be important as background to the Mulberry inquiry. What they would not be able to do, in the circumstances, was to show the folder to the Chief Constable. The matter was supposed to have been left to him.

At the back of the folder was an envelope. Culpeper flipped it open. It contained a series of photographs.

Farnsby came back into the room. 'Sorry about that, sir. I didn't expect her to come round with information. I'd just been trawling, really, as we'd agreed—'

'Get her back here,' Culpeper snapped.

'What?'

'Don't let her leave the premises. Get her back here, *now!*' Farnsby hesitated for a moment, and then turned and hurried back into the corridor. Culpeper heard his feet clattering on the stairs. He stood there behind his desk, staring at the photograph in his hand. A few minutes later Farnsby came back into the room, with Eileen Sharman in tow. The social worker looked somewhat alarmed. Culpeper gestured her to a chair.

Culpeper sat down and smiled supportively at her. 'I wonder,' he said ingratiatingly, 'whether you'd mind telling me a little more about these . . . allegations. You say there were two complainants?'

'That's right.' His smile seemed to have made her more nervous than ever.

'And the allegations were of sexual abuse?'

'That's right.' She flickered a nervous tongue over dry lips. 'They were both fifteen. They told me, separately, of incidents that had occurred over a period of some three years — since they were twelve. They had both come from broken homes, where there had already been evidence of abuse. They had been put into care, but had absconded, got into trouble . . . the usual story. Finally, they were sent to secure accommodation at Spittal.' Her voice began to tremble with rage. 'And they said the abuse had started again, at the home.

They'd moved from one evil environment to another. And this time they had had to submit to it, because the abuser was a person in authority.'

'They named him?'

'Of course. I . . . I'm unable to do so, of course, because the allegations were never proceeded with. No charges were ever brought. I was extremely angry at the time — I thought of leaking the story to the newspapers—'

'There were rumours around at the time,' Farnsby suggested.

She nodded. 'Some of us were extremely upset. We talked among ourselves, there were case conferences, but the Director of Social Services, he persuaded us that there was simply no point in pursuing the matter once the two boys dropped their complaints.'

'What happened to them?' Culpeper asked curiously.

'I lost track of them; they left our registers after they reached the age of sixteen. One went to London, I believe. I've had no contact with them since those days. But I've always kept the file, my personal notes.' Her eyes darted to the folder on Culpeper's desk. 'I wouldn't want them used publicly, of course, but I don't mind . . . Well, I think there was some sort of cover-up at that time; I think the boys were pressured. Something should have been done about it, but management was so weak . . . I was spitting mad about that.'

'What were the boys called? You know their names, I imagine?'

She nodded. 'The names are in the file notes. One was called Charlie Lawes. The other . . . he was called Dennis. William Dennis.'

Culpeper nodded. Farnsby was watching him curiously, not certain what was going on. Tell me,' Culpeper said slowly, reaching across the desk to show Eileen Sharman the photograph he held in his hand. 'I took this out of your folder. Is this one of the boys who made the complaints you were telling us about?'

She leaned forward to inspect it. Culpeper realized she was a little short-sighted. She nodded. 'Yes, that's one of them. He was about fourteen when that was taken.'

'And which of the two boys was he?'

'Charlie Lawes.' She hesitated. 'I think . . . I got the impression he had been . . . corrupted at an early age. Maybe he'd had latent tendencies, but certainly he had been seduced at home, by an uncle it seems, before he ever got brought into care. He was more streetwise than William Dennis, but whether he was complaisant or not with regard to the events at the home, it was wrong and he *was* prepared to bring charges, until suddenly both of them withdrew their allegations . . .'

'Charlie Lawes . . .' Culpeper mused. He passed the photograph to Farnsby and watched as the detective inspector's features changed after a few seconds. Wordlessly, he handed the photograph back to Culpeper, but his eyes were alight.

'Charlie Lawes,' Culpeper repeated quietly, almost to himself. Then he smiled grimly at Eileen Sharman. 'We know him as Steven Quaid.'

'He always wanted to be an actor,' Eileen Sharman said. 'That's probably why he changed his name.'

* * *

It had been a breakthrough, Culpeper thought as he and Farnsby were driven out of Ponteland, north towards the fells beyond Alnwick, and west towards Haggburn Hall. He recalled the way his blood had started to course more rapidly as they questioned Eileen Sharman. She had lost touch with Charlie Lawes once he had been removed from the register, but she understood he had stayed in the area while the other boy — William Dennis — had drifted south, to London. She had no doubt that he would have got into bad company down there.

Maybe not as bad as Charlie Lawes, Culpeper thought grimly.

But it had not been the end of the assistance that Eileen Sharman had been able to provide. They had gone through the other photographs: William Dennis, a few other boys who had also been questioned and whom Eileen Sharman had been able to persuade to be photographed. And Culpeper had shown her the formal photograph, of a group of men and two women, standing, soberly dressed, on a lawn in front of a large house, shaded by trees on either side.

'And what's this?' he had asked.

'It's the home at Spittal. It was owned by Mr Mulberry, though I understand he had little to do with the running of it. It's where Dennis and Lawes were kept . . . and abused . . .'

Culpeper had pointed with his finger. It was trembling slightly. 'And who's this?'

She had been silent a moment. At last, in a nervous voice, she had said, 'What made you pick *him* out?'

There was a cold excitement in Culpeper's veins. 'Why do you ask, Miss Sharman?' he countered.

'Because . . .' She licked dry lips. 'Because that's the man the boys accused of abusing them. How did you know it was him? I didn't tell you — it would have been a breach of . . . well, no charges were ever brought, and he left the home later, anyway, before it was sold by Mr Mulberry to the consortium . . .'

'What was his name, Miss Sharman?'

She hesitated. 'He was called Sinclair . . . Anthony Sinclair.' Vartek.

* * *

Culpeper wound down the car window. His face was burning; he was aware he was flushed. It must have been satisfaction. 'You know,' he said to Farnsby, 'I keep thinking about what that feller Landon's looking for up here. The Shape-Shifter legend. He told us about it at his interview, remember? What's been bothering us is that there are too many bloody shape-shifters around. Charlie Lawes, abused as a child, then put into the hands of an evil man at the home. When he gets out, he changes his name, takes a new identity as Steven Quaid, actor.'

'And Anthony Sinclair,' Farnsby agreed. 'Another shape-shifter. He told us his real name was Nicholson — attempting to change his identity again. And to Mrs Delaney . . . he was Vartek.' He glanced curiously at Culpeper. 'So how do you think it works out, sir?'

Culpeper grunted. 'I would have thought it was pretty obvious. Pressure was put on Charlie Lawes — or Quaid, as we know him — to withdraw the allegations against Anthony Sinclair, who was on the care staff at the home. *Care!*' Culpeper humphed in contempt. 'But it wasn't the end of the story when Lawes finally got out of the home. There was probably a certain amount of mud sticking to Sinclair, enough to prevent him getting another job as a carer, so he reinvented himself. He became a scam merchant, called himself Vartek, and eventually battened on to Mrs Delaney. I've no doubt once we question him, we'll find he's been involved in all sorts of cons over the intervening years. But he must have thought he was on to a good thing with Mrs Delaney.'

'And Charlie Lawes?'

Culpeper shrugged. 'We don't know for certain whether the relationship with Sinclair/Vartek ended when he left the home. Maybe it continued — Dr Demos suggested to me that he thought Quaid had homosexual tendencies. But my own guess is that Charlie Lawes tried to take up acting and changed his name, then drifted until he came into contact with Sinclair again. By which time he wasn't Sinclair, but Vartek, and trying to get money out of Mrs Delaney. I think young Quaid saw his chance. He put the squeeze on Vartek. He came up to stay at the Drover's Rest so he could be close to Vartek, a thorn in his side. Vartek paid him money — Quaid used cash to pay his hotel bills. He probably threatened Vartek. If he didn't pay, he'd expose Vartek to Mrs Delaney, and Vartek's scam would go down the drain.'

'And the killing?'

Culpeper shrugged. 'Maybe he got too pressing . . . or Vartek had just had enough. So he agreed to meet him at the hall, near the stables, to hand over some more cash . . . And then he clobbered him.'

Farnsby frowned. 'It didn't seem a particularly well-planned crime. I mean, why at the stables? Why not more secretly, in the woods or somewhere?'

Culpeper shrugged. 'Vartek was at the dinner party; Quaid might have been hanging around, waiting until he emerged. It could have been a regular rendezvous, of course — perhaps Vartek didn't like the idea of wandering in the woods. And when Quaid did, he carried a shotgun. That could have been for protection, in case Vartek turned nasty. So I wonder why he didn't have it the night he died?'

'Maybe he did, sir. Vartek could have got rid of it, after he killed Quaid.'

'Hmmm. We'll find out more when we've got that bastard Vartek in the cells. I don't like paedophiles . . .'

'It's likely to have been a panic, a fury, a spur of the moment killing when Quaid got too demanding,' Farnsby suggested.

'Could be,' Culpeper agreed. 'Somehow Quaid must have hit a raw spot, the spot that turned Vartek from a sexual abuser and scam merchant into a murderer. We'll find out, bonny lad; we'll find out once we get our hands on him!'

They drove on in silence. A vein was beating in Culpeper's forehead. He was conscious of the steady thudding as he was of the conflicting emotions that had been aroused in him. He didn't like child abusers and he recalled Vartek's appearance, the smooth elegance of the man, the way he had sweated when he was questioned. He must have realized then that the panic, or the fury, that had led him to kill the young man he had abused six years earlier would lead to his exposure, eventually. He had been sweating, and he had given a false name again, shifting his identity, blurring the shape . . .

* * *

197

They passed Haggburn village and proceeded onwards to the hall. As they swung into the gravel drive, to Culpeper's surprise he saw Arnold Landon standing by his car, parked near the entrance to the hall. He got out of his own car, hesitated, then turned to Farnsby. 'You go on in. I'll give you the pleasure of arresting the bastard. Make sure you caution him, of course.'

Farnsby hesitated, slightly taken aback, then nodded and walked towards the entrance with quick, nervous strides.

Culpeper walked slowly across to Arnold Landon, who seemed surprised to see him. 'I thought you'd finished here, Chief Inspector.'

'Hardly.' Culpeper squinted around him. 'And I thought you'd moved down to the Drover's Rest. What brings you back here?' Landon's eyes were bleak. 'Mrs Delaney . . . She died, at four o'clock this morning. I came here as soon as I heard.'

Culpeper felt uncomfortable. He was unable to find words that seemed suitable. 'I'm sorry to hear that. I didn't really get to know her — I mean, I only spoke to her once. She seemed . . .'

'A woman . . .' Landon paused, as though correcting himself. 'A lady of quality . . . and of conscience.'

'Ahh,' Culpeper added wisely. After a moment he said, 'It comes to us all, of course, in the end . . .'

Landon was getting into his car. He looked up, about to say something, but at that moment Farnsby came spilling out of the hall, running across the gravel. 'He's gone!' he shouted angrily. 'Scarpered!'

'Who's gone?' asked Landon, alarmed.

'Vartek!' Culpeper snarled. 'Bastard!'

3

The manhunt took the headlines for the rest of the week. While Vartek was not named, the local newspapers carried lead stories on the death of Steven Quaid and the search being conducted for the man who had stayed at Haggburn Hall as a guest of Mrs Delaney.

Gossip was also rife at the dig. Arnold managed to spend some time at the site, although he was called away for two days on business connected with his agreement to become Mrs Delaney's executor. Her solicitors were extremely helpful: they had acted as trustees for some of the estate and were able to give him a great deal of information concerning the investments she had held.

He had one confrontation with Rick Newton.

'I hear you've been given the task of winding up the estate,' Newton said bitterly, buttonholing him at the hall. 'I can't understand how you wheedled your way into that position, but no matter — when can we expect to get what's coming to us?'

'It's going to take me a couple of weeks to get everything in order for distribution, quite apart from the need to get probate,' Arnold explained patiently. 'But I can assure you that you're a major beneficiary under the will.'

'But how *much* do I get?' Newton insisted.

'I can't tell you until the valuations are completed,' Arnold replied.

'And Mahoney — what about him?'

'There is a legacy to George Mahoney, but I need to discuss that with him, not you,' Arnold said, somewhat nettled by Newton's manner. He brushed past him, refusing to discuss the matter further.

Later in the week he received a phone call from Jane. She had managed to get some information on the Carnforths. It seemed the aunt had died in 1970, and Jane was still trying to trace the children, but there were one or two leads she could follow. She hoped to get the information for him within a few days.

And things were progressing at the dig. The grave site Arnold's team were working on proved to be what he had imagined: a ritual burial, with no great collection of artefacts or grave goods. But Karen Stannard's group had come up with a more interesting discovery: another crouched body burial, clearly a man of some consequence — which clarified the fact that the area was not set out for the burial of outcasts. This grave had included a ritual dagger, pottery items and pig bones — meat designed to provide succour for the dead man in the underworld. The man had been a warrior of some standing in the community. And near his left hand had been placed a torso with an eagle's head.

'It's another symbol of the Shape-Shifter,' Rena Williams declared. 'It's clear that what we have here is a cult that swept through the area, and remained here for perhaps two hundred years, maybe more. The absence of other icons would suggest that it was a relatively late entrant into the area, as religions went, but was taken up, perhaps because of some catastrophe that occurred on these fells. Arnold, you were telling me you've now got some sort of theory . . .'

He nodded. 'From the study of the old legends I found in the library at Haggburn Hall, and the commentaries I received from Newcastle, I think I can suggest what might have happened. I don't think we'll ever know the truth, because of the general absence of written evidence — we only have oral traditions that were finally written down in the seventeenth century, and, of course, the evidence that we take from the earth. I suspect, however, that the cult of the Mórrigan came to these fells about a thousand years ago.'

'From the west?' Karen Stannard asked.

'Almost certainly. It may well have been that the cult was not unknown in the north — there was enough commerce between Ireland and England to permit us to guess that knowledge of the cult would have been available here. But I suspect that the cult really took root some time after societies had become settled on these fells. Something happened to bring them face to face with the Mórrigan; face to face with the fear the Shape-Shifter produced. It was climactic enough to persuade the settlements that lay around here to begin to pay homage to the war deity, to embrace the cult, maybe for several generations.'

'What sort of event are you suggesting?' Fred Harkness asked.

Arnold shrugged. 'Difficult to say. But since the Mórrigan was a war deity, it has to have a connection with violence and death . . . so it could well have been a war party from the west. If you take a look at these maps you'll see how the cult could have spread. We know, for instance, that no icons of this kind have been found so far, east of the Pennines. They may exist of course, but no digs have discovered anything of that nature. West of the Pennines . . . well, let's propose a hypothesis. Let's assume a war party of some strength, maybe driven from Ireland — or from the Isle of Man, whose Neolithic history has been well recorded, with a strong hunter-gatherer, tool-making tradition — landing here on the west coast. It would have had to be a party of significant size, but mainly young men, uprooted, seeking land. They could have landed at any of a number of places along this coastline, but I favour the thought that they may have beached up here, near Carlisle.'

'Why would you suggest that?' Rena Williams asked.

'Because it gives feasible support to the finds we've made. You see, if the war party beached there, in time they would be able to infiltrate, move inwards, eastwards, along the River Eden, and then across into Northumberland with their long boats, then climbing up the river valleys, to the fells along roads which had been drover roads . . .And as they moved inland, ravishing the settlements, taking what they willed, the people would have believed it to be the time of the Mórrigan, the female war deity, and evil and mischief would have soured their lives . . .'

Arnold thought about it a good deal when he worked at the site, and later, when he attended the funeral of Mrs Delaney. It was held at the small church at Haggburn, on the hill overlooking the village. The church itself had been built in the fifteenth century, but Arnold suspected it would have been a site of much greater age in terms of religious significance. It was not uncommon for Christian churches to be built upon sites that were already invested with significance. The fact that it would have been the site of a pagan, sacrificial cult made no difference. The Church would have needed to establish itself in the hearts and minds of men and it was politic to feed off whatever religious reputation a site might enjoy.

He caught sight of George Mahoney at the funeral. The estate manager came over to speak to him after the service. 'Good to see you here, Landon.'

'We came as a group,' Arnold replied, nodding towards the others from the dig, who were making their way back down the hill. 'We all liked her . . . enjoyed her hospitality.'

George Mahoney smiled wryly. 'Even if it was somewhat . . . eccentric.'

The smile faded. There was a haggard look about the man's face, and his eyes seemed blank, as though life had been drawn from them. The death of Mrs Delaney seemed to have hit him hard.

'She was a generous woman,' Arnold said. 'She told me you and she had become quite close.'

Mahoney lifted his head and his nostrils flared, as though he were sniffing the wind. He looked back to the church tower, reflectively. 'I saw her just as an employer, at first. But she seemed to enjoy my company. We talked a lot.'

'But never about her private life.'

'What do you mean by that?'

Arnold shrugged, avoided the question. 'I think I ought to come to see you soon. Newton's been chasing me, but you haven't. Nevertheless, I imagine you'll be aware that you've been left a significant amount in her will.'

'She said she'd look after me,' he replied dully. He seemed to be about to add something, but lapsed into silence. 'Well, you know where to find me, when you want a chat. I'll be around for a while. Then, I guess I'll move on.'

'Where to?'

Mahoney shrugged. 'I don't know. I'm past fifty now. I've a fancy to go to the States. Anyway, I'll see you around . . .' There was a strange uncertainty in the man's bearing as he walked away.

* * *

Next morning the news was on television in the Drover's Rest, it was announced on local radio and even the newspapers picked it up in their later editions. The man Arnold and the others had known as Vartek had been picked up in Suffolk, living under an assumed name. He was in custody, the Northumberland police had travelled down to Suffolk for some initial questioning, but he was now to be brought up to the north to be charged.

That evening Jane rang Arnold. She had obtained the information, such as it was, that Arnold had requested. It was enough for him to determine how, in general terms, the estate was to be divided.

Next day he called in to see the solicitors who were dealing with the probate for him. He gave them the information and then he drove along to Haggburn Hall, to tell the Newtons. The result was predictable. Rick Newton was viciously angry. He had hoped to obtain the whole estate — to take only half the residue did not suit him at all.

'So one of Joe Delaney's kids is dead,' he snapped. 'And you've yet to find the other. But as far as can be ascertained, the other one's still alive.'

'It seems so. There's no record of death. So I'm afraid there will be a further delay until things can be sorted out. There's no reason, of course, why I shouldn't be able to release some money, if you need it for the upkeep and management of the hall—'

'It'll be cheaper now that I've sacked that bastard Mahoney,' Newton raged. 'Why the hell she left money to him I'll never know — she should have seen through him. It was all he was ever after, sucking up to her . . .'

Gabriella Newton was more controlled, more sanguine. Arnold felt she was reasonably satisfied. They had enough. She plucked at her husband's arm. 'Let it go, Rick. It's over now, so let it go.' He glared at her in fury and stalked out of the room.

Arnold left them to the shards of their marriage. It was time to give George Mahoney details of his good fortune.

He was told that Mahoney was at his cottage, near the main entrance to the estate. He found him in the small garden at the back. He was leaning on the stone wall, staring aimlessly out across the fells. He turned his head as Arnold joined him.

'They've got Vartek, then.'

'So it seems,' Arnold replied. 'Apparently they can show some sort of connection between him and the dead man.' He glanced curiously at the estate manager, and then went on, 'I thought I'd better come round and tell you that things are being cleared up now, with regard to the estate. I've already told you that Mrs Delaney left you a very large sum of money, by way of a legacy. I think I should be able to pay it out soon — probate's next week, and I've got most things in order with the help of the solicitors. You'll have more than enough money to live comfortably for the rest of your life. Even in the States.'

Mahoney flickered a quick glance in his direction. 'I haven't really decided what to do, yet,' he said dully.

'I would have thought it would be very much in your interests to go there.'

There was a short silence. Mahoney's back had stiffened. After a while, he said, 'Why do you think it would be in my best interests?'

Arnold hesitated, watching Mahoney carefully. At last, in a quiet tone he said, 'I don't know. Maybe to stake a claim.'

The silence grew around them. A light breeze sprang up, whispering down from the fells; at last Mahoney turned to face Arnold. His features were shadowed. 'I don't know what you're talking about.'

'Perhaps not,' Arnold replied diffidently. 'But, since you're a legatee, there's no reason why I shouldn't tell you what I told the Newtons, earlier this morning. About the terms of the will, I mean. Did you know that she made me executor because there was bad blood between you and the Newtons, by the way? That, and the fact that she believed Rick Newton would do his best to destroy her intentions, after her death.'

'He always was a greedy bastard,' Mahoney said grimly.

'I think I can agree with that. Anyway, there are a number of legacies under the will, yours being the largest by far. She regarded you as a close friend — you'd been working for her for what . . .'

'Seven years.'

'Right. So she's provided handsomely for you. Then, after all the legacies are paid, there are a few charitable donations, and under the will the intention was for the residue to be divided between her nephew Rick, and Joe Delaney's children by his first wife.'

Arnold hesitated, his eyes still on Mahoney's wooden features. 'I've been in contact with a friend of mine who happens to be in New York at the moment. She's been helping me to trace the two children. Vita never told you the story, but when she married Joe Delaney, after his divorce, they cut away from the children . . .'

Mahoney stood stiffly, staring at Arnold.

'She admitted to me last week,' Arnold continued, 'how selfish she and Joe had been. But she'd decided to put things right, in the end. Anyway, Jane's been running a trace for me . . . She found that Miss Carnforth died in 1970, of cancer. Miss Carnforth was the aunt — the first Mrs Delaney's sister — who never married, but brought up Joe's children. A boy, and a girl. The girl — she was called Teresa — was killed in 1989. An overdose of heroin, Jane tells me. She'd fallen into bad company, been on the slide for years. Her brother turned up for the funeral, but then disappeared. It's been assumed he went back to where he had been living and working for some years. Canada. But apparently, he'd resigned from the Army there, and there seems to be no trace thereafter . . . the trail goes cold, so to speak. But Jane's still trying. I guess we'll find him in due course. To tell him he's entitled to half the residue of—'

'You know, don't you?' Mahoney's voice was harsh, and bitter.

Arnold was silent for a little while. 'I guessed . . .'

'When?'

'After the last phone call from Jane. Pieces of a jigsaw. A man called John Carnforth, who had lived in Canada for years, had been in the Canadian Army, who had disappeared about seven or eight years ago — just about the time you came to work for Vita Delaney. You were about the right age, the right background . . . And there was an old photograph — she faxed it to me. Not easy to make out, but . . . I guessed. So what was it all about, in the end?'

Mahoney began to pace in a tight circle, head down. He was frowning, twisting his mouth. He shook his head. 'You can't appreciate what it was like. We were brought up, Teresa and I, by an aunt whom I regarded as a mother until Teresa put me right. I had been born just before my father went to

England, where he met Vita. And when he came back it was to divorce my mother, so I never got to know Joe, or my grandfather. Or my mother, for that matter: it wasn't long before she was in an asylum, where she died. A pretty grim picture, hey?'

He glared at Arnold. 'No, you can't imagine what it was like. My aunt was a bitter woman. She never failed to drum into us how we had been denied what was rightfully ours. Our mother was dead; our aunt had little money, and she was forced to look after us while Vita Delaney lived in luxury in England. It was a constant theme throughout our teenage years. I fled from it, in the end, went to Canada, had a career in the Army. Teresa wrote to me occasionally, but I wasn't interested. I was married for a while, but it didn't work out. I had difficulty relating to anyone. A blighted, soured childhood, I guess . . .'

'Did you go to your aunt's funeral?'

'No. Teresa wrote me after the funeral. I don't think I would have gone anyway. There was no affection between us. I disliked her mean, petty ways, her constant harping . . . And I didn't see Teresa again until I heard she had died, in 1989. When I came back and saw the conditions she had been living in, and how she'd died, something snapped. I decided I had to seek out the woman who had stolen everything from us. I wanted to face her, challenge her . . . I went back to Canada; resigned from the Army; came to England.'

'And assumed a new identity.' Shades of the Mórrigan again, Arnold thought.

Mahoney laughed bitterly. 'Can you imagine what Vita would have done if I'd arrived at the hall announcing myself as a Carnforth? She'd have thrown me out on my neck!'

'Perhaps not.'

'Well, that's what I thought she would have done. So I turned up and managed to get a job with her — I had reasonable credentials, from forestry work, and then the Army — and I settled in.'

'What did you hope to achieve?' Arnold asked curiously. Mahoney grunted.

'Revenge, I think. I wanted my birth right. I wanted to find some way to hurt her, the way I'd been hurt. For the first year or so I seethed, plotted, worked on ways that I could get my own back on her for her indifference, wondered how I could get my hands on her money . . . And then, gradually, things changed.' He shook his head. 'I infiltrated her camp, crept in with a deliberate intention, to ingratiate myself with her. To that extent at least, Rick Newton was right. He and I were alike — we wanted the same things. And he saw through me.' Mahoney's voice was bitter, his eyes ravaged with the memories. 'But slowly, subtly, it changed. I grew to like her. We became friends. And somehow the pain receded. Revenge became less important to me. I . . . perhaps for the first time in my life, I began to feel settled, and happy, relaxed. The old darkness had gone.'

'You were never tempted to tell her?' Arnold asked. Mahoney shook his head. 'Too late. To tell her would have been to admit my reasons for coming to work for her. We had built a friendship. I didn't want that destroyed. And my identity . . . somehow, I felt it had become unimportant. But now . . .'

They were both silent for a while. Arnold could understand how the man felt. In the end it had been more important to allow Vita to keep the image of a friendship than go to her grave with the knowledge that she had been used, if only in the beginning.

'Do you think Vartek will be prosecuted?' Arnold asked quietly.

Mahoney stopped pacing. He leaned against the wall. 'I've no idea.'

'How will you feel if he is?' Arnold persisted. 'What if he's found guilty of killing Steven Quaid?'

Mahoney was silent.

'You see,' Arnold went on, 'I've got some doubts about whether he is guilty. It's partly because a few things have been bothering me, and partly because of an absurd theory Chief Inspector Culpeper came up with. You know what he suggested? He said maybe Gabriella Newton killed Quaid.'

Mahoney turned his head to stare at Arnold. After a moment he said, 'As you suggested — absurd.'

'He thought — Culpeper, that is — the killing could have been a mistake.' Arnold hesitated. 'It was a thought he planted in my mind. I churned it around a bit. And then the other little things that had been bothering me, they came back into my mind.'

'What things?'

'When I joined you beside Quaid's body, you made out you didn't recognize him. And you also told Culpeper you didn't know him. Yet you'd told me that night down by the ruins that you'd caught glimpses of someone wandering, shooting in the woods. Maybe you'd been too far off to identify him, I thought. But then I remembered, you'd also said you thought it was a townie staying in the village. So did you recognize him . . . and if so, why deny ever having seen him before?'

Mahoney was silent, his shoulders stiff, his features without expression. But his eyes were haunted.

'Then there was the matter of Newton's assignation with Karen Stannard. You don't know Karen Stannard as I do although I was a bit puzzled by her flirtatious behaviour. You may well have assumed she really intended to meet Newton clandestinely that night. I'd have been surprised had she done so . . . but I wondered whether you might have thought she intended to.'

He paused for a while. 'And there was the matter of your dislike of Rick Newton. I'd been struggling with a hypothesis, without much conviction, I admit — and then I got Jane's phone call . . . and I wondered . . .'

'Just what exactly are you trying to say?' Mahoney asked heavily.

'I'm just wondering,' Arnold said quietly, 'whether they've got the right man for Quaid's killing. I'm wondering whether Culpeper was right in suggesting it might have been a mistake. I'm wondering whether you thought Newton was meeting Karen Stannard and hid in the stable; then, when the man you thought was Newton came past, you hit him from behind. Except it wasn't Newton. It was Quaid . . . And then I'm wondering whether, if what I suggest is the truth, you'll be able to let Vartek go to prison for something he didn't do.'

There was a long silence. 'You have no proof of this,' Mahoney said at last, with a strange edge to his voice.

'No,' Arnold agreed. 'And I've no real motive I can impute to you, really. It's all pure supposition. But I can't stop . . . wondering.'

They stood there in the sunshine and a plane passed high overhead, scratching a white vapour trail against the intense blue of the sky. Mahoney craned his neck to look at it: there was a greyness in his cheek, a slackness about his mouth and jawline, and he seemed older than his fifty years. He sighed.

'He was carrying a shotgun.'

'Who?'

'Quaid. It was the first thing I realized, after I hit him and he began to go down. The shotgun. It clattered on the cobbles. I was startled, scared. I picked it up; I suppose I was dazed, incredulous at what I'd done. Then I thought about fingerprints, so I took it into the woods, buried it. I was shaking.' He took a deep breath. 'I think it was the worst moment of my life. But maybe there'll be worse to come.'

'But why did you attack him?' Arnold asked, puzzled. Mahoney turned his head. His eyes were scarred with pain. 'I told you — Newton and I had much in common. We had both been after her money. I had changed. Newton hadn't. He was suspicious; always trying to find some way to break my friendship with Vita. He gnawed away at it. He was afraid that Vita would leave the bloody estate to me. He never understood . . .'

Mahoney shook his head, as though trying to get rid of memories. 'And he knew that I'd checked on him, guessed that I'd discovered he'd been milking the accounts. He wanted to discredit me with her, the way I had discredited him. He was checking on my background. And that last day . . . I intercepted a package intended for him, from Canada. He'd been nosing around in Army records. I saw red; all the old bitterness came back.' He turned a ravaged glance on Arnold. 'You see, I was fond of Vita — in a way I saw in her the mother I'd never known. The stepmother, in reality, who'd discarded me and my sister — but whenever were emotions rational? Yet . . . I was fond of her. I went to the stables — I thought he would be coming down to meet Miss Stannard. I think I just wanted to warn him — scare the life out of him. But when he came past the stable it got to me, everything went red, I hated him maybe for being just like me and I picked up the stone and lashed out at him . . . and it wasn't him. It was Quaid . . .'

He was silent for a while. He shook his head slowly. 'What motive, you asked. I didn't want him to expose me to Vita; I didn't want him to find out I was her stepson, and tell her, destroy the relationship we'd established, put worms in her mind about me. It wasn't the money; it was no longer anything to do with money. And I had no idea she was going to split the estate between Newton and the surviving child of Joe Delaney . . . God, what a mess!'

He grimaced, and then slowly folded his arms and stared at Arnold dispassionately. His features seemed to have relaxed somewhat now he had unburdened himself. He would have been churning over the events in his mind. And now Vita was dead; it had all been pointless.

The irony was that, in Arnold's view, Vita Delaney would have accepted the situation, had she known. She had tried to put things right at the end, in any case. She might even have enjoyed knowing, at last, that the man she'd become close to over the last seven years had been Joe's son.

'So, what are you going to do?' Mahoney asked. 'Now you know.'

'Do?' Arnold shrugged, uncertainly. 'What should I do? As you've already said, I have a theory but no proof. And you could always deny this conversation. I don't see there's

211

anything for me to do. It's not my business. It's yours.' He watched Mahoney through narrowed eyes. 'I suppose it's really a matter for your conscience.'

Mahoney was silent. Arnold hesitated, then slowly turned away. He walked as far as the gate, then stopped, and looked back at the silent man standing against the wall.

'At least you'll have plenty of money. You'll be able to brief the best lawyers in the business for your defence.'

The final gift of Vita Delaney.

4

Culpeper had requested an audience with the Chief Constable. The Chief was surprised when he saw that Farnsby was in attendance. He sat behind his desk as the two men stood in front of him. He raised an interrogative eyebrow. 'Well?'

'There's been a new development in the Quaid killing, sir.' The Chief Constable seemed pleased. 'Vartek — or Sinclair, or whatever his name is — has confessed?'

'No, sir. The estate manager who worked for Mrs Delaney man called George Mahoney, or at least his real name is John Carnforth—'

'What the hell is going on here?' the Chief Constable snapped irritably. 'Everyone seems to be changing their names!'

'He's been in to make a statement. Says it was he who killed Steven Quaid. Or Charlie Lawes. If you understand what I mean, sir. Quaid had been up to the Hall, trying to squeeze more money out of Vartek, and Mahoney killed him. By mistake.'

'Is he a crazy?' the Chief Constable snorted.

'He made the statement in the company of a solicitor. It looks as though he will be using the defence that he did it when the balance of his mind was disturbed. And he'll be instructing a top QC.'

'He seems serious, sir,' Farnsby added.

The Chief Constable wrinkled his nose in thought. 'You've got the statement, Culpeper?'

'In this file, sir.' Culpeper handed the manila folder to the Chief Constable, who flipped quickly through it. At last he looked up, frowning.

'If his story holds water, it leaves this Vartek character—'

'In the clear. As far as the charge of murder is concerned. That's really why I thought it best to come in to see you. With Farnsby.'

'I don't understand,' the Chief Constable said warily.

Culpeper was standing to attention. 'It's just that we feel that if the charges stick against Mahoney — or Carnforth, as he really is — there might be a temptation to take no further action against Vartek — or Sinclair. Or Councillor Mulberry. Sir.' Culpeper paused. 'You see, I appreciate that you wanted information on Mulberry's business activities as a "Mulberry Defence" but it's gone beyond that now, sir.'

'How do you mean?'

'There's evidence to suggest,' Farnsby intervened, 'that allegations were suppressed six years ago, allegations of sexual abuse that should have been proceeded with against Vartek — Sinclair, I mean, sir.'

'Call him what the bloody hell you want,' the Chief Constable snapped irritably. 'What are you getting at?'

'We think it would be unwise if there were *another* cover-up, Chief Constable.'

A short silence followed. There was an apoplectic look about the Chief Constable's ruddy features. He leaned forward menacingly across his desk. 'What exactly are you saying, Culpeper — and choose your words with care.'

'It's like this, sir.' Culpeper had already chosen his words with rehearsed care. In front of Farnsby. 'Six years ago, it seems, Mulberry enlisted assistance from his friends, the ones supporting him for election to the council. He let it be known that some embarrassing revelations might appear, regarding allegations of sexual abuse, made by a couple of . . . expendable tearaways at one of his homes. It could damage the prospects of his sale of care and nursing businesses to the consortium making a bid. And it could embarrass the individuals, and the party, supporting him for election. So, a deal was struck. Money exchanged hands. Allegations were withdrawn.'

The Chief Constable's eyes narrowed with suspicion. 'You have proof of this?'

'I think there will be social workers who will give evidence. And while one of the two complainants is dead — Quaid, or rather, Charlie Lawes—'

'Culpeper . . .' the Chief Constable warned.

'The other one, William Dennis, is in London. Brixton, in fact. Banged up. He would be available to give evidence.'

'Consequently, sir,' Farnsby suggested, 'it might not be a good idea to think in terms of a Mulberry Defence. It should be more in the nature of . . . a formal investigation. You had, after all, originally asked us to consider whether any criminal prosecutions might, or should be, in the offing.'

The Chiefs eyes were glittering. 'I also told you that I'd be handling this business, personally.'

'The result would be the same, of course,' Culpeper said affably, ignoring the Chief Constable's anger. 'Your . . . ah . . . friends would not be under attack anymore, because once the scandal emerged, I doubt whether the Mulberry committee could sensibly continue its deliberations. And if we start an investigation . . . well, we couldn't be accused of a cover-up . . .' He paused. 'As we might be, if we merely used the Mulberry Defence and did nothing about the allegations arising out of the sexual abuse at Spittal, six years ago.' He raised his chin, defiantly. 'It's true some politicians other than Mulberry might also be severely embarrassed by an investigation. But I . . . we . . . don't think we can now keep this under wraps — no matter who might be embarrassed . . .'

The Chief Constable had got the message. They could see it in his eyes.

* * *

The news ripped around the Department of Museums and Antiquities the day Arnold returned to work. The assistance of Jerry Picton in its dissemination was not required. Miss Sansom was as near to smiling as Arnold had ever seen her. The short-term contract for Elliott Scarisbrick to work as replacement director had been cancelled — with appropriate compensation. Simon Brent-Ellis was back at his desk — the suggestions that he had put in false claims for expenses quietly dropped — and Karen Stannard had been reinstated, with the winding up of the Mulberry inquiry.

Councillor Mulberry was officially away sick, but it was rumoured that discussions were being held with the police and with the Department of Social Services with regard to certain charges surrounding the sale of the Mulberry care homes to a consortium, some years ago. Details were scarce, but it was rumoured that Mulberry was finished, and the likelihood of his standing at the forthcoming election was slim.

Arnold was called into Karen Stannard's office. She had pushed her chair back from her desk and she was staring at him, a slight smile on her wide mouth. Her eyes were triumphant.

'I don't know whether you've heard the news,' she said. 'Cossman International are not proceeding with the lawsuit. The television people have settled out of court, and the local authority has been let off the hook.'

'I'm sure Powell Frinton will be relieved.'

Her eyes were glittering. 'I told you I'd be back,' she said.

'Of course.'

She observed him carefully for a moment, then gestured towards her desk. 'The files have piled up in your absence, Landon. With the director and me both suspended, you should really have been here to take on the burden . . . I'm still not sure of your motivation, so, provided you get down to the backlog, we'll say no more about it. But we really must get them cleared quickly. I take it you have no objection to working late, because I'm going to be at committee meetings most of the week. The burden therefore must largely fall on you.'

Arnold came forward and picked up the bundle of files. '*Plus ça change, plus c'est la même chose,*' he muttered.

For a moment he thought she hadn't heard him. Then she smiled. It was a beautiful, mocking smile. 'You're absolutely right, Arnold,' she said. 'Around here, nothing ever really changes . . .'

5

It was an ancient wind that ripped across the fell. It had torn its way from the west in the same manner for a thousand years and the locals called it the Holm wind. They had forgotten the origins of the name, that it came from the west, from the dark island offshore. The island that had spawned the Northman.

It brought with it rain, and grew to gale strength, lashing the hill, tearing at the rocks, uprooting trees. On the rock scar above the field at Haggburn an old oak lurched, its roots being dragged from the clinging earth as the Holm wind raged through its heavy branches. Slowly, agonizingly, the roots gave way, sucked from the black earth until the tree itself leaned, and slowly fell, collapsing across the face of the rocky outcrop.

The rain bore down for hours, leaching away the earth, washing rivulets of mud from the base of the ancient oak, coursing down to the field below. And in a while the brittle bones appeared, pale against the darkness of the earth, exposed again after centuries of interment.

The man who had brought the Mórrigan to the land had lain in a deep sleep for a thousand years, but now his bones were exposed to the open sky and the wind raged across a fell black as a raven's wing. Men had said over the centuries that the Northman was still there, somewhere up on the fell, and that there would be a time again when the Shape-Shifter would return, to spread her confusion, and her promises, and her betrayals, and her death across the wide dark fells.

Perhaps she had returned; perhaps she had never gone away, from Haggburn. And as the rain poured down, more of the Northman's skeleton was exposed, awaiting the hands of the searcher . . .

THE END

Thank you for reading this book.

If you enjoyed it please leave feedback on Amazon or Goodreads, and if there is anything we missed or you have a question about, then please get in touch. We appreciate you choosing our book.

Founded in 2014 in Shoreditch, London, we at Joffe Books pride ourselves on our history of innovative publishing. We were thrilled to be shortlisted for Independent Publisher of the Year at the British Book Awards.

www.joffebooks.com

We're very grateful to eagle-eyed readers who take the time to contact us. Please send any errors you find to corrections@joffebooks.com. We'll get them fixed ASAP.